StartUp™ Assessment

Pre/Post Assessment Instructions

Step 1

☐ Make a copy of the teacher record for each student and place it in his or her file.

Teacher Record

Step 2

☐ Administer tests on a one-to-one basis. Use the examples provided with the directions to ensure students understand what to do.

Student Sheet

Step 3

☐ Analyze results to determine where to place students in the kit and how to group them for small-group instruction. If students lack phonological and letter awareness skills, you may wish to review these by completing the Level 1 lessons before moving on to the Level 2 phonics units.

Letter Recognition Pre- and Post-Tests

Student: _____

Directions: Ask the student to point to each letter, moving across the page, and name each one. If the student comes to a letter he or she doesn't know, say the letter name, put an X next to the letter in the column, and have the student continue. If the student says an incorrect letter name, record what he or she says in the column.

	Pre-Test Date ___	Post-Test Date ___		Pre-Test Date ___	Post-Test Date ___		Pre-Test Date ___	Post-Test Date ___		Pre-Test Date ___	Post-Test Date ___
e			f			L			B		
h			l			u			K		
m			g			N			J		
c			z			T			X		
o			j			A			P		
a			p			D			M		
y			k			V			G		
b			q			Z			C		
x			r			R			Y		
i			v			F			Q		
d			s			O			E		
n			w			W			I		
u			H			S					
t											

Letter Recognition

e h m c o a y b x

i d n u t f l g z

j p k q r v s w

H L U N T A D V Z

R F O W S B K J X

P M G C Y Q E I

Student Name: _____

Word Awareness

Directions: Say the sentence. Have the student repeat the sentence and tell you the number of words. **Example:** *This is my dog. I can hear four words in this sentence.*

	Pre-Test Date _____	Post-Test Date _____
I see my cat.	/4	/4
Can you do this?	/4	/4
This book is fun to read.	/6	/6
Please sit on the chair.	/5	/5
Where do you live?	/4	/4
Score	**/23**	**/23**

Observations: _____
_____
_____

Identify Rhyme

Directions: Say the word pairs and ask the student if the words rhyme. **Example:** Roast/toast. *Yes, these words rhyme.* Roast/ran. *No, these words don't rhyme.*

	Pre-Test Date _____	Post-Test Date _____
bug/rug		
pink/sink		
big/box		
hop/hip		
jump/pump		
Score	**/5**	**/5**

Observations: _____
_____
_____

Syllable Awareness

Directions: Say the word. Have the student repeat the word and clap for the number of syllables. **Example:** Engine. *I hear two syllables in* engine.

	Pre-Test Date _____	Post-Test Date _____
happy	/2	/2
Saturday	/3	/3
book	/1	/1
sunshine	/2	/2
experiment	/4	/4
Score	**/12**	**/12**

Initial Sounds

Directions: Say the word. Have the student repeat the word and tell you the sound at the beginning. **Example:** Hat. *I hear /h/ at the beginning of the word* hat.

	Pre-Test Date _____	Post-Test Date _____
turtle		
man		
sink		
pudding		
leg		
Score	**/5**	**/5**

Student Name: _____

Final Sounds

Directions: Say the word. Have the student repeat the word and tell you the sound at the end. **Example:** Hat. *I hear /t/ at the end of the word* hat.

	Pre-Test Date _____	Post-Test Date _____
park		
noise		
rabbit		
trap		
head		
Score	**/5**	**/5**

Observations: _____
_____
_____

Differentiating Sounds

Directions: Say the words. Have the student repeat the words and say which word starts with a different sound. **Example:** Mix, man, nose. Nose *starts with a different sound.*

	Pre-Test Date _____	Post-Test Date _____
bag, bug, cup		
table, nut, tent		
cup, cat, bat		
fish, pan, pin		
sun, sit, man		
Score	**/5**	**/5**

Observations: _____
_____
_____

Medial Sounds

Directions: Say the word. Have the student repeat the word and tell you the sound in the middle. **Example:** Hat. *I hear /a/ in the middle of the word* hat.

	Pre-Test Date _____	Post-Test Date _____
pet		
sack		
hit		
stop		
cut		
Score	**/5**	**/5**

Onset and Rime

Directions: Say the word. Have the student repeat the word, say the first sound in the word, and then say the rest of the word. **Example:** dig: /d/ /ig/.

	Pre-Test Date _____	Post-Test Date _____
cat: /k/ /at/		
run: /r/ /un/		
pop: /p/ /op/		
hen: /h/ /en/		
rid: /r/ /id/		
Score	**/5**	**/5**

Student Name: _____

Phoneme Segmentation

Directions: Say the word. Have the student tell you all the sounds in the word. **Example:** *If I say* run, *you will say* /r/ /u/ /n/.

	Pre-Test Date _____	Post-Test Date _____
cat: /k/ /a/ /t/	/3	/3
top: /t/ /o/ /p/	/3	/3
said: /s/ /e/ /d/	/3	/3
jumps: /j/ /u/ /m/ /p/ /s/	/5	/5
rugs: /r/ /u/ /g/ /z/	/4	/4
Score	**/18**	**/18**

Observations: _____
_____
_____

Blending Phonemes

Directions: Say the word sound by sound. Then have the student say the word. **Example:** *I will say the sounds of some words. I want you to blend the sounds and say the words: for example, /r/ /u/ /t/:* rut.

	Pre-Test Date _____	Post-Test Date _____
/n/ /u/ /t/ : nut		
/j/ /e/ /t/: jet		
/w/ /i/ /g/: wig		
/s/ /a/ /t/: sat		
/m/ /o/ /p/: mop		
Score	**/5**	**/5**

Observations: _____
_____
_____

Initial Sound Substitution

Directions: Say the word. Ask the student to replace the first sound in the word with the new sound. **Example:** *I can change the /b/ in* bat *to /k/ to make the word* cat.

	Pre-Test Date _____	Post-Test Date _____
tin: change /t/ to /b/ [bin]		
mug: change /m/ to /r/ [rug]		
hop: change /h/ to /b/ [bop]		
pen: change /p/ to /t/ [ten]		
lake: change /l/ to /k/ [cake]		
Score	**/5**	**/5**

Student Name: _____

Consonant Sounds Assessment

Directions: Have students point to each letter and tell you the sound each consonant stands for. Some letters stand for more than one sound. Note whether students say both sounds. Circle any letters they miss on the recording sheet.

	Pre-Test Date _____	Post-Test Date _____
m: /m/		
s: /s/, /z/		
c: /k/, /s/		
v: /v/		
l: /l/		
g: /g/, /j/		
n: /n/		
d: /d/		
t: /t/		
j: /j/		
w: /w/		
p: /p/		
r: /r/		
b: /b/		
q: /kw/		
h: /h/		
z: /z/		
f: /f/		
k: /k/		
x: /ks/		
n: /n/		
Score	**/21**	**/21**

Vowel Sounds Assessment

Directions: Have the student point to each word and tell you the sound each vowel stands for in the word. Record the student's responses in the column.

	Pre-Test Date _____	Post-Test Date _____
mat		
rub		
get		
hot		
fit		
Score	**/5**	**/5**

Blending Sounds Assessment

Student Name: _____

Directions: Explain to the student that these are nonsense words that you want him or her to sound out. Have the student put his or her finger on the example word on the student sheet. **Say:** *I can sound out this nonsense word:* /m/ /i/ /n/: min. Have the student say each sound in the nonsense word and then blend the sounds.

	Pre-Test Date _____	Post-Test Date _____		Pre-Test Date _____	Post-Test Date _____
fam: /f/ /a/ /m/			yad: /y/ /a/ /d/		
tif: /t/ /i/ /f/			hep: /h/ /e/ /p/		
wug: /w/ /u/ /g/			bab: /b/ /a/ /b/		
pof: /p/ /o/ /f/			ven: /v/ /e/ /n/		
rac: /r/ /a/ /k/			sut: /s/ /u/ /t/		
zot: /z/ /o/ /t/			gom: /g/ /o/ /m/		
jun: /j/ /u/ /n/			dat: /d/ /a/ /t/		
sot: /s/ /o/ /t/			nex: /n/ /e/ /ks/		
rog : /r/ /o/ /g/			leb: /l/ /e/ /b/		
mic: /m/ /i/ /k/			quet: /kw/ /e/ /t/		
pum: /p/ /u/ /m/			sil: /s/ /i/ /l/		
cof: /k/ /o/ /f/			kif: /k/ /i/ /f/		

Score   _____/24   _____/24

Observations: _____

_____

Consonant Sounds

m   s   c   v   l

g   n   d   t   j

w   p   r   b   q

h   z   f   k   x

n

Vowel Sounds

mat   rub   get   hot   fit

Blending Sounds

Example: min /m/ /i/ /n/

fam	tif	wug	pof
rac	zot	jun	sot
rog	mic	pum	cof
yad	hep	bab	ven
sut	gom	dat	nex
leb	quet	sil	kif

 Benchmark Phonics • StartUp Level 1 • Phonological Awareness & Letter Awareness

Sight Words

Student Name: _____

Directions: Have the student put his or her finger on the first word on the student sheet and then read across the line, saying the words as quickly as possible. Count as incorrect any word the student misses or hesitates on before reading.

	Pre-Test Date _____	Post-Test Date _____		Pre-Test Date _____	Post-Test Date _____
is			look		
a			he		
the			go		
has			put		
and			want		
of			this		
with			she		
see			saw		
for			now		
no			like		
cannot			do		
have			home		
are			they		
said			went		
I			good		
you			was		
me			be		
come			we		
here			there		
to			then		
my			out		
			Score _____/42	_____/42

Observations: _____

_____

Sight Words

is	a	the	has	and
of	with	see	for	no
cannot	have	are	said	I
you	me	come	here	to
my	look	he	go	put
want	this	she	saw	now
like	do	home	they	went
good	was	be	we	there
then	out			

 Benchmark Phonics • StartUp Level 1 • Phonological Awareness & Letter Awareness

1

2

3

Dear Parent/Guardian,

This year your child will learn all about sounds, letters, and words. There are many ways you can help your child learn to read. In class we will read many stories. I will send copies of these books home. Please listen to and help your child read the books to you. I will also send home some fun activities and games for your family to enjoy together.

I look forward to an exciting year of learning. Thank you in advance for the important part you play in helping your child learn to read.

Sincerely,

_____

Estimado padre de familia:

En el curso de este año escolar, su hijo aprenderá sobre sonidos, letras y palabras. Hay muchas maneras en que usted puede ayudar a su hijo a aprender a leer. En el aula leeremos muchos cuentos. Enviaré copias de los textos a su casa. Tenga la amabilidad de escuchar y ayudar a su hijo a leer los libros. También enviaré algunos juegos y actividades divertidas a su casa para que los disfruten juntos.

Será un año de aprendizaje emocionante. Le agradezco de antemano el apoyo que aportará al ayudar a su hijo a aprender a leer. Sin más por el momento, me despido cordialmente.

Atentamente,

_____

Glossary

Closed Syllable	a syllable or morpheme that precedes one or more consonants, as in /a/ in hat
Diphthong	a vowel sound produced when the tongue moves or glides from one vowel sound to another vowel or semivowel sound in the same syllable. Example: bee, bay, boo, boy, and bough
Formal Assessments	the collection of data using standardized tests or procedures under controlled conditions
Formal Assessment	an assessment that is both an instructional tool that a teacher and student use while learning is occurring and an accountability tool to determine if learning has occurred. Note: Benchmark Literacy Formal Assessments include Comprehension Strategy Assessment Handbooks for grades K-6.
Grapheme	a written or printed representation of a phoneme, as b for /b/ and oy for /oi/ in boy
High-frequency Word	a word that appears many more times than most other words in spoken or written language
Homonym	a word with different origin and meaning but the same oral or written form as one or more other words, as bear (an animal) vs. bear (to support) vs. bare (exposed)
Homophone	a word with different origin and meaning, but the same pronunciation as another word, whether or not spelled alike, as hare and hair
Homograph	a word with the same spelling as another word whether or not pronounced alike, as pen (a writing instrument) vs. pen (enclosure).
Informal Assessments	evaluations by casual observation or by other nonstandardized procedures. Note: Benchmark Literacy Informal Assessments include Informal Assessment Handbooks for reading comprehension, writing, spelling, fluency, vocabulary and English Language development provide teacher observation checklists, forms, and rubrics for ongoing assessment.
Initial Blend	the joining of two or more consonant sounds, represented by letters that begin a word without losing the identity of the sounds, as /bl/ in black, /skr/ in scramble.
Listening Center	a place where a student can use a headset to listen to recorded instructional material
Miscue	a term to describe a deviation from text during oral reading or a shift in comprehension of a passage

Modeling	teacher's use of clear demonstrations and explicit language
Open Syllable	a syllable ending in a vowel sound rather than a consonant
Oral Reading	the process of reading aloud to communicate to another or to an audience
Phonological Awareness	awareness of the constituent sounds of words in learning to read and spell (by syllables, onsets and rimes, and phonemes)
Print Awareness	a learner's growing recognition of conventions and characteristics of a written language, including directionality, spaces between words, etc.
Sight Word	a word that is immediately recognized as a whole and does not require word analysis for identification
Teacher Resource Web Site	a free Benchmark Education Web site that provides a searchable database of titles, levels, subject areas, themes, and comprehension strategies; the site contains downloadable resources including literacy texts and teacher's guides, comprehension question cards, oral reading records, take-home books, and assessment resources
Teacher Resource System	the analysis of the structural characteristics of the text, coherence, organization, concept load, etc.

Baumann, J. F., E. C. Edwards, G. Font, C. A. Tereshinksi, E. J. Kame'enui, and S. Olejnik. "Teaching Morphemic and Contextual Analysis to Fifth-Grade Students." Reading Research Quarterly: 37 (2), pp. 150–176. 2002.

Bear, D. R., M. Invernizzi,, S. Templeton, and F. Johnston. Words Their Way: Word Study for Phonics, Vocabulary, and Spelling Instruction. Columbus, OH: Merrill Publishing Company, 1995.

Blevins, W. Teaching Phonics & Word Study in the Intermediate Grades. New York: Scholastic, 2001.

Cunningham, Patricia M. Phonics They Use: Words for Reading and Writing. Boston: Allyn & Bacon, 2005.

Cunningham, Patricia M., and Dorothy P. Hall. Making Words. Torrance, CA: Good Apple, 1994.

Ganske, K. Mindful of Words: Spelling and Vocabulary Explorations 4-8. New York: Guilford Press, 2008.

Ganske, K. Word Journeys: Assessment-guided Phonics, Spelling, and Vocabulary Instruction. New York: Guilford Press, 2000.

Ganske, K. Word Sorts and More: Sound, Pattern, and Meaning Explorations K–3. New York: Guilford Press, 2006.

Gill, S. "Teaching Rimes with Shared Reading." The Reading Teacher 60, pp. 191–193. 2006.

Moats, L. "How Spelling Supports Reading—And Why It Is More Regular and Predictable than You May Think." American Educator, pp. 12-16, 20-22, 42-43. Winter 2005/2006.

Moats, L. C. "Teaching Decoding." American Educator, pp. 42–49. Spring/Summer 1998.

Schreiber, P. A., and C. Read. "Children's Use of Phonetic Cues in Spelling, Parsing, and—Maybe—Reading." Bulletin of the Orton Society, 30, pp. 209–224. 1980.

Tunmer, W. E. and Nesdale, A. R. "Phonemic Segmentation Skill and Beginning Reading." Journal of Educational Psychology, 77, pp. 417–427. 1985.

Zutell, J. "Word Sorting: A Developmental Spelling Approach to Word Study for Delayed Readers." Reading & Writing Quarterly, 14, pp. 219–238. 1998.

StartUp PHONICS Level 1 Assessment & Appendix

StartUp PHONICS Level 1 **Program Overview**

Introduction

Introduction

Components at a Glance

Getting Started

Using the Components

Managing Instruction in the Phonics Block

Phonics Instruction in a Balanced Literacy Program

StartUp™ Skills

Core Kit Materials Correlated to Units

StartUp™ *Phonics* is a complete kit designed for use in the phonics block within the Benchmark Literacy balanced core reading program. It presents a research-based, explicit, and systematic approach to teaching the phonics skills students need when learning to read.

Welcome to *BENCHMARK PHONICS*™ *StartUp*™ Levels 1 and 2

Thank you for selecting *StartUp*™ *Phonics* from Benchmark Education Company. *StartUp*™ *Phonics* supplies all the lesson resources, books, posters, and support tools needed to provide whole-group instruction, guided practice, and support in small groups, as well as independent practice opportunities. Teachers and students alike will find the lessons and materials engaging, hands-on, and motivating. Level 1 begins with phonological awareness and letter awareness, and Level 2 expands to cover short vowels and consonants, and introduces the concept of long vowels.

Why Teach Explicit Phonemic Awareness and Phonics?

A good reader is like a builder who is able to reach into a toolbox of familiar tools and pull out the right tool at the right moment. Like tools, each reading skill or strategy has an important use in the complex cognitive process of reading.

Think about a young student who is in the beginning stages of learning to read. He meets a large number of unfamiliar words in his environment. His brain is very busy trying to categorize, integrate, compare, and analyze the graphophonic information about letters, sounds, and words. Without the keys to this decoding process, the student cannot move quickly to other reading skills.

The Goals of *StartUp*™ *Phonics*

In order to shape young students' development of phonemic knowledge, *StartUp*™ *Phonics* creates opportunities to provide students at different stages of literacy growth with varied experiences that promote automatic and flexible control of letters and words. The systematic lessons will:

• **Build a foundation for successful phonemic awareness and phonics instruction**
Most students are expected to begin phonics instruction in kindergarten, but many of these students still need reinforcement in readiness skills to ensure success. *StartUp*™ *Phonics* provides explicit lessons to teach and review phonological awareness skills. There is also explicit hands-on instruction to teach and/or review letter recognition and formation.

- **Explicitly teach short vowels and consonants**

  Once students have developed the readiness skills for phonics, each five-day unit focuses on a single phonetic element and its sound. Instruction over the five days moves from direct whole-group modeling and guided practice to real reading of decodable books, and skill review through independent literacy center activities. Each day includes explicit instruction for phonemic or phonological awareness, sound/symbol relationships, blending, spelling, and sight words.

- **Support and motivate all learners**

  Some students grasp phonics skills quickly and easily. Others need more time to practice each new skill. Every *StartUp™ Phonics* unit helps teachers tailor instruction to their students' needs with hands-on small-group activities for additional practice; independent extension activities; support tips for English Language Learners; motivating, multisensory manipulatives; and take-home practice activities.

- **Make systematic phonics instruction manageable in a comprehensive literacy classroom**

  Phonics is only one of the many daily literacy events in a comprehensive literacy classroom. *StartUp™ Phonics* is designed to help teachers maximize their time in the phonics block. The explicit teacher's guides in this book can support teachers who have little or no phonics experience. This program provides all the information teachers need to be successful.

The Research Behind *StartUp*™ *Phonics*

StartUp™ *Phonics* reflects the most current research on how to teach phonemic awareness and phonics effectively. The bibliography on page xlvi summarizes this research.

Phonological and Phonemic Awareness

Phonological awareness is the ability to hear and orally manipulate sounds in spoken language. It includes the recognition of words within sentences, the ability to hear rhyming units within words, the ability to hear syllables within words, and the ability to hear and manipulate phonemes, or individual sounds, within words, which is known as phonemic awareness. Phonemic awareness is the understanding that the sounds of spoken language work together to make words.

What the Research Says About Phonological and Phonemic Awareness Instruction	What *StartUp*™ *Phonics* Provides
• Before children learn to read print, they need to become aware of how the sounds in words work.	• Fifty Level 1 lessons reinforce students' awareness of sounds so that they can more easily move to sound/symbol relationships.
• If children do not know letter names and shapes, they need to be taught them along with phonemic awareness.	• The Level 1 lessons also reinforce letter recognition and formation through explicit modeling and guided practice.
• Children who have phonemic awareness skills are likely to have an easier time learning to read and spell.	• As short vowel and consonant phonics instruction begin with Level 2, Unit 1, phonemic awareness instruction continues on a daily basis.
• Blending and segmenting phonemes in words is likely to produce greater benefits to students' reading than teaching several types of manipulation.	• Students practice orally blending and segmenting sounds in every phonics unit.

Benchmark Phonics • StartUp Level 1 • Phonological Awareness & Letter Awareness ©2012 Benchmark Education Company, LLC

Phonics Instruction

Phonics instruction focuses on teaching students the relationships between the sounds of the letters and the written symbols. In phonics instruction, students are taught to use these relationships to read and write words. Phonics instruction assumes that these sound/symbol relationships are systematic and predictable and that knowing these relationships will help students read words that are new to them.

What the Research Says About Phonics Instruction	What *StartUp*™ *Phonics* Provides
• Systematic and explicit phonics instruction is more effective than nonsystematic or no phonics instruction.	• *StartUp*™ *Phonics* units provide direct, explicit teaching of letter/sound relationships in a clearly defined sequence that schedules high-utility letter sounds early in the sequence.
• Students need frequent and cumulative review of taught letter sounds.	• Every *StartUp*™ *Phonics* unit incorporates review of previously taught letters and sounds.
• Effective phonics programs provide ample opportunities for students to apply their knowledge of letters and sounds to the reading of words, sentences, and stories.	• Within each unit, students progress from blending individual words to reading word lists to reading decodable texts that contain only words built on the phonics elements students have been taught. A carefully controlled number of sight words are introduced in each unit, as needed to read meaningful decodable texts.
• Approximately two years of phonics instruction is sufficient for most students.	• For most students, *StartUp*™ *Phonics* provides a year of beginning phonics instruction. *BuildUp*™ *Phonics*, for extending phonics instruction, also provides a year's worth of instruction. However, both kits can be paced to speed up or slow down instruction as needed.

Components at a Glance

Lesson Resources

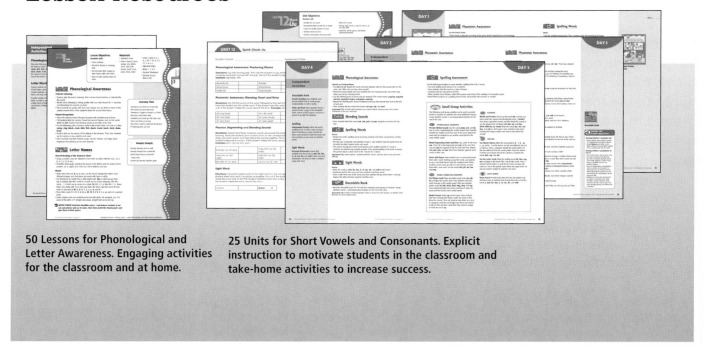

50 Lessons for Phonological and Letter Awareness. Engaging activities for the classroom and at home.

25 Units for Short Vowels and Consonants. Explicit instruction to motivate students in the classroom and take-home activities to increase success.

Books and Posters

Front

26 Start Up™ Poetry Posters (double-sided; 17"x 23")

Back

26 Decodable Titles (6-packs) (8 pages; 5 7/8" x 6")

Take-Home Books (available on the resource site)

Support Tools

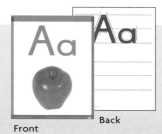

Front   Back

Alphabet Frieze Cards/ Letter Formation Cards
(set of 26; 8$\frac{1}{2}$" x 11")

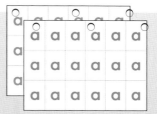

Front   Back

Front   Back

StartUp™ Picture Word Cards
(set of 129; 5" x 7")

Phonetic Letter Card Set

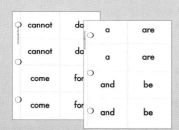

StartUp™ Sight Word Card Set
(set of 42; 8$\frac{1}{2}$" x 11")

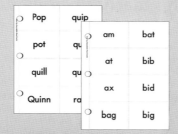

StartUp™ Decodable Word Card Set
(set of 153; 8$\frac{1}{2}$" x 11")

Alphabet Charts
(one 17$\frac{1}{2}$"x 23")

Student Alphabet Strips
(set of 20; 17$\frac{1}{2}$" x 23")

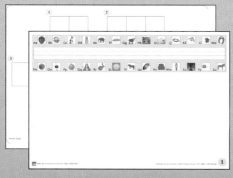

Student Workmats
(set of 20; 14" x 19$\frac{1}{2}$")

- **StartUp™ Song and Rhyme CD**
- **StartUp™ Poetry CD**

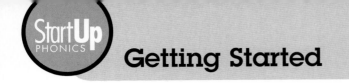

Getting Started Checklist

Use the following checklist to help you get ready to use *StartUp™ Phonics.*

❑ **Unpack your program components.** Use the *StartUp™ Phonics* Components at a Glance on pages viii–ix to make sure you have everything.

❑ **Organize your classroom.**

❑ **Familiarize yourself with how to use the program.** Read Using the Components on pages xii–xxi and review the *StartUp™* skills on pages xxiv-xxvii. Visit http://phonicsresources.benchmarkeducation.com to familiarize yourself with the digital tools available.

❑ **Study the teacher's guides.** Examine the posters, decodable texts, support tools, and assessments.

❑ **Prepare for assessment.**

- Download and print one copy of each student assessment page (laminate, if desired).

- Make one copy per student of the teacher record forms.

❑ **Prepare for instruction.**

- Create the spelling transparency (using the blackline master on page xli).

- Make copies of the parent letter (on pages xlii–xliii) if you wish to establish a home connection at the beginning of the year.

- Make student copies of lesson activities for upcoming lessons (using the downloadable blackline masters on the resource site).

❑ **Administer the pre-assessment** and analyze the results to determine your students' starting point in the *StartUp™ Phonics* skill sequence and how to group students for small-group instruction.

Setting Up Your Classroom

StartUp™ Phonics instruction accommodates whole-group and small-group instruction as well as center activities. Use the model below to help you prepare your classroom.

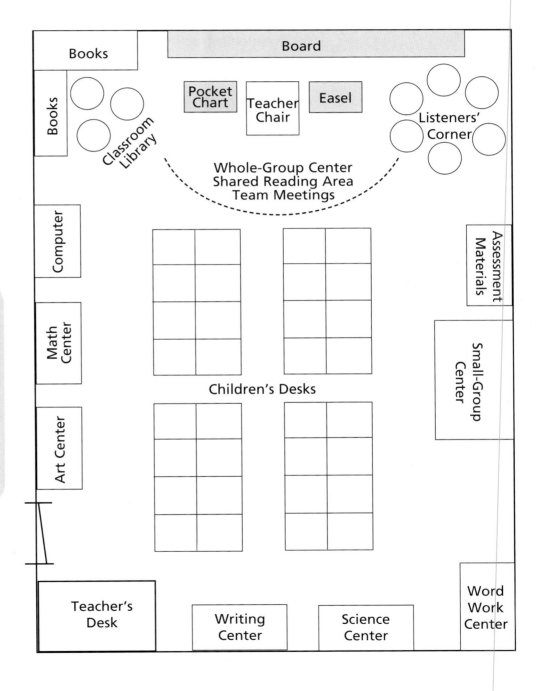

StartUp Level 1 Teacher's Guides for Phonological and Letter Awareness

Fifty Level 1 lessons begin the instructional sequence in *StartUp*™ *Phonics*. These explicit lessons are intended for students who need beginning-of-the-year instruction or review in phonological and letter awareness before they move to phonemic awareness and phonics instruction. Use the pre/post assessments to determine whether or not to use these lessons with your students.

Phonological awareness instruction follows a systematic sequence that moves from simple to more complex phonological tasks.

Two explicit phonological awareness activities are provided in each lesson using the Song and Rhyme CD, picture cards, and other support tools.

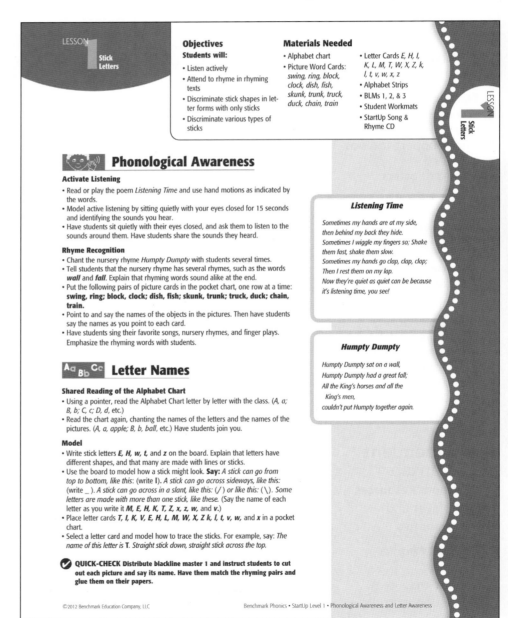

LESSON **1** Stick Letters

Objectives
Students will:
- Listen actively
- Attend to rhyme in rhyming texts
- Discriminate stick shapes in letter forms with only sticks
- Discriminate various types of sticks

Materials Needed
- Alphabet chart
- Picture Word Cards: *swing, ring, block, clock, dish, fish, skunk, trunk, truck, duck, chain, train*
- Letter Cards *E, H, I, K, L, M, T, W, X, Z, k, l, t, v, w, x, z*
- Alphabet Strips
- BLMs 1, 2, & 3
- Student Workmats
- StartUp Song & Rhyme CD

Phonological Awareness

Activate Listening
- Read or play the poem *Listening Time* and use hand motions as indicated by the words.
- Model active listening by sitting quietly with your eyes closed for 15 seconds and identifying the sounds you hear.
- Have students sit quietly with their eyes closed, and ask them to listen to the sounds around them. Have students share the sounds they heard.

Rhyme Recognition
- Chant the nursery rhyme *Humpty Dumpty* with students several times.
- Tell students that the nursery rhyme has several rhymes, such as the words **wall** and **fall**. Explain that rhyming words sound alike at the end.
- Put the following pairs of picture cards in the pocket chart, one row at a time: **swing, ring; block, clock; dish, fish; skunk, trunk; truck, duck; chain, train.**
- Point to and say the names of the objects in the pictures. Then have students say the names as you point to each card.
- Have students sing their favorite songs, nursery rhymes, and finger plays. Emphasize the rhyming words with students.

Letter Names

Shared Reading of the Alphabet Chart
- Using a pointer, read the Alphabet Chart letter by letter with the class. (*A, a; B, b; C, c; D, d,* etc.)
- Read the chart again, chanting the names of the letters and the names of the pictures. (*A, a, apple; B, b, ball,* etc.) Have students join you.

Model
- Write stick letters *E, H, w, t,* and *z* on the board. Explain that letters have different shapes, and that many are made with lines or sticks.
- Use the board to model how a stick might look. **Say:** *A stick can go from top to bottom, like this:* (write I). *A stick can go across sideways, like this:* (write _). *A stick can go across in a slant, like this:* (/) *or like this:* (\). *Some letters are made with more than one stick, like these.* (Say the name of each letter as you write it *M, E, H, K, T, Z, x, z, w,* and *v.*)
- Place letter cards *T, I, K, V, E, H, L, M, W, X, Z k, l, t, v, w,* and *x* in a pocket chart.
- Select a letter card and model how to trace the sticks. For example, say: *The name of this letter is* **T**. *Straight stick down, straight stick across the top.*

🕐 **QUICK-CHECK Distribute blackline master 1 and instruct students to cut out each picture and say its name. Have them match the rhyming pairs and glue them on their papers.**

Listening Time

*Sometimes my hands are at my side,
then behind my back they hide.
Sometimes I wiggle my fingers so; Shake them fast, shake them slow.
Sometimes my hands go clap, clap, clap;
Then I rest them on my lap.
Now they're quiet as quiet can be because it's listening time, you see!*

Humpty Dumpty

*Humpty Dumpty sat on a wall,
Humpty Dumpty had a great fall;
All the King's horses and all the King's men,
couldn't put Humpty together again.*

©2012 Benchmark Education Company, LLC

Benchmark Phonics • StartUp Level 1 • Phonological Awareness and Letter Awareness

To provide students with a quick beginning-of-the-year review of previously taught skills, complete each lesson in one day. To provide more intensive instruction and practice, spread the lessons over more than one day by slowing the pace, repeating some of the activities, and incorporating the small-group and independent activities.

Letter lessons begin with letter discrimination and then move through the alphabet from A to Z. All lessons include modeling, guided practice, and writing.

Independent Activities

Phonological Awareness

Place the following picture cards in the literacy center: **swing, ring, block, clock, dish, fish, skunk, trunk, truck, duck, chain, train.** Have students say the name of each picture card and match the picture cards that rhyme.

Letter Discrimination

Instruct students to sort individual sets of stick-letter cards according to their various attributes: long sticks, short sticks, and long and short sticks.

Provide models of the various types of sticks, as well as various stick letters, on a large sheet of butcher paper. Students can practice writing sticks and stick letters.

Guided Practice
- Ask individual students to select a letter card from the pocket chart, trace the sticks, and say the name of the letter. Provide support as needed.
- Provide additional support for students who need it by guiding their fingers over the sticks in the letter and telling them the letter name.
- Repeat the task until all the letter names have been identified and the students understand that all the letters are alike because they have sticks.
- Distribute individual sets of letter cards **H, K, L, M, t, v,** and **z**. Have students line up the cards on their workmats.
- Instruct students to pull down each stick letter.
- Ask them to trace the sticks of each letter and say the name of the letter if they can.
- Help individual students use a finger to trace the sticks in the letters or give them the name of the letter, if necessary.

Write
- Have students practice writing the different types of sticks on their workmats. Model each type of stick again on the board. Say: *Make some straight sticks on your workmats. Make them like this:* (l, l, l ,l). *Make some slanted sticks like this:* (/, /, /, /). *Make some slanted sticks like this:* (\, \, \, \). *Make some sticks like this:* (_, _, _, _).
- Distribute blackline master 2 and ask students to trace the different types of sticks. (The blackline master may be completed at this time or in a literacy center.)

 QUICK-CHECK Use blackline master 3. Instruct students to cut out each letter card and sort the letters into those that have short sticks and those that have long sticks.

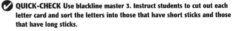 **Small Group Activities**

Select from the following small group activities to provide hands-on practice for students who need extra support.

LISTENING
Have students sit quietly with their eyes closed. Ask them to listen to the sounds around them for 15 seconds. Encourage students to discuss the sounds they heard. Then have students listen for an additional 15 seconds with their eyes open. Discuss the difference between what they heard with their eyes open and closed.

Small-group and independent activities help you support students at a range of levels.

RHYME RECOGNITION
Recite *Humpty Dumpty* to students, emphasizing the rhyming words by whispering them, saying them louder, or using crescendo. Recite the poem again. As you come to some of the rhyming couplets, stop and say each word of the couplet. Tell students to use a signal if the words rhyme. For example, ask: *Do the words* **wall** *and* **fall** *rhyme? If they do, show me by giving me a "thumbs up" signal.*

LETTER DISCRIMINATION
Use the board to show the different types of sticks and that some letters are made with more that one stick. Say the name of each letter as you form it. Distribute letter cards that have only sticks to students. Choose from **E, H, I, K, L, M, T, V, W, X, Z, k, l, t, v, w, x,** and **z**. As you model the task with letter cards in the pocket chart, have each student trace the sticks and say the letter name.

StartUp Level 2 Teacher's Guides for Phonemic Awareness and Phonics

The twenty-five Level 2 units in *StartUp™ Phonics* teach short vowels and consonants in a systematic sequence that supports current research on best practices. All teacher's guides follow a consistent sequence that provides five days of instruction targeting one phonetic element and its sound.

Start with phonological and phonemic awareness. (Days 1–4)

Move to quick sound/symbol relationship activities with word and picture sorts. (Days 1–2)

Provide blending practice daily with decodable word lists. (Days 1–4)

Introduce and practice six spelling words per unit. (Days 1-4)

Beginning with Unit 6, introduce and practice sight words. (Days 1–4)

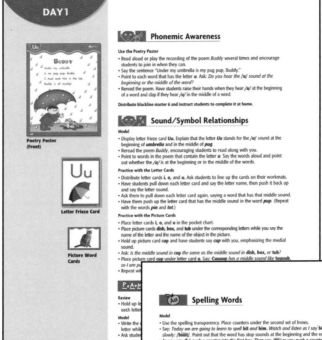

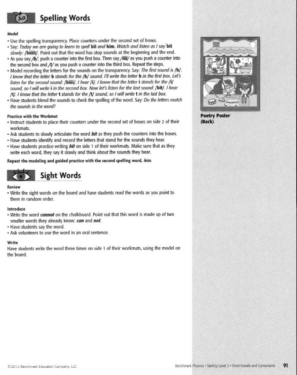

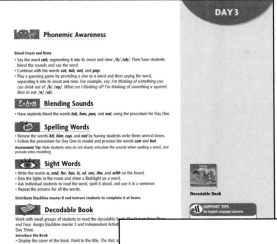

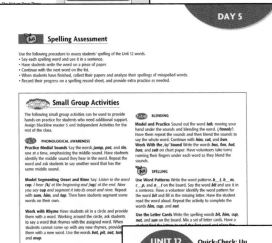

Work with small groups of students to read decodable texts. (Days 3–4) Students who are not reading the text complete a blackline master and independent activities.

Use the quick-checks provided on the last page of each unit to assess students' progress. Work with small groups of students who need extra support. (Day 5) Students who are not in the small group complete a blackline master and independent activities.

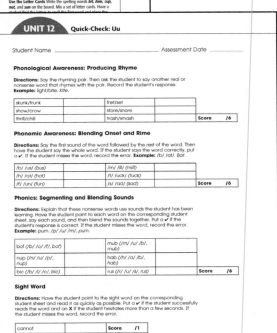

StartUp™ **Poetry Posters**

Twenty-six Poetry Posters—one for each letter of the alphabet—can be folded for easy storage. (Unit 1 has two Poetry Posters.) The posters are used for whole-group instruction as well as small-group activities to provide additional support.

The front of each poster features a playful, alliterative poem that emphasizes the target letter and sound. It is used to develop phonemic awareness and sound/symbol relationships.

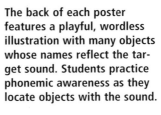

The back of each poster features a playful, wordless illustration with many objects whose names reflect the target sound. Students practice phonemic awareness as they locate objects with the sound.

Decodable Texts

StartUp™ Phonics follows best-practice research that recommends students have frequent opportunities to apply phonics skills in authentic reading contexts.

The *StartUp™ Phonics* decodable texts have been carefully written so that only phonics elements that students have learned and practiced appear in the books. A very limited number of sight words are also used in the decodable texts. New sight words are always explicitly taught before they appear in students' decodable text reading. Previously taught sight words are also reviewed.

20 Fiction Titles

Twenty engaging fiction titles introduce the new skills. Beginning in Level 2, Unit 6, one of these decodable titles is provided for each phonetic element that is introduced. Students will respond to the playful illustrations and the cast of characters they encounter from story to story.

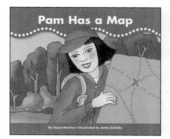  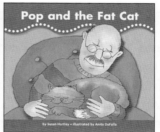

6 Nonfiction Titles

Six nonfiction, photo-illustrated decodable titles provide additional practice after all twenty-five Level 2 units of the StartUp™ Phonics skill sequence have been completed.

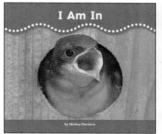  

Take-Home Books

allow you to send students home with a real book to share with family members. Available for download and printing on the resource site.

Support Tools

High-quality, durable, and motivating manipulatives are provided to support the instruction throughout *StartUp™ Phonics*.

StartUp™ Song and Rhyme CD

Twelve playful, familiar rhymes and twelve well-loved children's songs support the Level 1 phonological awareness lessons.

StartUp™ Poetry CD

Lively readings of all twenty-six *StartUp™ Phonics* Poetry Posters support the phonological awareness lessons and literacy center/independent activities in the Level 2 units.

26 Alphabet Frieze Cards/Letter Formation Cards

The uppercase and lowercase letters are displayed on the front of each laminated frieze card, along with a photo illustrating the target sound. The card fronts are used in Level 1 lessons and Level 2 units to teach letter recognition and sound/symbol relationships. On the back of each card are letter formation guides and writing lines. The card backs are used to model and provide practice with letter formation in the Level 1 lessons.

Front   Back

StartUp™ Picture Word Cards

All picture cards used in the Level 1 lessons and Level 2 units are provided in an alphabetically indexed box within the *StartUp™ Phonics* storage box. Because you will use these cards in many lessons, it is recommended that you store them alphabetically for easy reference. The cards have pictures on one side, for phonological awareness practice, and pictures with labels on the other side for picture and word sorts.

Front   Back

Front   Back

StartUp™ Sight Word Card Set

Two copies of every sight word explicitly taught in *StartUp™ Phonics* are provided on card stock to support whole-group instruction and small-group and independent activities. These cards are used in multiple lessons. Keep in mind that blackline master versions of these cards, organized by lesson, are also provided on the resource site.

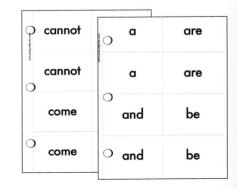

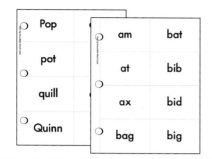
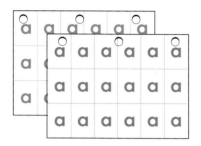

StartUp™ Decodable Word Card Set

One copy each of every decodable word used in *StartUp™ Phonics* lessons is also provided on card stock. These cards are also used in multiple lessons. Blackline master versions of these cards are provided on the resource site for each Level 2 unit.

Phonetic Letter Card Set

Multiple copies of each letter of the alphabet are provided on card stock for use in pocket chart, small-group, literacy center, and independent activities with Level 1 lessons and Level 2 units. Blackline master versions of these cards are also provided on the resource site for each Level 1 lesson and Level 2 unit.

Student Alphabet Strips

Twenty alphabet strips, sized for student use, support learning the alphabet and sound/symbol relationships.

Alphabet Charts

A large alphabet chart is included in the kit. It is a useful resource for the Level 1 letter-awareness lessons.

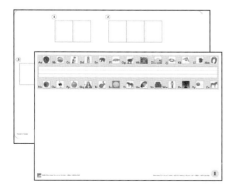

Student Workmats

The twenty laminated Student Workmats are double-sided. Side one has an alphabet strip at the top and a blank space on the bottom for practice in writing letters and words with a dry-erase marker. Side two has elkonian boxes for two-, three-, four-, five-, and six-letter words. Students can practice hearing and recording sounds with counters or by writing letters in the boxes.

Reproducible Tools, Activities, and Home Connections Resources

Every Level 1 lesson and Level 2 unit has corresponding reproducibles needed for instruction. They are all available for download and printing at http://phonicsresources.benchmarkeducation.com. You may also choose to display these resources on your whiteboard.

am	bat
cot	cub
fat	fit
ham	mat
mop	nip
nut	Sam
sip	sub
tip	tub

is	has
a	the
and	of
with	see
for	no
cannot	

All lesson-specific tools are provided in reproducible form for literacy center and independent activities. Once you make reproducible versions, save them in envelopes.

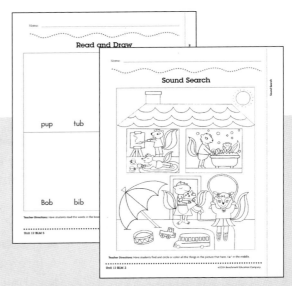

Activity blackline masters, referenced in each lesson or unit, are available.

Level 1 lessons have one take-home activity.

Level 2 units have three take-home activities.

Use the parent letter in English or Spanish on pages xlii–xliii to establish a home connection at the beginning of the year.

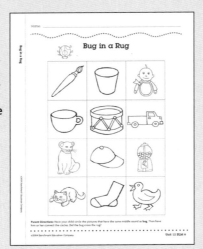

Four in a Row

cannot	the	and
with	see	for
no	cannot	of
is	a	has

is	the	with	no
a	and	see	cannot
has	of	for	cannot

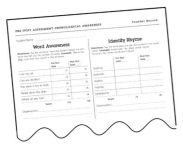

All assessments have teacher records for documenting individual student progress.

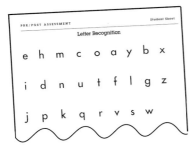

Letter, phonics, and sight word assessments have student pages. You may wish to laminate these for reuse.

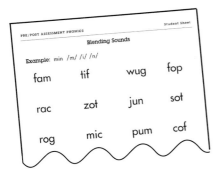

Phonics assessments require students to decode nonsense words in order to truly assess their knowledge of sound/symbol relationships.

Assessment

This *StartUp™ Phonics* Teacher Resource System provides a variety of methods for you to gather, record, and evaluate information about your students' knowledge of sound/symbol relationships. Based on this information, you can decide what skill instruction your students need and whether they would benefit from small-group instruction.

Pre/Post Assessments

Pre/Post Assessments cover all skills taught in the kit. All assessments are administered on a one-to-one basis. They are located behind the Assessment tab in this TRS.

Quick-Checks

Quick-Check Assessments, included after each week of instruction, include phonological awareness, segmenting and blending, and sight-word recognition. As you analyze student responses, note which sounds or sight words give students difficulty. You may decide to provide further practice in the skill by using the small-group activities in each unit. The student sheets are available on the resource site.

Informal Observation

It is recommended that in addition to the Pre/Post and Quick-Check Assessments, you use informal observation to note whether students are mastering the skills. If you are uncertain about how a student is performing on a skill, call on that student to perform the task during the lesson and observe what he/she does. If you feel the student requires more practice, use the small-group mini-lessons provided within each unit. Throughout the unit, teacher assessment tips are provided to help you make observations about student progress.

Quick-Check Teacher Record

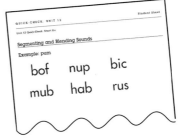

Quick-Check Student Sheet

A sight word assessment measures all the words that are not decodable.

Managing Instruction in the Phonics Block

Grouping Students

Use the pre-test to determine where in the kit you will begin instruction (Level 1 lessons or Level 1 units). The pre-test will also help you determine whether or not you need to do all sections of the unit lessons, and it will help you identify students who will need more support in learning the sounds. The independent activities for each unit allow you to provide meaningful learning for the larger group while you work with a small group or individual students who have not mastered the skills.

Most of the Level 2 unit instruction can be done with a whole class, using a pocket chart or chalkboard for demonstration purposes. Assessment tips throughout the unit help you determine whether students need further support in a small group. It is recommended that decodable texts be read with small groups of students so that you can more easily monitor students' reading.

Pacing the Instruction

StartUp™ Phonics has been designed for use with a whole group during the phonics block of your comprehensive literacy program. Each day's lesson is designed to fit within a 20–30 minute instructional block of time. During this time, students will practice sounding out words in a controlled, decodable format. They should have the opportunity to apply their decoding skills, along with other reading strategies, during the small-group reading block of your literacy program.

Each unit spans a five-day period. In other words, you will introduce one skill per week. You can choose to use some or all of the activities, depending on the needs of your students. For example, you may find that you want students to work more quickly and learn a new skill every three days. If this is the case, you may select from any of the activities that you feel will most benefit your students.

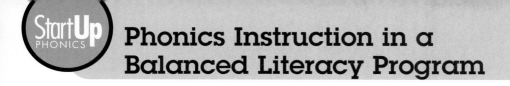
Introducing Benchmark Literacy for Grades K–6

Benchmark Education Company is known for its pedagogically sound, research-proven literacy solutions. Now Benchmark Education is proud to put these carefully developed, scientifically tested components into one comprehensive, easy-to-implement reading program for Grades K–6. Benchmark Literacy supports all the daily components of high-quality reading instruction, including the research-based, systematic approach found in StartUp Phonics.

You will find:

- **Assessment** to drive instruction and help teachers monitor progress

- **Interactive read-alouds** to model good-reader strategies with award-winning trade literature

- **Shared reading mini-lessons** to explicitly model comprehension, vocabulary, and fluency

- **Differentiated small-group reading** that builds seamlessly on shared-reading instruction and addresses the needs of above-, on-, and below-level readers, as well as English learners and special-needs students

- **Independent reading** to encourage the transfer of skills and strategies

- **Phonemic awareness, phonics, and word study** to build strong decoding and word-solving strategies

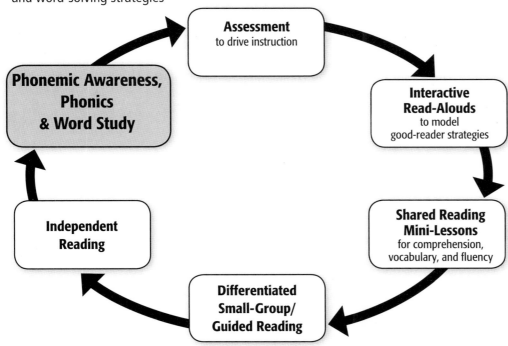

 **Skills**

LEVEL 1 Phonological and Letter Awareness Lessons

Week 1	Day 1	Day 2	Day 3	Day 4	Day 5
Phonological Awareness Skill	• Listening • Rhyme recognition	• Listening • Rhyme recognition	• Listening • Rhyme recognition	• Listening • Rhyme recognition	• Listening • Rhyme recognition
Letter Recognition and Formation	Letter Discrimination • Stick letters	Letter Discrimination • Straight sticks	Letter Discrimination • Slanted Sticks	Letter Discrimination • Straight and slanted sticks	Letter Discrimination • Review stick letters
Week 2	**Day 1**	**Day 2**	**Day 3**	**Day 4**	**Day 5**
Phonological Awareness Skill	• Listening • Rhyme recognition	• Listening • Rhyme recognition	• Listening • Rhyme recognition	• Listening • Rhyme recognition	• Listening • Rhyme recognition
Letter Recognition and Formation	Letter Discrimination • Circles and curves	Letter Discrimination • Sticks and curves	Letter Discrimination • Sticks and circles	Letter Discrimination • Letters that look alike	• Review letter discrimination
Week 3	**Day 1**	**Day 2**	**Day 3**	**Day 4**	**Day 5**
Phonological Awareness Skill	• Word discrimination • Rhyme recognition	• Word discrimination • Concept of words	• Listening • Rhyme recognition	• Word discrimination • Concept of words	• Word discrimination • Rhyme recognition
Letter Recognition and Formation	A	a	B	b	Cc
Week 4	**Day 1**	**Day 2**	**Day 3**	**Day 4**	**Day 5**
Phonological Awareness Skill	• Word discrimination • Rhyme recognition	• Listening • Concept of words	• Word discrimination • Concept of words	• Word discrimination • Concept of words	• Word discrimination • Concept of words
Letter Recognition and Formation	D	d	E	e	F
Week 5	**Day 1**	**Day 2**	**Day 3**	**Day 4**	**Day 5**
Phonological Awareness Skill	• Rhyme recognition • Concept of words	• Word discrimination • Concept of sentences	• Listening • Concept of sentences	• Rhyme recognition • Concept of words	• Listening • Producing rhyme
Letter Recognition and Formation	f	G	g	H	h

Week 6	Day 1	Day 2	Day 3	Day 4	Day 5
Phonological Awareness Skill	• Producing rhyme • Segmenting words by syllables	• Identifying rhyme • Segmenting words by syllables	• Listening • Segmenting words by syllables	• Segmenting initial sounds • Identifying repeated sounds	• Segmenting initial sounds • Segmenting compound words
Letter Recognition and Formation	Ii	J	j	Kk	L

Week 7	Day 1	Day 2	Day 3	Day 4	Day 5
Phonological Awareness Skill	• Producing rhyme • Segmenting compound words	• Producing rhyme • Segmenting initial sounds	• Listening • Producing rhyme	• Identifying rhyme • Segmenting initial sounds	• Sound discrimination • Segmenting words by syllables
Letter Recognition and Formation	l	M	m	N	n

Week 8	Day 1	Day 2	Day 3	Day 4	Day 5
Phonological Awareness Skill	• Producing rhyme • Segmenting initial sounds	• Sound discrimination • Segmenting words into syllables	• Performing steps in a sequence • Identifying rhyme	• Segmenting initial sounds • Segmenting words by syllables	• Segmenting initial sounds • Segmenting words into syllables
Letter Recognition and Formation	Oo	Pp	Q	q	R

Week 9	Day 1	Day 2	Day 3	Day 4	Day 5
Phonological Awareness Skill	• Producing rhyme • Segmenting words into syllables	• Blending syllables • Segmenting initial sounds	• Blending syllables • Segmenting words into syllables	• Sound discrimination • Blending syllables	• Segmenting initial sounds • Segmenting words into syllables
Letter Recognition and Formation	r	Ss	T	t	Uu

Week 10	Day 1	Day 2	Day 3	Day 4	Day 5
Phonological Awareness Skill	• Producing rhyme • Segmenting initial sounds	• Blending syllables • Segmenting initial sounds	• Blending syllables • Segmenting initial sounds	• Blending syllables • Segmenting initial sounds	• Segmenting initial sounds • Segmenting words by syllables
Letter Recognition and Formation	Vv	Ww	Xx	Yy	Zz

LEVEL 2 Phonemic Awareness and Phonics Units

Unit/ Phonics Skill	Phonological Awareness Skill	Phonemic Awareness Skill	Sight Words	Spelling Words
1/Mm and Short Aa	listening for rhyme	• initial /m/ • medial /a/	N/A	am
2/Ss	listening for rhyme	• initial /s/ • listening for initial sounds	N/A	am, Sam
3/Tt	listening for rhyme	• initial /t/ • listening for initial consonant sounds	N/A	am, Sam, mat, sat, Tam
4/Nn	listening for rhyme	• initial /n/ • differentiating consonant sounds	N/A	man, Nat, mat, sat, Tam, tan
5/ Short Ii	listening for rhyme	• medial /i/ • differentiating medial sounds	N/A	man, Nat, tan, am, in, sit
6/Ff	listening for rhyme	• initial /f/ • listening for initial consonants	is	man, mat, fan, fit, if, fin
7/Pp	identifying and producing rhyme	• initial /p/ • blending and segmenting onset and rime	a, has	tin, fat, tap, pat, pin, sip
8/ Short Oo	identifying and producing rhyme	• medial /o/ • discriminating medial sounds	the	nap, fit, on, pot, mop, not
9/Cc	identifying and producing rhyme	• initial /k/ • discriminating sounds	and, of	pit, top, cat, can, cot, cap
10/Hh	identifying and producing rhyme	• initial /h/ • blending and segmenting onset and rime	with, see	nip, can, hat, him, hit, hop
11/Bb	identifying and producing rhyme	• initial /b/ • identifying final consonants	for, no	hat, sap, bat, bib, bin, bit
12/ Short Uu	identifying and producing rhyme	• initial and medial /u/ • blending onset and rime	cannot	bit, him, cup, nut, sun, but
13/Rr	identifying and producing rhyme	• initial /r/ • differentiating final consonants	have, are	cup, hop, run, rub, rip
14/ Short Ee	identifying and producing rhyme	• initial and medial /e/ • segmenting and blending onset and rime	said	rap, cab, met, pen, let, ten
15/Gg	identifying and producing rhyme	• initial /g/ • segmenting and blending onset and rime	I, you, me	men, bin, tag, get, beg, rug

Unit/ Phonics Skill	Phonological Awareness Skill	Phonemic Awareness Skill	Sight Words	Spelling Words
16/Dd	identifying and producing rhyme	• initial /d/ • blending phonemes	come, here, to	bag, pen, dig, had, red, did
17/Ww		• initial /w/ • blending phonemes • blending and segmenting onset and rime	my, look, he	bed, pat, wet, win, wig, wed
18/Ll		• initial /l/ • differentiating final consonants • blending and segmenting onset and rime	go	bag, dad, let, lap, lid, lip
19/Jj		• initial /j/ • initial sound substitution • blending and segmenting phonemes	put, want	lab, bin, job, jam, Jim, Jen
20/Kk		• initial /k/ • initial sound substitution • blending and segmenting sounds	this, she, saw	led, bad, kiss, Kit, jam, Kim
21/Yy		• initial /y/ • vowel substitution • blending and segmenting sounds	now, like, do	jog, but, yes, yap, yell, yet
22/Vv		• initial /v/ • vowel substitution • blending and segmenting sounds	home, they, went	yet, tip, vet, van, Val, hug
23/Qq		• initial /kw/ • initial sound substitution • blending and segmenting sounds	good	jam, bad, quit, yet, quip, quill
24/Xx		• final /ks/ • vowel substitution • blending and segmenting sounds	was, be, we	sip, did, mix, box, fox, wax
25/Zz		• initial and final /z/ • final sound substitution • blending and segmenting sounds	there, then, out	fox, quiz, zip, buzz, zap, fuzz

Core Kit Materials Correlated to Units

Level 2 Unit	Decodable Title	Poetry Posters	Alphabet Frieze Cards
1	N/A	Melons and Muffins; Apple Pie	Mm; Aa
2	N/A	Seven Silly Sailors	Ss
3	N/A	Turtles	Tt
4	N/A	Nip the Newt	Nn
5	N/A	Baking	Ii
6	Fit	Fuzzy Fox and Fiddle	Ff
7	Pam Has a Map	Pet Parade	Pp
8	Pop	Oliver and Dot	Oo
9	Pop and the Fat Cat	Camping	Cc
10	The Hot Pan	Happy Thoughts	Hh
11	The Bib	Baby Bird	Bb
12	The Nut	Buddy	Uu
13	Rob	The Race	Rr
14	Mem the Hen	The Red Hen	Ee
15	Get the Gum	By the Garden Gate	Gg
16	The Red Pen	Dot	Dd
17	The Wig	Worm	Ww
18	Pop and Len	Lenny Lion	Ll
19	The Job	Jumping	Jj
20	Kit and Kim	King Karl's Kangaroo	Kk
21	Yip and Yap	Yellow	Yy
22	The Vet	Violins and Violets	Vv
23	Quinn	The Queen's Nap	Qq
24	The Sax	Max	Xx
25	Buzz, Buzz	Baby Zigzag	Zz

Lessons

LESSON
1
Stick
Letters

LESSON
1
Stick
Letters

Objectives

Students will:

- Listen actively
- Attend to rhyme in rhyming texts
- Discriminate stick shapes in letter forms with only sticks
- Discriminate various types of sticks

Materials Needed

- Alphabet chart
- Picture Word Cards: *swing, ring, block, clock, dish, fish, skunk, trunk, truck, duck, chain, train*
- Letter Cards *E, H, I, K, L, M, T, W, X, Z, k, l, t, v, w, x, z*
- Alphabet Strips
- BLMs 1, 2, & 3
- Student Workmats
- StartUp Song & Rhyme CD

 # Phonological Awareness

Activate Listening

- Read or play the poem *Listening Time* and use hand motions as indicated by the words.
- Model active listening by sitting quietly with your eyes closed for 15 seconds and identifying the sounds you hear.
- Have students sit quietly with their eyes closed, and ask them to listen to the sounds around them. Have students share the sounds they heard.

Rhyme Recognition

- Chant the nursery rhyme *Humpty Dumpty* with students several times.
- Tell students that the nursery rhyme has several rhymes, such as the words **wall** and **fall**. Explain that rhyming words sound alike at the end.
- Put the following pairs of picture cards in the pocket chart, one row at a time: **swing, ring; block, clock; dish, fish; skunk, trunk; truck, duck; chain, train.**
- Point to and say the names of the objects in the pictures. Then have students say the names as you point to each card.
- Have students sing their favorite songs, nursery rhymes, and finger plays. Emphasize the rhyming words with students.

Letter Names

Shared Reading of the Alphabet Chart

- Using a pointer, read the Alphabet Chart letter by letter with the class. (*A, a; B, b; C, c; D, d*, etc.)
- Read the chart again, chanting the names of the letters and the names of the pictures. (*A, a, apple; B, b, ball*, etc.) Have students join you.

Model

- Write stick letters *E, H, w, t,* and *z* on the board. Explain that letters have different shapes, and that many are made with lines or sticks.
- Use the board to model how a stick might look. **Say:** *A stick can go from top to bottom, like this:* (write **I**). *A stick can go across sideways, like this:* (write _). *A stick can go across in a slant, like this:* (/) *or like this:* (\ ). *Some letters are made with more than one stick, like these.* (Say the name of each letter as you write it *M, E, H, K, T, Z, x, z, w,* and *v.*)
- Place letter cards *T, I, K, V, E, H, L, M, W, X, Z k, l, t, v, w,* and *x* in a pocket chart.
- Select a letter card and model how to trace the sticks. For example, say: *The name of this letter is* **T**. *Straight stick down, straight stick across the top.*

✓ **QUICK-CHECK** Distribute blackline master 1 and instruct students to cut out each picture and say its name. Have them match the rhyming pairs and glue them on their papers.

Listening Time

*Sometimes my hands are at my side,
then behind my back they hide.
Sometimes I wiggle my fingers so; Shake
them fast, shake them slow.
Sometimes my hands go clap, clap, clap;
Then I rest them on my lap.
Now they're quiet as quiet can be because
it's listening time, you see!*

Humpty Dumpty

*Humpty Dumpty sat on a wall,
Humpty Dumpty had a great fall;
All the King's horses and all the
  King's men,
couldn't put Humpty together again.*

Independent Activities

Phonological Awareness

Place the following picture cards in the literacy center: **swing, ring, block, clock, dish, fish, skunk, trunk, truck, duck, chain, train.** Have students say the name of each picture card and match the picture cards that rhyme.

Letter Discrimination

Instruct students to sort individual sets of stick-letter cards according to their various attributes: long sticks, short sticks, and long and short sticks.

Provide models of the various types of sticks, as well as various stick letters, on a large sheet of butcher paper. Students can practice writing sticks and stick letters.

Guided Practice

- Ask individual students to select a letter card from the pocket chart, trace the sticks, and say the name of the letter. Provide support as needed.
- Provide additional support for students who need it by guiding their fingers over the sticks in the letter and telling them the letter name.
- Repeat the task until all the letter names have been identified and the students understand that all the letters are alike because they have sticks.
- Distribute individual sets of letter cards **H, K, L, M, t, v,** and **z.** Have students line up the cards on their workmats.
- Instruct students to pull down each stick letter.
- Ask them to trace the sticks of each letter and say the name of the letter if they can.
- Help individual students use a finger to trace the sticks in the letters or give them the name of the letter, if necessary.

Write

- Have students practice writing the different types of sticks on their workmats. Model each type of stick again on the board. Say: *Make some straight sticks on your workmats. Make them like this:* (I, I, I ,I). *Make some slanted sticks like this:* (/, /, /, /). *Make some slanted sticks like this:* (\, \, \, \, \). *Make some sticks like this:* (_, _, _, _, _).
- Distribute blackline master 2 and ask students to trace the different types of sticks. (The blackline master may be completed at this time or in a literacy center.)

 QUICK-CHECK Use blackline master 3. Instruct students to cut out each letter card and sort the letters into those that have short sticks and those that have long sticks.

 # Small Group Activities

Select from the following small group activities to provide hands-on practice for students who need extra support.

LISTENING
Have students sit quietly with their eyes closed. Ask them to listen to the sounds around them for 15 seconds. Encourage students to discuss the sounds they heard. Then have students listen for an additional 15 seconds with their eyes open. Discuss the difference between what they heard with their eyes open and closed.

RHYME RECOGNITION
Recite *Humpty Dumpty* to students, emphasizing the rhyming words by whispering them, saying them louder, or using crescendo. Recite the poem again. As you come to some of the rhyming couplets, stop and say each word of the couplet. Tell students to use a signal if the words rhyme. For example, ask: *Do the words* **wall** *and* **fall** *rhyme? If they do, show me by giving me a "thumbs up" signal.*

LETTER DISCRIMINATION
Use the board to show the different types of sticks and that some letters are made with more that one stick. Say the name of each letter as you form it. Distribute letter cards that have only sticks to students. Choose from **E, H, I, K, L, M, T, V, W, X, Z, k, l, t, v, w, x,** and **z.** As you model the task with letter cards in the pocket chart, have each student trace the sticks and say the letter name.

LESSON 2
Straight Stick Letters

Objectives
Students will:
- Listen for the direction or source of sounds
- Recognize words that rhyme
- Discriminate letters made of straight lines or sticks
- Write different types of straight sticks

Materials Needed
- Alphabet Chart
- Picture Word Cards: *plant, ring, swing, blouse, house, claw, saw, vest, nest, pan, fan, feet, wheat, ant, skate, gate*
- Letter Cards *E, F, H, I, L, T, t, l*
- Alphabet Strips
- BLMs *1, 2 & 3*
- Student Workmats
- StartUp Song & Rhyme CD

Phonological Awareness

Activate Listening
- Read or play the recording of the poem *Listening Time* and use hand motions as indicated by the words.
- Have one student go to another part of the room. Close your eyes and show students you are listening quietly.
- Ask the student to make a sound. Point to the part of the room where the sound is coming from and open your eyes.
- Have students say the "Fe-fi-fo-fum" verse. Ask them to close their eyes and listen quietly. Go to another part of the room and make a sound. Have students keep their eyes closed and point in the direction of the sound.

Rhyme Recognition
- Chant the nursery rhyme *Hey Diddle Diddle* with students several times.
- Point out that the nursery rhyme has two pairs of rhyming words.
- Ask students to repeat the pairs of rhyming words.

Letter Discrimination

Shared Reading of the Alphabet Chart
- Using a pointer, read the Alphabet Chart letter by letter with the class. (*A, a; B, b; C, c; D, d,* etc.)
- Read the chart again, chanting the names of the letters and the names of the pictures. (*A, a, apple; B, b, ball,* etc.) Have students join you.

Model
- Write stick letters *E, H, I,* and *t* on the chalkboard. Explain that letters have different shapes, and that many are made only with straight sticks.
- Use the chalkboard to model how straight sticks might look. Say: *A straight stick can go from top to the bottom, like this:* (write **|**). *A straight stick can go across sideways, like this:* (write **_**). *Some letters are made with more than one straight stick, like these.* (Say the name of each letter as you write it: *E, F, H, I, L, T, t*)
- Place letter cards *E, F, H, I, L, T, l,* and *t* in the pocket chart.
- Select a letter card and model how to trace the straight sticks. For example, say: *The name of this letter is* **H**. *Straight down, straight down, and straight across the middle.*

✓ **QUICK-CHECK Distribute blackline master 1. Instruct students to say the name of each picture. Then have them draw lines to match the pictures whose names rhyme.**

Listening Time
Sometimes my hands are at my side.
Then behind my back they hide.
Sometimes I wiggle my fingers so;
Shake them fast, shake them slow.
Sometimes my hands go clap,
*   clap, clap;*
Then I rest them on my lap.
Now they're quiet as quiet can be
Because it's listening time, you see!

Fe-fi-fo-fum
Where is that sound coming from?
Listen, listen! (whisper this line)

Hey Diddle Diddle
Hey diddle diddle,
The cat and the fiddle,
The cow jumped over the moon.
The little dog laughed to see
*   such a sport,*
And the dish ran away with
*   the spoon.*

Independent Activities

Phonological Awareness

Place the following picture cards in the literacy center: **pan, fan, feet, wheat, skate, gate.** Have students say the name of each picture card and match the picture cards that rhyme.

Letter Discrimination

Instruct students to look through a set of letter cards and pick out the letters that are made with straight sticks.

Provide models of the types of straight sticks, as well as straight stick letters, on a large sheet of butcher paper. Students can practice writing straight sticks and straight stick letters.

Have students use clay or another modeling material to form straight stick letters.

Guided Practice

- Ask individual students to select a letter card from the pocket chart, trace the straight sticks, and say the name of the letter. Provide support as needed.
- Provide additional support for students who need it by guiding their fingers over the straight sticks in the letter and telling them the letter name.
- Repeat the task until all the letter names have been identified and students understand that all the letters are alike because they have only straight sticks.
- Distribute individual sets of letter cards **E, F, H, I, L, T, l,** and **t.** Have students line up the cards on their workmats.
- Instruct students to pull down each straight stick letter.
- Ask them to trace the straight sticks of each letter and say the name of the letter if they can.
- Help individual students use a finger to trace the straight sticks in the letters or give them the name of the letter, if necessary.

Write

- Have students practice writing the different types of straight sticks on their workmats. Model each type of straight stick again on the chalkboard. Say: *Make some straight sticks on your workmats. Make them like this:* (|, |, |, |). *Make some straight sticks like this:* (_, _, _, _).
- Distribute blackline master 2 and ask students to practice writing the different types of straight sticks. (The blackline master may be completed at this time or in a literacy center.)

 QUICK-CHECK Use blackline master 3. Instruct students to look at the circled letter in each row. Have them draw a line under the matching letter.

 Small Group Activities

Select from the following small group activities to provide hands-on practice for students who need extra support.

LISTENING

Have students sit quietly with their eyes closed. Make the same sound in different parts of the room. For example, ring a bell several times. Have students point in the direction of the sound as they say the "Fe-fi-fo-fum" verse.

RHYME RECOGNITION

Recite or play the recording of *Hey Diddle Diddle* with students. Have them shout the rhyming words and whisper the rest of the words. Then display the following pairs of picture cards in the pocket chart: **ring/swing, blouse/house, claw/plant, saw/ant, vest/nest.** Say each pair of picture names with students. Have them tell whether the words in each pair rhyme or not.

LETTER DISCRIMINATION

Use the chalkboard to show how a straight stick might look and how some letters, such as *E, F, H, I, L, T,* and *t,* are made with more than one straight stick. Say the name of each letter as you form it. Distribute letter cards for straight stick letters. Choose from **E, F, H, I, L, l, T,** and **t.** As you model the task with letter cards in the pocket chart, have students trace the sticks in the letters and say the letter names.

Lesson Objectives
Students will:

- Listen to and remember the sequence of sounds
- Distinguish rhyming words from nonrhyming words
- Discriminate letters made of slanted stick shapes
- Write different types of slanted stick shapes

Materials Needed

- Alphabet Chart
- Picture Word Cards: *fox, box, cat, snake, cake, bell, fan, pan, feet, chick, stick, ant, duck, truck, saw, clock, block, pan*
- Letter Cards *X, x, V, v, W, w, y*
- Alphabet Strips
- BLMs *1, 2 & 3*
- Student Workmats

 Phonological Awareness

Activate Listening

- Close your eyes and choose a student to make a sound. Then try to identify the sound.
- Have students close their eyes. Make a knocking sound and tell students to open their eyes. Ask them to identify the sound they heard.
- Ask students to listen carefully. Make two distinct sounds, such as coughing and dropping a book. Have students open their eyes, identify the sounds, and tell which they heard first and last. Repeat with two other sounds (sneeze, finger snapping).

Rhyme Recognition

- Put picture cards **cat, fox,** and **box** in the pocket chart.
- Ask students to name each picture as you point to it. If students name the picture incorrectly, tell them the correct name of the picture.
- Explain that one of the pictures does not belong with the others. Tell students to listen to the names of the pictures and tell which picture does not belong.
- Say the names of the pictures again, emphasizing the rhyme. Repeat with the following sets of picture cards: **snake, cake, bell; fan, pan, feet; chick, stick, ant; duck, truck, saw.**
- If students have difficulty, explain that words rhyme because they have the same middle and ending sounds.

Aa Bb Cc **Letter Discrimination**

Shared Reading of the Alphabet Chart

- Using a pointer, read the Alphabet Chart letter by letter with the class. (*A, a; B, b; C, c; D, d,* etc.)
- Read the chart again, chanting the names of the letters and the names of the pictures. (*A, a, apple; B, b, ball,* etc.) Have students join you.

Model

- Write the slanted stick letters *X, x, V, v, W, w,* and *y* on the chalkboard. Explain that letters have different shapes and that many are made with only slanted sticks.
- Use the chalkboard to model how a letter that has only slanted sticks might look. Say: *A stick can go across in a slant, like this:* (write /) *or this:* (write \). *Some letters are made with more than one slanted stick, like these.* (Say the name of each letter as you write it: *W, X, V, w, x, v, y*)
- Place letter cards **W, X, V, w, x, v,** and **y** in the pocket chart.
- Select a letter card and model how to trace the slanted sticks. For example, say: *The name of this letter is* **V**. *Slant down and in, slant down and in.*

 QUICK-CHECK Distribute blackline master 1. Ask students to say the name of each picture in each row. Then have them circle the picture that does not rhyme with the others.

Independent Activities

Phonological Awareness

Place the following picture cards in the literacy center: **chick, stick, fox, box, duck, truck, snake, cake.** Have students say the name of each picture card and match the picture cards that rhyme.

Letter Discrimination

Have students look through a set of letter cards and pick out the letters that are made with slanted sticks.

Provide models of the types of slanted sticks, as well as various slanted stick letters, on a large sheet of butcher paper. Students can practice writing slanted sticks and slanted stick letters.

Have students use clay or another modeling material to form slanted stick letters.

Have students look around the room or in a book and locate letters that have only slanted sticks.

Guided Practice

- Ask individual students to select a letter card from the pocket chart, trace the slanted sticks, and say the name of the letter. Provide support as needed.
- Provide additional support for students who need it by guiding their fingers over the slanted sticks in the letter and telling them the letter name.
- Repeat the task until all the letter names have been identified and students understand that all the letters are alike because they have only slanted sticks.
- Distribute individual sets of letter cards **V, W, X, v, w, x,** and **y.** Have students line up the cards on their workmats.
- Tell students to pull down each slanted stick letter.
- Ask them to trace the slanted sticks of each letter and say its name if they can.
- Help individual students use a finger to trace the slanted sticks in the letters or give them the name of the letter, if necessary.

Write

- Have students practice writing the different types of slanted sticks on their workmats. Model each type of slanted stick again on the chalkboard. Say: *Make some slanted sticks on your workmats. Make them like this:* (). *Make some slanted sticks like this:* ().
- Distribute blackline master 2. Ask students to practice writing the different types of slanted sticks. (The ` master may be completed at this time or in a literacy center.)

✔ **QUICK-CHECK Use blackline master 3. Tell students to draw a line to match each slanted stick letter.**

Small Group Activities

Select from the following small group activities to provide hands-on practice for students who need extra support.

LISTENING

Have students sit quietly with their eyes closed. Make two different sounds. Ask students to identify the sounds and the order in which they heard them (first and last). Make any of the following sounds: shut a door, sharpen a pencil, knock, clap, stomp your foot, open a drawer, cut paper with scissors, write on the chalkboard.

RHYME RECOGNITION

Have students sort the picture cards from the lesson into categories—words that rhyme and words that do not rhyme. Have them explain their choices. If they cannot explain, show that the nonrhyming card has different sounds in the middle and at the end than the other two cards.

LETTER DISCRIMINATION

On the chalkboard, show how a slanted stick might look and how some letters, such as **V, W, X, v, w, x,** and **y,** are made with more than one slanted stick. Say the name of each letter as you form it. Distribute letter cards for slanted stick letters. Choose from **V, W, X, v, w, x,** and **y.** As you model the task with letter cards in the pocket chart, have students trace the sticks in the letters and say the letter names.

Objectives

Students will:

- Listen to and remember the sequence of sounds
- Identify rhyming words
- Discriminate letters made of both straight and slanted sticks
- Write straight and slanted sticks

Materials Needed

- Alphabet Chart
- Picture Word Cards: *car, jar, top, mop, vest, nest, soap, rope, ski, tree, blouse, house, claw, saw, clock, block*
- Letter Cards *A, K, M, N, Y, Z, k, z*
- Alphabet Strips
- BLMs *1, 2 & 3*
- Student Workmats

Phonological Awareness

Activate Listening

- Close your eyes. Have a student make three sounds. Try to identify the sounds.
- Have students close their eyes. Drop a book, then cough, then clap. Have students open their eyes and identify the sounds they heard, in order.
- Ask students to listen carefully. Make three distinct sounds. Tell students to identify the sound they heard first, next, and last. Once students can identify sounds in sequence, have them identify sounds out of order.

Rhyme Recognition

- Put picture cards **top, block, nest, ski, saw, jar, rope,** and **blouse** in the pocket chart.
- Ask students to name each picture as you point to it. If they name the picture incorrectly, tell them the correct name of the picture.
- Explain that you will play "I Spy." Say: *I spy a word that rhymes with* **vest**. Have students find the card in the pocket chart that rhymes with ***vest***.
- Repeat the sentence with each of the following prompts: ***house, claw, sock, mop, car, tree, soap***.
- If students have difficulty, explain that words rhyme because they have the same middle and ending sounds.

Letter Discrimination

Shared Reading of the Alphabet Chart

- Using a pointer, read the Alphabet Chart letter by letter with the class. (*A, a; B, b; C, c; D, d,* etc.)
- Read the chart again, chanting the names of the letters and the names of the pictures. (*A, a, apple; B, b, ball,* etc.) Have students join you.

Model

- Write the stick letters ***A, K, M, N, Y, Z, k,*** and ***z*** on the chalkboard. Explain that letters have different shapes and that many are made with both straight and slanted sticks.
- Use the chalkboard to model how a letter that has straight and slanted sticks might look. Say: *A stick can go across in a slant, like this:* (write /) *or this:* (write \). *A straight stick can go from top to bottom, like this* (write |). *A straight stick can go across sideways, like this* (write _). *Some letters are made with more than one type of stick, like these.* (Say the name of each letter as you point to the letters on the chalkboard.)
- Place letter cards **A, K, M, N, Y, Z, k,** and **z** in the pocket chart.
- Select a letter card. Model tracing the slanted and straight sticks. For example, say: *The name of this letter is* **K**. *Straight down, slant in to the middle, slant out to the bottom.*

✔ **QUICK-CHECK Distribute blackline master 1. Tell students to say the name of each picture and draw a line to match the rhyming words.**

Independent Activities

Phonological Awareness

Place the picture cards for Lesson 4 in the literacy center. Have students say the name of each picture card and match the picture cards that rhyme.

Letter Discrimination

Have students look through a set of letter cards and pick out the letters that are made with slanted and straight sticks.

Provide models of straight and slanted sticks, as well as various straight and slanted stick letters, on a large sheet of butcher paper. Students can practice writing various types of sticks as well as straight and slanted stick letters.

Have students use clay or another modeling material to form slanted stick letters.

Have students look around the room or in a book and locate letters that have only slanted sticks.

August Heat

In August, when the days are hot,
I like to find a shady spot
And hardly move a single bit—
And sit, and sit, and sit.

Guided Practice

- Ask individual students to select a letter card from the pocket chart, trace the straight and slanted sticks, and say the name of the letter. Provide support as needed.
- Provide additional support for students who need it by guiding their fingers over the straight and slanted sticks in the letter and telling them the letter name.
- Repeat the task until all the letter names have been identified and students understand that all the letters are alike because they have both slanted and straight sticks.
- Distribute individual sets of letter cards **A, K, M, N, Y, Z, k,** and **z.** Have students line up the cards on their workmats.
- Tell students to pull down each stick letter.
- Ask them to trace the slanted and straight sticks of each letter and say the name of the letter if they can.
- Help individual students use a finger to trace the straight and slanted sticks in the letters or give them the name of the letter, if necessary.

Write

- Have students practice writing the different types of sticks on their workmats. Model each type of stick again on the chalkboard. Say: *Make some straight sticks on your workmats. Make them like this:* (|, |, |). *Make some straight sticks that look like this.* (_, _, _). *Make some slanted sticks like this* (/, /, /) *and this* (\, \, \).
- Distribute blackline master 2 and ask students to practice writing the slanted and straight sticks. (The blackline master may be completed at this time or in a literacy center.)

 QUICK-CHECK Use blackline master 3. Tell students to circle the matching letter in each row.

 ## Small Group Activities

Select from the following small group activities to provide hands-on practice for students who need extra support.

LISTENING

Have students sit with their eyes closed. Make three different sounds. Ask students to identify the sounds and the order in which they heard them (first, second, or last). Use the following sound sequences: shut a door, ring a bell, drop a book; sharpen a pencil, stomp your feet, ring a bell; knock, clap, slap your thigh; clap, shut a door, cough.

RHYME RECOGNITION

Recite the poem *August Heat.* Recite it again and stop after each rhyming couplet. Ask students to tell you the two words that rhyme. Repeat with other nursery rhymes or poems.

LETTER DISCRIMINATION

Use the chalkboard to show how a slanted stick might look, how a straight stick might look, and how some letters are made with both straight and slanted sticks. Say the name of each letter as you form it. Distribute letter cards that have letters with both straight and slanted sticks to students. Choose from **A, K, M, N, Y, Z, k,** and **z.** As you model the task with letter cards in the pocket chart, have students trace the sticks and say the letter names.

Objectives

Students will:

- Listen to and remember the omitted sound in a sequence
- Identify rhyming words
- Discriminate straight and slanted sticks in letter forms with straight sticks, slanted sticks, and both straight and slanted sticks
- Write straight and slanted sticks

Materials Needed

- Alphabet Chart
- Picture Word Cards: *swing, ring, block, clock, dog, frog, chick, stick, skunk, trunk, truck, duck, goat, coat, chain, train*
- Letter Cards *E, H, I, L, M, T, V, W, X, Z, k, l, t, v, w, x, z*
- Alphabet Strips
- BLMs *1, 2 & 3*
- Student Workmats
- Start Up Song & Rhyme CD

 Phonological Awareness

Activate Listening

- Read or play the recording of *Listening Time*, using the hand motions indicated by the words.
- Close your eyes. Have a student make three sounds. Identify the sounds.
- Have students close their eyes. Make three sounds: whistle, scratch, and knock. Ask them to identify the sounds they heard, in order.
- Repeat the sequence, but omit a sound. Have students name that sound.
- Have students make sounds for the rest of the class to guess.

Rhyme Recognition

- Put picture cards **swing, ring, block, clock, dog, frog, chick, stick, skunk, trunk, truck, duck, goat, coat, chain,** and **train** into a bag.
- Have students, one at a time, pull two cards out of the bag and show them to the rest of the class. Have the class say the two picture names.
- Ask if the two words rhyme. If so, they should give a "thumbs up"; if not, a "thumbs down." If the words rhyme, the cards go in the pocket chart. If not, the student should put them back into the bag.
- Repeat the activity until all picture cards are matched.
- If students have difficulty, explain that words rhyme because they have the same middle and ending sounds.

> ### *Listening Time*
> *Sometimes my hands are at my side.*
> *Then behind my back they hide.*
> *Sometimes I wiggle my fingers so;*
> *Shake them fast, shake them slow.*
> *Sometimes my hands go clap,*
>   *clap, clap;*
> *Then I rest them on my lap.*
> *Now they're quiet as quiet can be*
> *Because it's listening time, you see!*

Aa Bb Cc **Letter Discrimination**

Shared Reading of the Alphabet Chart

- Using a pointer, read the Alphabet Chart letter by letter with the class. (*A, a; B, b; C, c; D, d,* etc.)
- Read the chart again, chanting the names of the letters and the names of the pictures. (*A, a, apple; B, b, ball,* etc.) Have students join you.

Model

- Write the stick letters *E, H, I, L, M, T, V, W, X, Z, k, l, t, v, w, x,* and *z* on the board. Explain that many letters are made with straight sticks or slanted sticks or both straight and slanted sticks.
- Use the board to model how slanted and straight sticks might look. Say: *A stick can go across in a slant, like this:* (write /) *or this:* (write \). *A straight stick can go from top to bottom, like this* (write |). *A straight stick can go across sideways, like this* (write _). *Some letters are made with more than one type of stick, like these.* (Say the name of each letter as you point to the letters written on the board.)
- Put letter cards **E, H, I, L, M, T, V, W, X, Z, k, l, t, v, w, x,** and **z** in the pocket chart.
- Select a card and model how to trace the sticks. For example, say: *This letter is* **K**. *Straight down, slant in to the middle, slant out to the bottom.*

✔ **QUICK-CHECK** Distribute blackline master 1. Have students cut out each picture card, name the picture, and match the rhyming pairs. Have students glue each rhyming pair on their papers.

Independent Activities

Phonological Awareness

Place the following picture cards in the literacy center: **swing, ring, block, clock, nose, rose, dish, fish, skunk, trunk, truck, duck, goat, coat, chain, train.** Have students say the name of each picture card and match the picture cards that rhyme.

Letter Discrimination

Have students sort a set of letter cards into straight stick, slanted stick, and straight and slanted stick letters. Use letter cards **E, H, I, L, M, T, V, W, X, Z, k, l, t, v, w, x,** and **z.**

Provide models of stick letters on a large sheet of butcher paper, as well as various stick letters. Students can practice writing various types of sticks.

The Itsy-Bitsy Spider

The itsy-bitsy spider
climbed up the water spout;
Down came the rain
and washed the spider out.
Out came the Sun
and dried up all the rain.
So the itsy-bitsy spider
climbed up the spout again.

Guided Practice

- Ask individual students to select a letter card from the pocket chart, trace the straight and slanted sticks, and say the name of the letter. Provide support as needed.
- Provide additional support for students who need it by guiding their fingers over the sticks in the letter and telling them the letter name.
- Repeat the task until all the letter names have been identified and students understand that all the letters are alike because they have sticks.
- Distribute individual sets of letter cards **E, H, I, L, M, T, V, W, X, Z, k, l, t, v, w, x,** and **z.** Have students line up the cards on their workmats.
- Tell students to pull down each stick letter.
- Ask them to trace the sticks of each letter and say the name of the letter if they can.
- Help individual students use a finger to trace the sticks in the letters or give them the name of the letter, if necessary.

Write

- Have students practice writing the different types of sticks on their workmats. Model each type of stick again on the board. Say: *Make some straight sticks on your workmats. Make them like this: (|, |, |). Make some straight sticks that look like this (_, _, _). Make some slanted sticks like this (/, /, /) and this (\, \, \).*
- Distribute blackline master 2 and ask students to practice writing the slanted and straight sticks. (The blackline master may be completed at this time or in a literacy center.)

 QUICK-CHECK Use blackline master 3. Have students cut out each letter and sort the letters into straight stick letters, slanted stick letters, and straight and slanted stick letters.

 # Small Group Activities

Select from the following small group activities to provide hands-on practice for students who need extra support.

LISTENING

Have students sit with their eyes closed. Make three animal sounds. Ask students to identify the sounds. Then make sounds again, omitting one of the three. Ask students which sound is missing. Use combinations of these animal sounds: *meow, woof, neigh, oink, cluck, baa.*

RHYME RECOGNITION

Recite or play the recording of *The Itsy-Bitsy Spider*. Emphasize the rhyming words. Ask students to tell you two words that rhyme in the poem. Chant the poem again until all the rhyming words have been identified. Repeat the activity with other nursery rhymes or poems.

LETTER DISCRIMINATION

Use the board to show how a slanted stick might look (write /, \) and how a straight stick might look (write |, _). Show how some letters, such as *E, H, I, L, M, T, V, W, X, Z, k, l, t, v, w, x,* and *z,* are made with sticks. Say the name of each letter as you form it. Distribute stick letter cards, choosing from those on the board. Model the task with letter cards in the pocket chart. Have students trace the sticks in the letters and say the letter names.

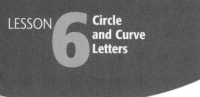

LESSON 6 — Circle and Curve Letters

Objectives
Students will:

- Listen to a sequence of sounds and duplicate the pattern
- Identify rhyming words
- Discriminate letters made of circles or curves
- Write circles and curves

Materials Needed
- Alphabet Chart
- Picture Word Cards: *swing, ring, chain, coat, skunk, trunk, fish, clock, block, duck, truck, car, jar, shell, bell, dish*
- Letter Cards *C, O, S, c, o, s*
- Alphabet Strips
- BLMs *1, 2 & 3*
- Student Workmats
- StartUp Song & Rhyme CD

Phonological Awareness

Activate Listening
- Clap once, then twice (clap, clap-clap). Demonstrate how to copy the pattern by tapping with a pencil the pattern you clapped.
- Repeat with a few simple patterns.
- Tell students to listen carefully and duplicate your pattern after you clap it. Begin with simple patterns: *clap-clap, clap; clap, clap-clap, clap; clap-clap, clap, clap.*
- Make the sequences more difficult by adding finger snapping and foot stomping.
- Stop after each pattern to let students try to duplicate it. Then let individual students create patterns for the rest of the group to mimic.

Rhyme Recognition
- Chant the poem *My Nose* to students.
- Say the following word groups from the poem: ***breathe, smell, well; nose, it, blows.*** Have students tell which two words in each group rhyme.
- Repeat the activity with other nursery rhymes or poems.
- If students have difficulty, explain that words rhyme because they have the same middle and ending sounds.

> ### My Nose
> It doesn't breathe;
> It doesn't smell;
> It doesn't feel
> So very well.
>
> I am discouraged
> With my nose.
> The only thing it
> Does is blows.

Letter Discrimination

Shared Reading of the Alphabet Chart
- Using a pointer, read the Alphabet Chart letter by letter with the class. (*A, a; B, b; C, c; D, d,* etc.)
- Read the chart again, chanting the names of the letters and the names of the pictures. (*A, a, apple; B, b, ball,* etc.) Have students join you.

Model
- Write circle and curve letters ***O, C, s,*** and ***u*** on the board. Explain that letters have different shapes and that many are made with circles and curves.
- Use the board to model how a curve might look. Say: *A curve can go up from the bottom of the board, then across and down, like this* (write ∩). *A curve can go from near the top of the board, down and across, like this* (write U). *A curve can go from the top toward the bottom, like this* (write ⊂) *or this* (write ⊃). *Some letters are made with curves, like these.* (Say the name of each letter as you point to the letters written on the board.)
- As you review each kind of curve, have students write each one on their workmats.
- Model how a circle looks. For example, say: *A circle goes all the way around, like this.* (write O O O O o o o) Have students practice writing circles on their workmats.

> ✓ **QUICK-CHECK** Distribute blackline master 1. Tell students to say the name of each picture in each row. Then have them draw a circle around the picture that does not rhyme with the other two.

Independent Activities

Phonological Awareness

Place the following picture cards in the literacy center: **skunk, trunk, duck, truck, swing, ring, fish, dish.** Have students say the name of each picture card and match the picture cards that rhyme.

Letter Discrimination

Have students look through a set of letter cards and pick out the letters that are made with circles and curves.

Provide models of circles and curves, as well as circle and curve letters, on a large sheet of butcher paper. Students can practice writing circle and curve letters.

Have students use clay or another modeling material to form circle and curve letters.

Hey, Diddle Diddle

Hey diddle diddle,
The cat and the fiddle,
The cow jumped over the moon.
The little dog laughed to see
such a sport,
And the dish ran away with
the spoon.

Guided Practice

- Place letter cards **C, O, S, c, o,** and **s** in the pocket chart. Select a card and trace the curves or circles. Say: *The letter name is C. Down and around.*
- Ask individual students to select a card from the pocket chart, trace the curves or circles, and say the name of the letter.
- Provide support for students who need it by guiding their fingers over the circles and curves in the letter and telling them the letter name.
- Repeat until all the letter names have been identified and students understand that the letters are alike because they have circles or curves.
- Distribute individual sets of letter cards **C, O, S, c, o,** and **s.** Have students line up the cards on their workmats.
- Tell students to pull down each circle or curve letter.
- Ask them to trace the circles and curves of each letter and say its name.
- Help individual students use a finger to trace the circles or curves in the letters or give them the name of the letter, if necessary.

Write

- Have students practice writing circles and curves on their workmats. Model each type of curve and circle again on the board. Say: *A curve can go up from the bottom of the board, then across and down, like this:* (write ∩) *A curve can go from near the top of the board, down and across, like this (*write U*). A curve can go from the top toward the bottom, like this* (write ⊂) *or this* (write ⊃) *Some letters are made with curves, like these.* (Say the name of each letter as you point to the letters written on the board.)
- Distribute blackline master 2 and ask students to practice writing the circles and curves. (The blackline master may be completed at this time or in a literacy center.)

 QUICK-CHECK Use blackline master 3. Instruct students to look at the circled letter in each row. Have them draw a circle around the matching letter.

 # Small Group Activities

Select from the following small group activities to provide hands-on practice for students who need extra support.

LISTENING

Have students close their eyes. Make the same sound in different parts of the room. For example, ring a bell several times. Have students point in the direction of the sound as they say the "Fe-fi-fo-fum" verse.

RHYME RECOGNITION

Recite or play the recording of *Hey, Diddle Diddle*. Have students shout the rhyming words. Then display the following pairs of picture cards in the pocket chart: **swing/ring, chain/ train, skunk/trunk, fish/dish, clock/block, duck/truck, car/jar, shell/bell.** Say each pair of picture names with students. Have them tell whether the words in each pair rhyme or not.

LETTER DISCRIMINATION

Model how curves might look. Say: *A curve can go up from the bottom of the board, then across and down, like this* (write ∩). *A curve can go from near the top of the board, down and across, like this (*write ∩*). A curve can go from the top toward the bottom, like this* (write ⊂) *or this* (write ⊃). *Some letters are made with curves, like these.* (Say the name of each letter as you point to the letters written on the board.) Distribute letter cards **C, c, O, o, S,** and **s.** As you model the task with letter cards in the pocket chart, have students trace the circles and curves and say the letter names.

Objectives

Students will:

- Identify changes in familiar spoken text
- Identify rhyming words
- Discriminate letter forms that have sticks and curves
- Write sticks and curves

Materials Needed

- Alphabet Chart
- Picture Word Cards: *house, trunk, truck, horn, saw, coat, car, plant, blouse, skunk, duck, corn, claw, goat, jar, ant*
- Letter Cards *B, D, G, J, U, e, f, h, j, m, n, r, u*
- Alphabet Strips
- BLMs *1, 2 & 3*
- Student Workmats
- StartUp song & rhyme CD

Phonological Awareness

Activate Listening

- Sing or play the recording of *The Itsy-Bitsy Spider* and have students perform the finger movements with you.
- Explain that you need help with the song's words. Say the words in each line and tell students to clap if they think you say an incorrect word.
- Say a line of the song. Then say the line again with an incorrect word. Clap at this point and say the correct word. Say: *The itsy-bitsy spider climbed up the water spout.* Then say: *The itsy-bitsy spider went down . . .* Clap and say *up.*
- Repeat with another line from the song until students understand the task.

Rhyme Recognition

- Explain that you will say all but the last word of a rhyming phrase and hold up a picture card. Ask students to complete each phrase with the name of the card.

The Itsy-Bitsy Spider

The itsy-bitsy spider
climbed up the water spout;
Down came the rain
And washed the spider out.
Out came the Sun
And dried up all the rain.
So the itsy-bitsy spider
climbed up the spout again.

Letter Discrimination

Shared Reading of the Alphabet Chart

- Using a pointer, read the Alphabet Chart letter by letter with the class. (*A, a; B, b; C, c; D, d,* etc.)
- Read the chart again, chanting the names of the letters and the names of the pictures. (*A, a, apple; B, b, ball,* etc.) Have students join you.

Model

- Write the stick and curve letters **B, h, R,** and **f** on the board. Explain that letters have different shapes and that many are made with sticks and curves.
- Use the board to model how letters with sticks and curves might look. Say: *Some letters have sticks and curves.* Say the name of each of the following letters as you write it: **B, J, Q, R, e, f, h, u.**
- Place letter cards **B, D, G, J, U, e, f, h, j, m, n, r,** and **u** in the pocket chart. Select a card and trace the sticks and curves in the letter. Say: *The name of this letter is* **B.** *Straight down, around and down to the middle, around and down to the bottom.*

A **blouse** that is in a _____.
    (**house**)
A **skunk** who lives in a _____.
    (**trunk**)
A **duck** who drives a _____.
    (**truck**)
A **thorn** that is blowing a _____.
    (**horn**)
A **claw** that is using a _____.
    (**saw**)
A **goat** who is eating a _____.
    (**coat**)
A **star** who is driving a _____.
    (**car**)
An **ant** who is eating a _____.
    (**plant**)

✓ **QUICK-CHECK Distribute blackline master 1. Tell students to draw lines to match the rhyming words.**

Phonological Awareness

Place the following picture cards in the literacy center: **house, trunk, truck, horn, saw, coat, car, plant, blouse, skunk, duck, corn, claw, goat, jar, ant.** Have students say the name of each picture card and match the picture cards that rhyme.

Letter Discrimination

Tell students to look through a set of letter cards and pick out the letters that are made with sticks and curves.

Provide models of sticks and curves, as well as various stick and curve letters, on a large sheet of butcher paper. Students can practice writing various types of sticks and curves as well as stick and curve letters.

Give each student a small notebook. Have students search the room to find and write letters that have sticks and curves.

Let students use pipe cleaners to form stick and curve letters.

Guided Practice

- Place letter cards **B, D, G, J, U, e, f, h, j, m, n, r,** and **u** in the pocket chart.
- Ask individual students to select a letter card from the pocket chart, trace the sticks and curves, and say the name of the letter. Provide support as needed.
- Provide additional support for students who need it by guiding their fingers over the sticks and curves in the letter and telling them the letter name.
- Repeat until all of the letter names have been identified and students understand that all of the letters are alike because they have sticks and curves.
- Distribute individual sets of letter cards **B, D,** and **e.** Have students line up the cards on their workmats.
- Tell students to pull down each letter.
- Ask them to trace the sticks and curves of each letter and say the name of the letter if they can.
- Help individual students use a finger to trace the sticks and curves in the letters or give them the name of the letter, if necessary.

Write

- Have students practice writing letters that have sticks and curves on their workmats. Say: *Some letters are made with sticks and curves, like these.* Say the name and shape(s) of the letters *B, D, G, J, R, U, e, f, h, j, m, n, r,* and *u.*
- Distribute blackline master 2 and ask students to trace the sticks and curves. (The blackline master may be completed at this time or in a literacy center.)

 QUICK-CHECK Use blackline master 3. Have students cut out all of the letters that are made of sticks and curves. They should then glue them into the boxes.

 # Small Group Activities

Select from the following small group activities to provide hands-on practice for students who need extra support.

LISTENING

Recite or play the recording of *Hickory, Dickory, Dock* with students. Recite the poem again, making some changes in each line. Have students indicate each incorrect word and say the correct word.

RHYME RECOGNITION

Place the following pairs of picture cards in the pocket chart: **house/ trunk, corn/horn, saw/claw, ant/plant, blouse/skunk, duck/truck, coat/ goat, jar/car.** Say the names of each picture pair and have students repeat them. Have students tell you if the pair rhymes.

LETTER DISCRIMINATION

Distribute cards for letters that have sticks and curves. Choose from **B, D, G, J, R, U, e, f, h, j, m, n, r,** and **u.** As you model the task with letter cards in the pocket chart, have students trace the sticks and curves in the letters and say the letter names.

Objectives
Students will:
- Identify changes in familiar spoken text
- Identify rhyming words and nonrhyming words
- Discriminate letters made of sticks and circles
- Write sticks and circles

Materials Needed
- Alphabet Chart
- Picture Word Cards: *ant, plant, coat, bat, cat, light, nest, vest, duck, gate, skate, skunk, train, chain, frog*
- Letter Cards *P, p, a, b, d, g, q, Q*
- Alphabet Strips
- BLMs *1, 2, & 3*
- Student Workmats
- StartUp Song & Rhyme CD

Phonological Awareness

Activate Listening
- Sing or listen to the recording of *Baa, Baa Black Sheep* with students.
- Recite the poem and make several changes to the words, as shown at right. Tell students to clap if they think you say an incorrect word.
- Repeat the process with other poems and songs, and have students identify the changes you make.

Rhyme Recognition
- Say: *The skunk lives in the trunk.* Have students repeat the sentence. Ask: *Do any words rhyme?* Help students name the rhyming words, **skunk** and **trunk**. Then say: *The skunk lives in the tree. Do any words rhyme?* Point out that there are no rhyming words.
- Repeat with the sentences shown (below right). Have students clap two times and name the words if they hear rhyming words. Have them clap one time and say nothing if they do not.

Letter Discrimination

Shared Reading of the Alphabet Chart
- Using a pointer, read the Alphabet Chart letter by letter with the class. (*A, a; B, b; C, c; D, d,* etc.)
- Read the chart again, chanting the names of the letters and the names of the pictures. (*A, a, apple; B, b, ball,* etc.) Have students join you.

Model
- Write the stick and circle letters *a, b,* and *Q* on the board. Explain that letters have different shapes and that many are made with sticks and circles.
- Use the board to model how letters with sticks and circles might look. Say: *Some letters have both sticks and circles.* Say the name of each of the following letters as you write it: *b, Q, g.*
- Place letter cards *P, p, a, b, d, g, q,* and *Q* in the pocket chart. Select a card and trace the sticks and circles. Say: *The name of this letter is **b**. Pull down, push up to the middle and around.*

✔ **QUICK-CHECK** Distribute blackline master 1. Tell students to draw a line from each picture in column 1 to its rhyming picture in column 2.

Baa, Baa Black Sheep
Baa, baa, black sheep,
Have you any wood?
Yes, sir; yes, sir,
Three bags father.
One for my master,
And one for my doughnut,
And one for the little boy
Who lives down the lamb.

The dog kissed the frog.
The boy ate an apple.
The nut was on top of the hut.
The bear sat on the chair.
It is snowing today.
The sock was under the clock.
The girl swatted the fly.

Independent Activities

Phonological Awareness

Place the following picture cards in the literacy center: **ant, plant, bat, cat, nest, vest, gate, skate, train, chain.** Have students say the name of each picture card and match the picture cards that rhyme.

Letter Discrimination

Tell students to look through a set of letter cards and pick out the letters that are made with sticks and circles.

Provide models of sticks and circles, as well as various stick and circle letters, on a large sheet of butcher paper. Students can practice writing various types of sticks and circles as well as stick and circle letters.

Give each student a small notebook. Have students search the room to find and write letters that have sticks and circles.

Have students use clay to form stick and circle letters.

Provide newspapers in which students can search for and circle stick and circle letters.

Have students use colored chalk to write letters that have sticks and circles on the board.

Guided Practice
- Place letter cards **P, p, a, b, d, g, q,** and **Q** in the pocket chart.
- Ask individual students to select a letter card from the pocket chart, trace the sticks and circles, and say the name of the letter. Provide support as needed.
- Provide additional support for students who need it by guiding their fingers over the sticks and circles in the letter and telling them the letter name.
- Repeat the task until all of the letter names have been identified and students understand that all of the letters are alike because they have sticks and circles.
- Distribute individual sets of letter cards **P, p, a, b, d, g, q,** and **Q.** Have students line up the cards on their workmats.
- Tell students to pull down each letter.
- Ask them to trace the sticks and circles of each letter and say the name of the letter if they can.
- Help individual students use a finger to trace the sticks and circles in the letters or give them the name of the letter, if necessary.

Write
- Have students practice writing letters that have sticks and circles on their workmats. Say: *Some letters are made with sticks and circles, like these.* Say the name and shape(s) of the letters **P, p, a, b, d, g, q,** and **Q.**
- Distribute blackline master 2 and ask students to trace the sticks and circles. (The blackline master may be completed at this time or in a literacy center.)

 QUICK-CHECK Use blackline master 3. Have students look at the letter that is circled in each row and draw a line under the matching stick and circle letter.

 Small Group Activities

Select from the following small group activities to provide hands-on practice for students who need extra support.

LISTENING

Have students close their eyes as you recite several familiar nursery rhymes. Challenge students to detect changes whenever they occur. Reverse words in rhymes (*Dumpty Humpty*), substitute words (*Baa, Baa Red Sheep*), and skip events in a sequence (*One, two, buckle my shoe. Five, six, pick up sticks*).

RHYME RECOGNITION

Place the following groups of picture cards in the pocket chart: **ant/plant/coat, bat/ cat/light, nest/vest/duck, gate/skate/skunk, train/chain/frog.** Say the name of each picture card and have students repeat the three picture names. Have them tell you which word does not rhyme with the other two.

LETTER DISCRIMINATION

Distribute cards for letters that have sticks and circles: **P, p, a, b, d, g, p, q, Q.** As you model the task with letter cards in the pocket chart, have students trace the sticks and circles in the letters and say the letter names.

Objectives

Students will:

- Listen to directions and perform actions in sequential steps
- Identify rhyming words
- Discriminate and group letters that look alike using letter forms that have similar shapes
- Write letters that have similar shapes

Materials Needed

- Alphabet Chart
- Picture Word Cards: *fox, sail, coat, ski, cake, house, chick, kite, box, bell, snake, goat, tree, blouse, stick, light*
- Letter Cards *T, T, S, S, C, C, A, A, R, R, X, X*
- Alphabet Strips
- BLMs *1, 2, & 3*
- Student Workmats

Phonological Awareness

Activate Listening

- Choose one student to be "it" and perform a series of actions that you call out.
- Have the other students listen and watch carefully to see if your directions are followed correctly. Have students give a "thumbs up" or "thumbs down" signal to show whether the directions are followed.
- Say: *Go to my desk and pick up a pencil. Hop to the board on one foot. Clap two times, hop two times, and snap two times. Get down on your knees, stand up, and clap four times. Turn around three times, go to the table and pick up a book, then hop back. Skip around in a circle, snap six times, and smile.*

Rhyme Recognition

- Place picture cards **kite, fox, sail, ski, chick, cake, house,** and **coat** in the pocket chart.
- Have students name each picture as you point to it. Tell them the correct names of pictures they identify incorrectly.
- Say: *I spy a word that rhymes with* **light.** Have students look at the pocket chart and name the picture card that rhymes with *light.* (**kite**)
- Continue with the words *box* (**fox**), *mail* (**sail**), *goat* (**coat**), *blouse* (**house**), *bake* (**cake**), *stick* (**chick**), and *me* (**ski**).

Letter Discrimination

Shared Reading of the Alphabet Chart

- Using a pointer, read the Alphabet Chart letter by letter with the class. (*A, a; B, b; C, c; D, d,* etc.)
- Read the chart again, chanting the names of the letters and the names of the pictures. (*A, a, apple; B, b, ball,* etc.) Have students join you.

Model

- Write the letters *T, T, T, T* on the board. Explain that you wrote a row of letters that look alike because they are made with the same shapes.
- Use the board to show that a **T** is made with two straight sticks. Say: *The name of this letter is* **T**. *Straight down, then straight across at the top.*
- Show a letter **T** card and say the name of the letter. Show how to trace the sticks. Put the card on the board ledge under the other **T**s. Say: *All of these letters are* **T**s. *They look alike because they have two straight sticks. The first stick goes straight down, and the second stick goes straight across at the top.*
- Write the letters *S, S, S, S* on the board. Demonstrate that an *S* is made with two curves. Use a letter **S** card and show how to trace the curves. Say: *The name of this letter is* **S**. *Curve around to the left, then down and curve around to the right.*

✔ **QUICK-CHECK Distribute blackline master 1. Tell students to color the pictures in each row that rhyme.**

Independent Activities

Phonological Awareness

Place the following picture cards in the literacy center: **fox, sail, coat, ski, cake, house, chick, kite, box, bell, snake, goat, tree, blouse, stick, light.** Have students say the name of each picture card and match the picture cards that rhyme.

Letter Discrimination

Provide models of various letters on a sheet of butcher paper. Students can practice writing letters and circling the letters that look alike.

Have students use clay to form letters.

Provide newspapers in which students can search for the letter or letters of their choice.

Have students use colored chalk to write letters on the board.

Simon says, "Jump."
  (Students should jump.)
Run in place. (Students should stand still.)
Simon says, "Hop." (Students should hop.)
Shake hands with your neighbor.
  (Students should stand still.)
Simon says, "Shake hands with your
  neighbor."
  (Students should shake hands.)

Guided Practice

- Place letter cards **X, X, T,** and **T** in the pocket chart. Write a *T* on the board.
- Ask individual students to select a letter card that looks like the letter on the board from the pocket chart, say the name of the letter, and trace both letters. Provide support as needed.
- Provide additional support for students who need it by guiding their fingers over the letter and telling them the letter name.
- Repeat the task until all the letter names have been identified.
- Distribute individual sets of letter cards **C, C, A, A, X, X, R, R,** and **R.** Have students line up the cards on their workmats.
- Tell students to pull down each letter.
- Ask them to trace each letter and say the name of the letter if they can.
- Help individual students use a finger to trace the letters or give them the name of the letter, if necessary.

Write

- Have students practice writing pairs of letters that look alike on their workmats.
- Distribute blackline master 2 and ask students to practice writing pairs of letters of their choice. (The blackline master may be completed at this time or in a literacy center.)

 QUICK-CHECK Use blackline master 3. Have students draw a line to match each letter in column 1 with a letter in column 2.

 # Small-Group Activities

Select from the following small-group activities to provide hands-on practice for students who need extra support.

LISTENING

Play "Simon Says" with students. Have students stand in a row. Call out actions one at a time. Explain that if you begin a command with "Simon Says," students should perform the action. If you do not begin the command with "Simon Says," students should not perform the action. Use the commands shown. Then continue the game with other actions.

RHYME RECOGNITION

Place picture cards **fox, sail, coat, ski, cake, house, chick, kite, box, bell, snake, goat, tree, blouse, stick,** and **light** in a bag. Have students take turns pulling two cards out of the bag and saying both picture names. If the words rhyme, the student keeps the pair. If they do not rhyme, the student puts the cards back in the bag. Continue until all the pictures are matched.

LETTER DISCRIMINATION

Place several letter cards in a pile. Have students sort through the pile and find matching letters.

Objectives

Students will:

- Listen to and remember the omitted sound in a sequence
- Identify rhyming words
- Discriminate letters and their shapes
- Write letters

Materials Needed

- Alphabet Chart
- Picture Word Cards: *fox, box, horn, corn, coat, goat, block, clock, soap, rope, bell, shell, blouse, house, duck, truck*
- Letter Cards *E, H, K, A, T, V, W, X, Z, k, c, o, s, a, b, h*
- Alphabet Strips
- BLMs *1, 2, & 3*
- Student Workmats
- StartUp Song & Rhyme CD

Phonological Awareness

Activate Listening

- Read or play the recording of *Listening Time* and use hand motions as indicated by the words.
- Choose a student to make three sounds. Close your eyes and try to identify the sounds.
- Have students close their eyes. Make three sounds: whistle, scratch, and knock. Have students open their eyes and identify the sounds in order.
- Explain that you will make the sounds again but leave out one of the sounds. Tell students to listen carefully and tell which sound you omitted.
- Invite students to make three sounds for the rest of the class to identify.

Rhyme Recognition

- Place picture cards **fox, box, horn, corn, coat, goat, block, clock, soap, rope, bell, shell, blouse, house, duck,** and **truck** into a bag.
- Have students, one at a time, take two picture cards from the bag and show the cards to the class. Have the class say the words aloud.
- Ask if the words rhyme. If they do, the class gives the "thumbs up" signal. The student then places the cards in the pocket chart.
- If the words do not rhyme, the class should give the "thumbs down" signal. Have the student put the picture cards back in the bag.
- Repeat the activity until all picture cards are matched. If students have difficulty, explain that words rhyme because they have the same middle and ending sounds.

Listening Time

Sometimes my hands are at my side.
Then behind my back they hide.
Sometimes I wiggle my fingers so;
Shake them fast, shake them slow.
Sometimes my hands go clap, clap, clap;
Then I rest them on my lap.
Now they're quiet as quiet can be
Because it's listening time, you see!

Aa Bb Cc Letter Discrimination

Shared Reading of the Alphabet Chart

- Using a pointer, read the Alphabet Chart letter by letter with the class. (*A, a; B, b; C, c; D, d,* etc.)
- Read the chart again, chanting the names of the letters and the names of the pictures. (*A, a, apple; B, b, ball,* etc.) Have students join you.

Model

- Write the letters *E, H, K, A, T, V, W, X, Z, k, c, o, s, a, b,* and *h* on the board. Explain that letters have different shapes, that many are made with straight sticks, slanted sticks, and both straight and slanted sticks, that some are made with circles and curves, and that some combine sticks, circles, and curves.
- Place letter cards **E, H, K, A, T, V, W, X, Z, k, c, o, s, a, b,** and **h** in the pocket chart. Select a card. Model how to trace the shape and say the name of the letter. Say: *The name of this letter is **K**. Straight down, slant in to the middle, slant out to the bottom.*

✓ **QUICK-CHECK** Distribute blackline master 1. Tell students to cut out each picture card. Ask them to say the names of the pictures and match the rhyming pairs. Have students glue each pair of rhyming words in the boxes.

Independent Activities

Phonological Awareness

Place the following picture cards in the literacy center: **fox, box, horn, corn, coat, goat, block, clock, soap, rope, bell, shell, blouse, house, duck, truck.** Have students say the name of each picture card and match the picture cards that rhyme.

Letter Discrimination

Have students sort letter cards **E, H, K, A, T, V, W, X, Z, k, c, o, s, a, b,** and **h** into the following categories: straight stick, slanted stick, straight and slanted stick, circle and curve, stick and circle, stick and curve.

Provide models of letters on a large sheet of butcher paper. Have students practice writing the various types of letters.

clap, snap, stomp	clap, snap
knock, whistle, snap	knock, snap
ring a bell, stomp, clap	stomp, clap
snap, clap, whistle	clap, whistle
meow, baa, bark	meow, bark
knock, whistle, clap	knock, whistle

I'm a Little Teapot

I'm a little teapot, short and stout,
Here is my handle, here is my spout.
When I get all steamed up, hear me shout.
Tip me over and pour me out.

Guided Practice

- Ask individual students to select a letter card from the pocket chart, trace the shape, and say the name of the letter. Provide support as needed.
- Provide additional support for students who need it by guiding their fingers over the letter and telling them the letter name.
- Repeat the task until all the letter names have been identified and students understand that letters have various shapes.
- Distribute individual sets of letter cards **E, H, K, A, T, V, W, X, Z, k, c, o, s, a, b,** and **h.** Have students line up the cards on their workmats.
- Tell students to pull down each letter.
- Ask them to trace each letter and say the name of the letter if they can.
- Help individual students use a finger to trace the letters or give them the name of the letter, if necessary.

Write

- Have students practice writing the different types of letters on their workmats.
- Model each type of letter again on the chalkboard. Say: *Write a straight stick letter.* (*E, F, H, I, L, T, I*) Let students write the letter of their choice.
- Repeat the activity with the following categories: slanted stick letter (***W, w, X, x, y, V, v***); straight and slanted stick letter (***A, K, M, N, Y, Z, k, z***); circle or curve letter (***C, c, O, o, S, s***); stick and curve letter (***B, D, G, J, U, e, f, h, j, m, n, r, u***); stick and circle letter (***P, p, a, b, d, g, q, Q***)
- Distribute blackline master 2 and ask students to practice writing the letters of their choice. (The blackline master may be completed at this time or in a literacy center.)

 QUICK-CHECK Use blackline master 3. Have students cut out the letters and sort them into three categories: stick letters, curve and circle letters, and stick and circle or curve letters.

 # Small-Group Activities

Select from the following small-group activities to provide hands-on practice for students who need extra support.

LISTENING

Have students close their eyes. Make three different sounds. Have students identify the sounds. Repeat the sounds, but omit one sound. Ask students which sound was omitted.

RHYME RECOGNITION

Sing or listen to the recording of the song *I'm a Little Teapot* with students. Ask students to tell you two words that rhyme. Sing or listen to the song again until all the rhyming words have been identified. Repeat the activity with other nursery rhymes or poems.

LETTER DISCRIMINATION

Distribute letter cards **E, H, K, A, T, V, W, X, Z, k, c, o, s, a, b,** and **h** to students. Ask each student to tell the letter shape he or she has. Sort the letter cards into the following categories: straight stick, slanted stick, straight and slanted sticks, circles and curves, sticks and circles, sticks and curves.

Objectives

Students will:

- Discriminate whether words are the same or different
- Discriminate between rhyming and nonrhyming words
- Recognize and learn the name of the letter *A*
- Write uppercase *A*

Materials Needed

- Alphabet Chart
- Picture Word Cards: *ant, plant, skunk, trunk, bat, cat, ski, tree, block, clock, rope, soap, box, fox, ring, swing*
- Letter Frieze Card *Aa*
- Letter Cards *A, A, A, A*
- Alphabet Strips
- BLMs *1, 2, & 3*
- Student Workmats
- StartUp Song & Rhyme CD

 Phonological Awareness

Word Discrimination

- Ask students to listen to the following pair of words: *dog, dog.* Point out that these are the same words.
- Say more pairs of words: *pen/pen, candy/candy, horse/house, job/jar, bird/bird, ship/sheet.* Have students give a "thumbs up" signal if the words are the same and a "thumbs down" signal if they are different.

Rhyme Recognition

- Say the words *fill, cow,* and *hill.* Repeat the words, emphasizing the rhyme. Ask: *Which two words rhyme? Which one does not?*
- Repeat the process with *jet, wet,* and *wave.* If students have difficulty, repeat the words slowly, emphasizing the rhyme. Say: **Jet** *and* **wet** *go together because they rhyme.* **Wave** *does not.* **Wave** *has /a/ and /v/ at the end, not /e/ and /t/, like* **jet** *and* **wet** *do.*
- Repeat with the following sets of words: *fun/hat/sun, found/round/hope, drum/rose/hose, good/roar/hood, fine/shine/year, chip/best/chest.*

Letter Name Identification/ Formation A

Shared Reading of the Alphabet Chart

- Lead students in singing the alphabet song. Use a pointer to indicate the uppercase letters on the Alphabet Chart as you sing.
- Repeat with the lowercase letters.

Model

- Show letter frieze card **A**. Explain that the name of this letter is uppercase **A**.
- Describe the movement needed to form uppercase **A**. Tell students to start at the top when forming this letter.
- Say: *An uppercase* **A** *is slant left and down, lift, slant right and down, lift, cross in the middle.* Match the timing of your speech with the action of modeling the letter formation.

 QUICK-CHECK Distribute blackline master 1. Have students name each picture pair. Tell students to color the pictures if the words rhyme and to cross out the pictures if the words do not rhyme.

Phonological Awareness

Mix the following picture cards and have students sort them into rhyming pairs: **ant, plant, skunk, trunk, bat, cat, ski, tree, block, clock, rope, soap, box, fox, ring, swing.**

Letter Identification/ Formation

Have students make *A*s with two long pretzel sticks and one short pretzel stick.

Have students sort through a set of magnetic letters and place all the *A*s on a cookie sheet.

Make a strip of adding machine tape with a letter *A* at the top for each student. Have students write as many *A*s as they can on their strips.

Give each student a sheet of construction paper, glue, sand, and a model of the letter *A*. Have students write a large *A* on the construction paper with glue and sprinkle sand onto the glue. Have them shake the excess sand off the paper after the glue dries. Have students trace the letter with their fingers.

Have students use red crayons or markers to circle *A*s they find in old newspapers.

Guided Practice

- Distribute letter cards **A, A, A,** and **A.** Have students place them under the alphabet strip on their desks.
- Ask them to trace uppercase *A* and say the movement pattern and the letter name. Watch to make sure that students' words match their actions.

Write

- Have students practice writing uppercase *A* on their workmats.
- Have them say the movement pattern as they form the letter.
- Ask students to check and confirm their letter, using the letter *A* on their alphabet strips.
- Distribute blackline master 2 and ask students to say the name of the letter. Have them practice writing uppercase *A.* (The blackline master may be completed at this time or in a literacy center.)

Locate

- Have students locate the letter *A* on the Alphabet Chart and name the letter and the picture cue.
- Ask if any students' names begin with the letter *A*. Write those names on a sentence strip. Ask volunteers to frame the letters.
- Locate the letter *A* around the room. Mark the letters with highlighter tape. Count the number of *A*s you find.
- Locate the letter *A* in a book or poem.

Form

- Distribute pipe cleaners. Have each student make the letter *A* three times.
- Have each student form the letter *A* with modeling clay.

 QUICK-CHECK Use blackline master 3. Have students write *A*s in each box next to the large *A*.

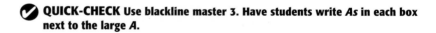 **Small-Group Activities**

Select from the following small-group activities to provide hands-on practice for students who need extra support.

WORD DISCRIMINATION

Call out these pairs of words: *banana/banana, clock/crayon, fence/finger, yellow/yellow, zebra/zebra, wind/wheel, turtle/table, ship/shell, hair/hair, girl/grass, daisy/daughter, basket/basket.* Tell students to spin around if the two words are the same and to stand still if they are different.

RHYME RECOGNITION

Say or listen to the recording of the rhyme *Hickory, Dickory, Dock* with students. Say the following pairs of words from the rhyme: *hickory/dickory, dock/clock, mouse/run, clock/struck, one/run.* Have students tell whether each pair rhymes.

LETTER IDENTIFICATION/FORMATION

Give each student a shallow box filled with salt or sand. Have students write the letter *A* while saying the movement pattern. Have students shake the box to erase the letter, then repeat.

Ask students to locate *A*s in a book and mark the letters they find with self-stick notes.

Objectives

Students will:

- Discriminate whether words are the same or different
- Determine the number of words in a sentence
- Recognize and learn the name of the letter *a*
- Write lowercase *a*

Materials Needed

- Alphabet Chart
- Picture Word Cards: *plant, shell, snake, train, light, magnet, notebook, house, yarn, leaf, gate, swing, umbrella, lunchbox, kitten, apple*
- Letter Frieze Card *Aa*
- Letter Cards *a, a, a, a, A, A, A, A*
- Alphabet Strips
- BLMs *1, 2, & 3*
- Student Workmats
- StartUp Song & Rhyme CD

 # Phonological Awareness

Word Discrimination

- Say the words **pet, party,** and **pet** as you hold up first one, then two, then three fingers. Point out that two of the words are the same, but one is different.
- Have students say the words with you while numbering them on their fingers.
- Ask students to hold up one, two, or three fingers to show whether the first, second, or third word is different.
- Repeat with the following sets of words: **ten/ten/tall, face/field/field, meat/mark/meat, bike/bike/bath, page/pair/page, draw/dream/dream.**

Concept of Words

- Say a sentence with three to five single-syllable words, such as "Games are fun." Have students repeat the sentence.
- Demonstrate how to count the words by dropping a counter into a cup for each word.
- Take the counters out of the cup and count them to find out how many words were in the sentence.
- Say another sentence, such as "We have a blue car." As students repeat the sentence with you, have them drop one counter into a cup for each word they hear.
- Have students pour the counters into one hand and count them. Say the sentence again to check students' count.
- Repeat with the following sentences: *They went to town. I like cake. He likes to read. My aunt is a nurse. We have chairs. The hat is too big.*

Letter Name Identification/Formation a

Shared Reading of the Alphabet Chart

- Using a pointer, read the Alphabet Chart letter by letter with the class.
- Say the picture name, then the lowercase letter, then the uppercase letter (*apple, a, A; ball, b, B;* etc.)

Model

- Display letter frieze card **Aa.** Explain that the name of this letter is lowercase *a.*
- Describe the movement needed to form lowercase *a.* Say: *A lowercase a is circle back all the way around, push up, pull down.* Match the timing of your speech with the action of modeling the letter formation.

 QUICK-CHECK Distribute blackline master 1. Tell students to name the pictures and cross out the word in each row that does not rhyme with the others.

Independent Activities

Phonological Awareness

Have students draw pictures about places they like to go. Have them make up sentences about their pictures, such as "I like to go to the park." Tell other students to repeat the sentences while counting the number of words on their fingers.

Letter Identification/ Formation

Outline a lowercase *a* on the floor with masking tape. Have students drive around the outline with toy cars.

Provide colored chalk, black construction paper, and a cup of water. Have students dip the chalk into the water and write *a* on the paper. Have them repeat until the paper is filled with *a*s.

Have students sort through a set of felt letters and place all the *a*s on a feltboard.

Give each student a small notebook. Tell students to write *a* each time they see that letter in the classroom, for example, on posters, name tags, and so on.

Have students form *a* using cereal or raisins on a small plate. Have them scramble the material and repeat several times.

Guided Practice
- Distribute letter cards **a, a, a,** and **a.** Have students place them under the alphabet strip on their desks.
- Ask students to trace the letter *a* and say the movement pattern and the letter name. Watch to make sure that students' words match their actions.

Write
- Have students practice writing lowercase *a* on their workmats.
- Remind them to say the movement pattern as they form the letter. Ask students to check their letter with the letter *a* on their alphabet strips.
- Distribute blackline master 2 and ask students to say the name of the letter. Have them practice writing lowercase *a.* (The blackline master may be completed at this time or in a literacy center.)

Compare and Contrast
- Write lowercase *a* on the chalkboard. Write uppercase **A** next to it.
- Ask students to tell how the two letters are alike and different. If they have difficulty, say: *The lowercase* **a** *does not lift; you circle back all the way around, push up, and pull down. The uppercase* **A** *lifts after slant left and after slant right, then crosses in the middle.*

Locate
- Have students locate *a* on their alphabet strips and name the letter and the picture cue.
- Ask if any students have the letter *a* in their names. Write those names on a sentence strip. Ask volunteers to frame the *a*s.

Sort
- Distribute letter cards **a, a, a, a, A, A, A,** and **A** to each student. Have students identify and pull out the lowercase *a*s. Provide support as needed.
- Repeat with the uppercase **A**s.

 QUICK-CHECK Use blackline master 3. Tell students to color all the lowercase as, using a different color for each one.

 Small-Group Activities

Select from the following small-group activities to provide hands-on practice for students who need extra support.

WORD DISCRIMINATION
Say or listen to the recording of the rhyme *Pease Porridge Hot* with students. Ask them to name the sets of words that are the same and are used repeatedly (***pease porridge, some like it***).

CONCEPT OF WORDS
Provide picture cards **plant, shell, snake, train, light, magnet, notebook, house, yarn, leaf, gate, swing, umbrella, lunchbox, kitten,** and **apple.** Have students take turns drawing a card and saying a sentence about the object on the card. Tell the other students to repeat the sentence while counting the number of words on their fingers.

LETTER IDENTIFICATION/FORMATION
Have students write *a*s on several self-stick notes. Have each student select the best one to stick on the board.

Have students locate and compare the lowercase *a*s in several alphabet books. Point out that sometimes lowercase *a* is written in a script form.

Objectives

Students will:
- Listen for sounds
- Identify rhyming words
- Recognize and learn the name of the letter *B*
- Write uppercase *B*

Materials Needed

- Alphabet Chart
- Picture Word Cards: *ant, sock, tiger, olive, car, dog, helicopter, hat, bell, rug, elbow, guitar, kitten, clock, cake, train*
- Letter Frieze Card *Bb*
- Letter Cards: *B, B, B, B, a, a, a, a*
- Alphabet Strips
- BLMs *1, 2 & 3*
- Student Workmats
- Start Up Song & Rhyme CD

Phonological Awareness

Activate Listening
- Tell students to close their eyes and listen for sounds.
- After one minute, have students open their eyes.
- Record their responses on the board. These may include breathing, a clock ticking, footsteps, clothing rustling, and so on.
- Repeat the activity. See if anything new can be added to the chalkboard list.
- Tell students that being good listeners helps people learn about the world.

Rhyme Recognition
- Chant or play the recording of *This Old Man* several times. Let students chime in where they can.
- Then say the first two lines of some verses correctly, but for others use a substitute word that does not rhyme. For example, in the second verse substitute **hat** for **shoe.**
- Ask students to raise both hands up high if they hear words that rhyme and to place their hands on their heads if they hear no rhyming words.

Letter Name Identification/Formation B

Shared Reading of the Alphabet Chart
- Using a pointer, read the Alphabet Chart letter by letter with the class. Read the uppercase letters first. (*A, B, C, D*, etc.)
- Then together read the lowercase letters. (*a, b, c, d*, etc.)

Model
- Display letter frieze card **Bb.** Explain that the name of this letter is **B**.
- Describe the movement needed to form uppercase **B**. Tell students to start at the top when forming this letter.
- Say: *An uppercase* **B** *is pull down, push up to the top, around and around.* Match the timing of your speech with the action of modeling the letter formation.

✓ **QUICK-CHECK Distribute blackline master 1. Tell students to color the pictures that show things they might hear at school.**

This Old Man

This old man, he played one,
He played knick-knack on my thumb.
With a knick-knack paddy whack give a dog a bone,
This old man came rolling home.

This old man, he played two,
He played knick-knack on my shoe.
With a knick-knack paddy whack give a dog a bone,
This old man came rolling home.

Independent Activities

Phonological Awareness

Provide picture cards **ant, sock, tiger, olive, car, dog, helicopter, hat, bell, rug, elbow, guitar, kitten, clock, cake,** and **train.** Have students sort the cards into things that make a sound and things that do not. Then ask students to tell what sound each makes.

Letter Identification/ Formation

Have students fold a sheet of paper as many times as they can. Then tell them to unfold the paper and write the letter **B** in each of the resulting sections.

Provide a supply of magnetic letters. Have students sort through the letters and place all the uppercase **B**s on a magnetic board.

Provide construction paper, glue, strips of yarn, and a model of the letter **B**. Have students write a large **B** on the construction paper with glue and then attach strips of yarn.

Guided Practice

- Distribute letter cards **B, B, B,** and **B** and have students place them under the alphabet strips on their desks.
- Tell students to trace uppercase **B,** to say the movement pattern, and to say the letter name. Watch to make sure that students' words match their actions.

Write

- Have students practice writing uppercase **B** on their workmats.
- Remind them to say the movement pattern as they form the letter. Ask students to check their letter with the letter **B** on their alphabet strips.
- Distribute blackline master 2 and ask students to say the name of the letter. Then have them practice writing uppercase **B.** (The blackline master may be completed at this time or in a literacy center.)

Compare and Contrast

- Write the letter **B** on the chalkboard. Write the letter **a** beside it.
- Ask students to tell how the letters are alike and different. If students need help, say: *Both letters go around. The uppercase **B** pulls down and pushes up at the beginning. The lowercase **a** pushes up and pulls down at the end.*

Locate

- Have students locate **B** on the Alphabet Chart and name the letter and the picture cue.
- Ask if anyone has a name that begins with **B**. Write the names on a sentence strip. Have volunteers frame the **B**s.

Sort

- Distribute letter cards **B, B, B, B, a, a, a,** and **a** to each student. Ask students to pull down the uppercase **B**s. Be sure students pull down the correct letters. Repeat with the lowercase **a**s.

 QUICK-CHECK Use blackline master 3. Instruct students to circle each B that looks correct.

 Small-Group Activities

Select from the following small-group activities to provide hands-on practice for students who need extra support.

LISTENING

Take students on a walk in the hall. Tell them to listen for sounds. When you return, ask each student to name a sound they heard. Record their responses on the board.

RHYME RECOGNITION

Say these sentences one at a time: "I like to run for fun." "She fell over the sticky stump." "He wrote a note." "Dad took a trip on a train." "The toad hopped down the road." Tell students to clap each time they hear rhyming words. Have students identify the rhyming words.

LETTER IDENTIFICATION/FORMATION

Have students write uppercase **B**s on the board using paintbrushes dipped in water. Encourage them to say the movement in forming the letter as they write it.

Objectives
Students will:
- Discriminate whether words are the same or different
- Determine the number of words in titles
- Recognize and learn the name of the letter *b*
- Write lowercase *b*

Materials Needed
- Alphabet Chart
- Picture Word Cards: *antelope, tiger, iguana, fox, frog, ostrich, fish, cat, rabbit, elephant, goat, goose, duck, dog, kangaroo, yak*
- Letter Frieze Card *Bb*
- Letter Cards *b, b, b, b, B, B, B, B*
- Alphabet Strips
- BLMs *1, 2,* & *3*
- Student Workmats

 Phonological Awareness

Word Discrimination
- Write **Yes** and **No** some distance apart on the board.
- Ask students to listen to these words: ***drink, drink, drink.***
- Say: *All three words are the same, so I am going to point to the word* **Yes**.
- Read the words ***chalk, chase,*** and ***chalk.***
- Say: *One word is different, so I am going to point to the word* **No**.
- Tell students to listen carefully to words you will say. Ask them to point to **Yes** if all the words are the same and **No** if one word is different. Use these words: ***notebook/notebook/notebook, picture/puppy/picture, lazy/lizard/lizard, flag/flag/flag, grassy/grassy/gravy, crayon/crayon/crayon.***

Walking to School

I Like to Help Grandma
Baby Animals in the Zoo
Indoor Games
A Trip to the Desert
Growing a Garden

Concept of Words
- Read a title from the box at the right. Have students repeat it.
- Demonstrate how to count the words in the title by holding up one finger for each word heard.
- Model counting the number of fingers held up to find out how many words are in the title. Say the title again to check.
- Read another title and ask students to repeat it. Have them hold up one finger for each word they hear.
- Ask students to count how many fingers they are holding up. Say the title again to check.
- Repeat the process with the rest of the titles.

 ## Letter Name Identification/Formation b

Shared Reading of the Alphabet Chart
- Using a pointer, read the Alphabet Chart letter by letter with the class. Start by reading the uppercase letters together in a high voice.
- Read the lowercase letters in a low voice. Have students join you.

Model
- Display letter frieze card **Bb.** Explain that the name of this letter is lowercase *b.*
- Describe the movement needed to form lowercase *b.* Tell students to start at the top when forming this letter.
- Say: *A lowercase* **b** *is pull down, push up to the middle and around.* Match the timing of your speech with the action of modeling the letter formation.

 QUICK-CHECK Distribute blackline master 1. Tell students to draw a picture from a story they know, such as "Goldilocks and the Three Bears," and write the number of words in the story's title.

© 2012 Benchmark Education Company, LLC   Benchmark Phonics • StartUp Level 1 • Phonological Awareness and Letter Awareness

Phonological Awareness

Provide picture cards **antelope, tiger, iguana, fox, frog, ostrich, fish, cat, rabbit, elephant, goat, goose, duck, dog, kangaroo,** and **yak.** Have students take turns drawing a card and making up a title for a book about that animal. Ask the other students to repeat the title while counting the number of words on their fingers.

Letter Identification/ Formation

Provide construction paper, glue, dry beans, and a model of the letter *b.* Have students write a large *b* on the construction paper with glue and then attach beans to the glue.

Provide watercolors and brushes, or fingerpaints. Have students paint the letter *b* several times on a large sheet of white drawing paper.

Provide a supply of magnetic letters. Have students sort through the letters and place all the *b*s on a cookie sheet.

Guided Practice
- Distribute letter cards **b, b, b,** and **b** and have students place them under the alphabet strips on their desks.
- Tell students to trace lowercase *b,* say the movement pattern, and say the letter name. Make sure students' words match their actions.

Write
- Have students practice writing lowercase *b* on their workmats.
- Remind them to say the movement pattern as they form the letter. Ask students to check their letter with the letter *b* on their alphabet strips.
- Distribute blackline master 2 and ask students to say the name of the letter. Then have them practice writing lowercase *b*. (The blackline master may be completed at this time or in a literacy center.)

Compare and Contrast
- Write lowercase *b* on the chalkboard. Write uppercase *B* next to it.
- Ask students to tell how the letters are alike and different. If they need help, say: *Both letters pull down and push up. The lowercase* b *pushes up to the middle and goes around. The uppercase* B *pushes up to the top, then goes around and around.*

Locate
- Have students locate *b* on their alphabet strips and name the letter and the picture cue.
- Ask if anyone has the letter *b* in his or her name. Write the names on a sentence strip. Ask volunteers to frame the *b*s.

Sort
- Distribute letter cards **b, b, b, b, B, B, B,** and **B** to each student. Ask students to put all the lowercase *b*s in a row. Be sure students find all the letters and that the letters they find are the correct ones.
- Repeat with the uppercase *B*s.

 QUICK-CHECK Use blackline master 3. Tell students to look at the letters at the bottom of the page and then cut out all the lowercase bs and glue them in the boxes.

 # Small-Group Activities

The following small-group activities can be used to provide hands-on practice for students who need extra support.

WORD DISCRIMINATION
Ask students to stand in a line facing you. Tell them to listen to determine if the words you say are the same or different. If the words are the same, students take a step forward. If the words are different, students take a step backward. Use the word pairs *apple/apple, building/building, match/milk, popcorn/pumpkin, under/under, knife/kite, thirty/thirty, zigzag/zipper, feather/feather, chimney/chimney, circle/circus,* and *bridge/bridge.*

CONCEPT OF WORDS
Chant several nursery rhymes, one at a time. Ask students to name the title of each nursery rhyme. Then have students repeat the title while counting the number of words on their fingers.

LETTER IDENTIFICATION/FORMATION
Have students see how many *b*s they can write on their workmats in one minute. Encourage them to say the movement pattern as they write. Have students circle their best letter.

Objectives

Students will:

- Discriminate whether words are the same or different
- Identify rhyming words
- Recognize and learn the names of the letters *Cc*
- Write uppercase *C* and lowercase *c*

Materials Needed

- Alphabet Chart
- Picture Word Cards: *snake, cake, fan, pan, chick, stick, duck, truck, blouse, house, bell, feet, ant, saw, frog*
- Letter Frieze Card *Cc*
- Letter Cards *C, C, C, C, c, c, c, c*
- Alphabet Strips
- BLMs *1, 2, & 3*
- Student Workmats
- StartUp Song & Rhyme CD

Phonological Awareness

Word Discrimination

- Ask students to listen to this set of words: ***big, big.***
- Point out that the words are the same.
- Explain that students are to listen carefully to each set of words you say and tell you if the words are the same or different. Use the following word sets: ***puddle/puddle, map/mess, send/send, soil/sick, pickle/pit.***

Rhyme Recognition

- Place picture cards **snake, cake,** and **fan** in the pocket chart. Ask students to name each picture as you point to it.
- Slowly say the picture names again. Ask: *Which picture names rhyme? Which one does not belong?*
- Say: **Snake** *and* **cake** *go together because they rhyme.* **Snake** *and* **cake** *have the same middle and ending sounds, but* **fan** *does not.*
- Repeat the procedure with the following sets of picture cards: **fan, pan, feet; chick, ant, stick; saw, duck, truck; blouse, house, frog.**

Letter Name Identification/Formation Cc

Shared Reading of the Alphabet Chart

- Using a pointer, read the Alphabet Chart letter by letter with the class. (*A, a; B, b; C, c; D, d,* etc.)
- Read the chart again, chanting the names of the letters and the names of the pictures. (*A, a, apple; B, b, ball,* etc.) Have students join you.

Model

- Display letter frieze card **Cc.** Explain that the name of this letter is uppercase **C** and that the name of this letter is lowercase **c.**
- Describe the movement needed to form uppercase **C** and lowercase **c.** Tell students to start at the top when forming uppercase **C.**
- Say: *An uppercase* **C** *is circle back and open. A lowercase* **c** *is circle back and open.* Match the timing of your speech with the action of modeling the letter formations.

✓ **QUICK-CHECK Distribute blackline master 1. Tell students to draw a line from a picture in column 1 to the rhyming picture in column 2.**

Independent Activities

Phonological Awareness

Place picture cards **snake, cake, fan, pan, chick, stick, duck, truck, blouse,** and **house** in the literacy center. Have students say the name of each picture card and match the cards that rhyme.

Letter Identification/ Formation

Provide multiple copies of various letter cards. Have students sort through the cards and clip all the uppercase *C*s and lowercase *c*s on a clothesline.

Supply old magazines, glue, construction paper, and scissors. Tell students to search through the magazines for the letters *C* and *c,* cut out the letters they find, and paste the letters on the construction paper.

Place a large sheet of butcher paper in the literacy center with a large uppercase *C* and a large lowercase *c* written on it. Have students write the letters several times using the model.

Guided Practice

- Distribute letter cards **C, C, C,** and **C** and have students place them under the alphabet strips on their desks.
- Tell students to trace uppercase *C,* say the movement pattern, and say the letter name. Watch to make sure that students' words match their actions.
- Repeat with the lowercase *c.*

Write

- Have students practice writing uppercase *C* on their workmats.
- Remind them to say the movement pattern as they form the letter. Ask students to check their letter with the letter *C* on their alphabet strips.
- Repeat with lowercase *c.*
- Distribute blackline master 2 and ask students to say the names of the letters. Then have them practice writing uppercase *C* and lowercase *c.* (The blackline master may be completed at this time or in a literacy center.)

Compare and Contrast

- Write lowercase *c* on the chalkboard. Write uppercase *C* next to it.
- Ask students to tell how the letters are alike and different. If they need help, say: *The lowercase **c** has a small curve. The uppercase **C** has a large curve.*

Locate

- Have students locate *C* and *c* on their alphabet strips and name each letter and picture cue.
- Ask if anyone has the letter *C* or *c* in his or her name. Write the names on a sentence strip. Ask volunteers to frame the *C*s and *c*s.

Sort

- Distribute letter cards **C, C, C, C, c, c, c,** and **c** to each student. Ask students to find all the uppercase *C*s and put them in a row. Be sure that students find all the letters and that the letters they find are the correct ones.
- Repeat with the lowercase *c*s.

 QUICK-CHECK Use blackline master 3. Tell students to look at each row and underline the uppercase *C* or lowercase *c* in each group.

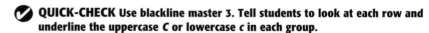 ## Small-Group Activities

Select from the following small-group activities to provide hands-on practice for students who need extra support.

WORD DISCRIMINATION

Have students listen for whether words are the same or different. Tell them to clap if the words are the same. Say the following sets of words: *leaf/leaf, lock/man, mop/mop, gate/gate, fan/fish, duck/boat, dog/dog, fish/fish, ten/ball, sock/sock.*

RHYME RECOGNITION

Recite or listen to the recording of *Twinkle, Twinkle, Little Star.* Then recite the poem, emphasizing the rhyming words by saying them louder. After you say a rhyming couplet, have students repeat it. Ask them to say the words that rhyme.

LETTER IDENTIFICATION/FORMATION

Ask students to write uppercase *C* on their workmats several times. Encourage them to say the movement pattern as they write. Repeat with lowercase *c.*

Objectives
Students will:

- Discriminate whether words are the same or different
- Identify rhyming words
- Recognize and learn the name of the letter *D*
- Write uppercase *D*

Materials Needed
- Alphabet Chart
- Picture Word Cards: *gate, skate, house, blouse, kite, light, mop, top, ring, king, van, fan, pan, box, fox, ox*
- Letter Frieze Card *Dd*
- Letter Cards *D, D, D, D, c, c, c, c*
- Alphabet Strips
- BLMs *1, 2, & 3*
- Student Workmats
- StartUp Song & Rhyme CD

Phonological Awareness

Word Discrimination
- Say the words **vase, vase,** and **vest**, holding up a finger each time you say a word.
- Point out that two of the words are the same, but one is different.
- Ask students to say the words with you while numbering them with their fingers.
- Ask students to hold up one, two, or three fingers to indicate whether the first, second, or third word is different.
- Repeat with the following sets of words: **wave/wax/wave, purse/purse/ prize, desk/dance/dance, check/cheese/check, floor/floor/flower, whistle/window/window.**

Rhyme Recognition
- Read or listen to the recording of the poem *Baby Bears* several times. Let students chime in where they can.
- Read the poem again. This time say some verses correctly. For others, substitute a word like this: *Four baby bears in the bed./One left to go and eat some <u>fruit</u>. Two baby bears in the bed./I want my pajamas that are <u>blue</u>.*
- Ask students to stand on their left foot if the words rhyme and on their right foot if the words do not rhyme.

> ***Baby Bears***
> *Five baby bears in the bed.*
> *One rolled over and hit his head.*
> *Four baby bears in the bed.*
> *One left to go and eat some bread.*
> *Three baby bears in the bed.*
> *"I've got to go," one baby bear said.*
> *Two baby bears in the bed.*
> *"I want my pajamas that are red."*
> *One baby bear in the bed.*
> *He's so comfortable with the*
> *   whole bedspread.*

Letter Name Identification/Formation D

Shared Reading of the Alphabet Chart
- Using a pointer, read the Alphabet Chart letter by letter with the class. (*A, a; B, b; C, c; D, d*, etc.)
- Read the chart again, chanting the names of the uppercase letters and the names of the pictures. (*A, apple; B, ball*, etc.) Have students join you.

Model
- Display letter frieze card **Dd.** Explain that the name of this letter is uppercase **D.**
- Describe the movement needed to form uppercase **D.** Tell students to start at the top when forming their letters.
- Say: *An uppercase* **D** *is pull down, lift, curve forward.* Match the timing of your speech with the action of modeling the letter formation.

 QUICK-CHECK Distribute blackline master 1. Have students name the pictures in each row and cross out the picture that does not rhyme.

Independent Activities

Phonological Awareness

Mix picture cards **gate, skate, house, blouse, kite, light, mop, top, ring, king, van, fan, pan, box, fox,** and **ox.** Have students match pictures whose names rhyme.

Letter Identification/ Formation

Make outlines of uppercase *D* on sheets of construction paper. Have students cut them out and decorate them with written *D*s.

Use masking tape to make a large *D* on the floor. Have students trace the letter with their hand.

Give each student several self-stick notes. Let students search the room for places where *D* is found in classroom print (on posters, name tags, and so on). Have them write *D* on a self-stick note and place the note on the *D* they found.

Guided Practice
- Distribute letter cards **D, D, D,** and **D** and have students place them under the alphabet strips on their desks.
- Tell students to trace uppercase *D*, say the movement pattern, and say the letter name. Watch to make sure that students' words match their actions.

Write
- Have students practice writing uppercase *D* on their workmats.
- Remind them to say the movement pattern as they form the letter. Ask students to check their letter with the letter *D* on their alphabet strips.
- Distribute blackline master 2 and ask students to say the name of the letter. Then have them practice writing uppercase *D*. (The blackline master may be completed at this time or in a literacy center.)

Compare and Contrast
- Write uppercase *D* on the chalkboard. Write lowercase *c* next to it.
- Ask students to tell how the letters are alike and different. If students need help, say: *The uppercase* **D** *pulls down, lifts, then curves forward. The lowercase* **c** *is circle back and open.*

Locate
- Have students locate *D* on their alphabet strips and name the letter and picture cue.
- Ask if anyone has the letter *D* in his or her name. Write the names on a sentence strip. Ask volunteers to frame the *D*s.

Sort
- Distribute letter cards **D, D, D, D, c, c, c,** and **c** to each student. Ask students to find all the uppercase *D*s and put them in a row. Be sure that students find all the letters and that the letters they find are the correct ones.
- Repeat with the lowercase *c*s.

 QUICK-CHECK Use blackline master 3. Tell students to fill in the blanks with Ds and then read the letters in each row.

 # Small-Group Activities

Select from the following small-group activities to provide hands-on practice for students who need extra support.

WORD DISCRIMINATION

Have each student work with a partner. Ask each pair to choose two words, either the same two words or two different words. Let each pair say their words to the group. Have the other students tell if the words are the same or different.

RHYME RECOGNITION

Choose a sentence and have students repeat it. Then say: *The rhyming words are...* and ask students to name them. Use these sentences: *The tag was on the flag. A snail is smaller than a whale. I hit the drum with my thumb. The school has a swimming pool. I put my hand in the sand. My sister took my book.*

LETTER IDENTIFICATION/FORMATION

Give each student a sheet of paper. Ask students to write the letter *D* in the middle and in each corner. Encourage them to say the movement pattern as they write.

Objectives

Students will:

- Listen to and duplicate sound patterns
- Determine the number of words in the line of a song
- Recognize and learn the name of the letter *d*
- Write lowercase *d*

Materials Needed

- Alphabet Chart
- Picture Word Cards: *cat, top, snake, pan, car, chick, coat, horn, apple, king, olive, umpire, hot dog, watch, mitten, queen*
- Letter Frieze Card *Dd*
- Letter Cards *d, d, d, d, D, D, D, D*
- Alphabet Strips
- BLMs *1, 2, & 3*
- Student Workmats
- StartUp Song & Rhyme CD

 # Phonological Awareness

Sound Patterns

- Explain that you will clap several times. Tell students to listen carefully so they can copy the way you clap.
- Start by clapping once, then twice. Let students clap the pattern.
- Continue, using simple patterns, such as clap-clap, clap; clap, clap-clap, clap; clap-clap, clap, clap.
- Finally, add another sound to the pattern, such as snapping your fingers, slapping your thighs, or stomping your feet. Use these sound patterns: clap, snap, snap; stomp, clap, stomp; slap, slap, clap; clap, stomp, clap, stomp. Let students repeat each pattern.

Concept of Words

- Sing or listen to the recording of *Do Your Ears Hang Low?* with students.
- Say a line from the song and have students repeat it with you. Demonstrate how to count the words by dropping a counter into a cup for each word heard.
- Show how to take the counters out of the cup and count them to find out how many words were in the line.
- Let students take turns dropping counters into a cup as you say a line. Let other volunteers count the counters to determine the number of words in the line.

Letter Name Identification/ Formation d

Shared Reading of the Alphabet Chart

- Using a pointer, read the Alphabet Chart letter by letter with the class. (*A, a; B, b; C, c; D, d*, etc.)
- Read the chart again, chanting the names of the lowercase letters and the names of the pictures. (*a, apple; b, ball*, etc.) Have students join you.

Model

- Display letter frieze card **Dd**. Explain that the name of this letter is lowercase ***d***.
- Describe the movement needed to form lowercase ***d***. Tell students to start in the middle when forming this letter.
- Say: *A lowercase* **d** *is circle back around, push up to the top, pull down.* Match the timing of your speech with the action of modeling the letter formation.

✔ **QUICK-CHECK Distribute blackline master 1. Tell students to color the shapes according to the key. They should then tap their pencils once on each red circle and twice on each blue square. Finally, have students put a check mark next to the two sound patterns that are the same.**

Do Your Ears Hang Low?

*Do your ears hang low, do they
waggle to and fro?
Can you tie them in a knot?
Can you tie them in a bow?
Can you throw them o'er your
shoulder
Like a continental soldier?
Do your ears hang low?*

*Do your ears stick out?
Can you waggle them about?
Can you flap them up and down
As you fly around the town?
Can you shut them up for sure
When you hear an awful bore?
Do your ears stick out?*

*Do your ears stand high?
Do they reach up to the sky?
Do they hang down when they're wet,
Do they stand up when they're dry?
Can you semaphore your neighbor
With a minimum of labor?
Do your ears stand high?*

Independent Activities

Phonological Awareness

Provide picture cards **cat, top, snake, pan, car, chick, coat, horn, apple, king, olive, umpire, hot dog, watch, mitten,** and **queen.** Have students sort the cards into things that make a sound and things that do not. Then ask students to tell what sounds are made. Have them create a sound pattern for each, such as *meow, meow-meow.*

Letter Identification/ Formation

Let students work in pairs. Have one partner write lowercase *d.* Then have the other partner trace the letter. Partners then switch roles.

Provide each student with a strip of adding machine tape and a model of the letter *d.* Tell students to write as many *d*s on their strips as they can.

Have students write the letter *d* on a large sheet of white paper with a red crayon or marker. Tell them to trace the letter with four other colors of their own choosing.

Guided Practice

- Distribute letter cards **d, d, d,** and **d** and have students place them under the alphabet strips on their desks.
- Tell students to trace lowercase *d,* say the movement pattern, and say the letter name. Watch to make sure that students' words match their actions.

Write

- Have students practice writing lowercase *d* on their workmats.
- Remind them to say the movement pattern as they form the letter. Ask students to check their letter with the letter *d* on their alphabet strips.
- Distribute blackline master 2 and ask students to say the name of the letter. Then have them practice writing lowercase *d.* (The blackline master may be completed at this time or in a literacy center.)

Compare and Contrast

- Write lowercase *d* on the chalkboard. Write uppercase *D* next to it.
- Ask students to tell how the letters are alike and different. If they need help, say: *The lowercase* **d** *has a circle back around, then push up to the top and pull down. The uppercase* **D** *has a pull down, lift, then curve forward.*

Locate

- Have students locate *d* on their alphabet strips and name the letter and picture cue.
- Ask if anyone has the letter *d* in his or her name. Write the names on a sentence strip. Ask volunteers to frame the *d*s.

Sort

- Distribute letter cards **d, d, d, d, D, D, D,** and **D** to each student. Ask students to find all the lowercase *d*s and put them in a row. Be sure that students find all the letters and that the letters they find are the correct ones.
- Repeat with the uppercase *D*s.

QUICK-CHECK Use blackline master 3. Ask students to find all the lowercase ds and color each one a different color.

 # Small-Group Activities

Select from the following small-group activities to provide hands-on practice for students who need extra support.

SOUND PATTERNS

Sing or listen to the recording of *This Old Man* with students. Pair students and have them invent a sound pattern for the refrain "knick-knack paddy whack" using clapping, tapping, snapping, patting, or stomping. Have pairs demonstrate their patterns as the group sings.

CONCEPT OF WORDS

Choose a song or use *This Old Man.* Sing the song with students. Then say a line. Have students repeat the line while counting the words on their fingers. To help students check, repeat the line as they count each finger.

LETTER IDENTIFICATION/FORMATION

Give each student a shallow box filled with salt or sand. Have students practice writing the letter *d* while saying the movement pattern. Tell them to gently shake the box to "erase" the letter. Then ask them to write *d* again.

Objectives
Students will:
- Discriminate whether words are the same or different
- Determine the number of words in the line of a rhyme or in a sentence
- Recognize and learn the name of the letter *E*
- Write uppercase *E*

Materials Needed
- Alphabet Chart
- Picture Word Cards: *sock, tub, nut, nest, ink, van, box, fish, pen, sun, mitten, house, ball, king, jam, leaf*
- Letter Frieze Card *Ee*
- Letter Cards *E, E, E, E, d, d, d, d*
- Alphabet Strips
- BLMs *1, 2, & 3*
- Student Workmats
- StartUp Song & Rhyme CD

 Phonological Awareness

Word Discrimination
- Write **Yes** and **No** some distance apart on the board.
- Ask students to listen to these words: **bush, bush, bush.**
- Say: *All three words are the same, so I am going to point to the word* **Yes.**
- Read the words **dentist, desert,** and **dentist.**
- Say: *One of the words is different, so I am going to point to the word* **No.**
- Ask students to listen carefully to each set of words you say. Tell them to point to **Yes** if all the words are the same and to **No** if one of the words is different. Use these sets of words: **honey/honey/honey, eagle/easel/easel, puppy/puppet/puppy, window/window/window, helmet/ helmet/helmet, square/square/star.**

Concept of Words
- Say or listen to the recording of *Pease Porridge Hot* several times with students.
- Say the first line of the rhyme. Demonstrate how to count the words by stacking one block for each word you say. Count the blocks to find out how many words are in the line.
- Distribute six blocks to each student. Say the next line of the nursery rhyme. As students repeat the line with you, have them stack one block for each word they hear. Then have students count the blocks. Say the line again to check.
- Repeat with the remaining lines of the nursery rhyme.

Pease Porridge Hot
Pease porridge hot!
Pease porridge cold!
Pease porridge in the pot
Nine days old.

Some like it hot.
Some like it cold.
Some like it in the pot
Nine days old!

Letter Name Identification/Formation E

Shared Reading of the Alphabet Chart
- Using a pointer, read the Alphabet Chart letter by letter with the class. (*A, a; B, b; C, c; D, d,* etc.)
- Read the chart again, chanting the names of the uppercase letters from **A** to **Z,** then from **Z** to **A.** Have students join you.

Model
- Display letter frieze card **Ee.** Explain that the name of this letter is uppercase **E.**
- Describe the movement needed to form uppercase **E.** Tell students to start at the top when forming this letter.
- Say: *An uppercase* **E** *is pull down, lift, on the top slide right, in the middle slide right, on the bottom slide right.* Match the timing of your speech with the action of modeling the letter formation.

✓ **QUICK-CHECK Distribute blackline master 1. Tell students to name the pictures in each row and color the smiley face if the picture names are the same or the frowning face if they are different.**

Independent Activities

Phonological Awareness

Recite the nursery rhyme *Baa, Baa, Black Sheep* several times with students. Ask them to listen for and name words and phrases that are the same, such as *Baa, baa; yes, sir, yes, sir; one for, one for, one for.*

Letter Identification/ Formation

Provide old newspapers and red markers. Ask students to circle *E*s they find in the headlines.

Have students form the letter *E* with coins or buttons. Then have them scramble the objects and form the letter again.

Provide pretzel sticks. Have students make *E*s by using one long and three short pretzel sticks.

Guided Practice

• Distribute letter cards **E**, **E**, **E**, and **E** and have students place them under the alphabet strips on their desks.
• Tell students to trace uppercase *E* and say the movement pattern and the letter name. Listen and watch to make sure that students' words match their actions.

Write

• Have students practice writing uppercase *E* on their workmats.
• Remind them to say the movement pattern as they form the letter. Ask students to check their letter with the letter *E* on their alphabet strips.
• Distribute blackline master 2 and ask students to say the name of the letter. Then have them practice writing uppercase *E*. (The blackline master may be completed at this time or in a literacy center.)

Compare and Contrast

• Write uppercase *E* on the board. Write lowercase *d* next to it.
• Ask students to tell how the letters are alike and different. If they need help, say: *Both letters pull down. The uppercase* **E** *begins with a pull down. The lowercase* **d** *circles back around and pushes up to the top before it pulls down.*

Locate

• Have students locate *E* on their alphabet strips and name the letter and picture cue.
• Ask if anyone has the letter *E* in his or her name. Write the names on a sentence strip. Ask volunteers to frame the *E*s.

Sort

• Distribute letter cards **E**, **E**, **E**, **E**, **d**, **d**, **d**, and **d** to each student. Ask students to find all the uppercase *E*s and to put them in a row. Be sure that students find all the letters and that the letters they find are the correct ones.
• Repeat with the lowercase *d*s.

 QUICK-CHECK Use blackline master 3. Tell students to color the pieces, cut them out, and glue them onto the paper to build an E.

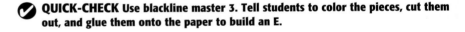 ## Small-Group Activities

Select from the following small-group activities to provide hands-on practice for students who need extra support.

WORD DISCRIMINATION

Have students listen for whether words are the same or different. Tell them to hop if all the words are the same. Use the following sets of words: *tight/tight, wood/wolf, teacher/teaspoon, slipper/slipper, rooster/rooster, pencil/penguin, dinner/dinner, marble/market, food/foot, drawing/drawing, garage/garden, eleven/eleven.*

CONCEPT OF WORDS

Use picture cards **sock, tub, nut, nest, ink, van, box, fish, pen, sun, mitten, house, ball, king, jam,** and **leaf.** Have a student take a card and say a sentence that includes the name of the object in the picture. Ask the other students to repeat the sentence while counting the number of words on their fingers.

LETTER IDENTIFICATION/FORMATION

Ask students to use self-stick notes to mark *E*s in words in library books. Let students show some of the words they found to the other students in the group.

Objectives

Students will:

- Discriminate whether words are the same or different
- Determine the number of words in the line of a song, category label, or sentence
- Recognize and learn the name of the letter *e*
- Write lowercase *e*

Materials Needed

- Alphabet Chart
- Picture Word Cards: *apple, sandwich, nut, napkin, fork, pumpkin, olive, cup, egg, dish, lunchbox, vegetables, jam, cake, corn, wheat*
- Letter Frieze Card *Ee*
- Letter Cards *e, e, e, e, E, E, E, E*
- Alphabet Strips
- BLMs *1, 2, & 3*
- Student Workmats
- StartUp Song & Rhyme CD

 Phonological Awareness

Word Discrimination

- Say the words **apple, apple,** and **apron,** holding up a finger each time you say a word.
- Point out that two of the words are the same, but one is different.
- Ask students to say the words with you while numbering them with their fingers.
- Tell students to hold up one, two, or three fingers to indicate whether the first, second, or third word is different.
- Repeat with the following sets of words: **carry/cart/carry, feathers/father/father, jump/jump/judge, lemon/leopard/lemon, picture/picnic/picnic, seesaw/season/seesaw.**

Row, row, row your boat
Gently down the stream.
Merrily, merrily, merrily, merrily,
Life is but a dream.

Concept of Words

- Prepare a sentence strip for each line of the song *Row, Row, Row Your Boat.*
- Sing or listen to the recording of the song with students several times.
- Say the first line of the song. Demonstrate how to count the words on your fingers. Check by holding up the sentence strip for the first line and counting the words.
- Say the next line of the song. As students repeat the line with you, have them count the number of words on their fingers. Help them check by counting the words on the sentence strip for the second line.
- Repeat with the remaining lines of the song.

Letter Name Identification/Formation e

Shared Reading of the Alphabet Chart

- Using a pointer, read the Alphabet Chart letter by letter with the class. (*A, a; B, b; C, c; D, d,* etc.)
- Read the chart again, chanting the names of the lowercase letters from *a* to *z*, then from *z* to *a*. Have students join you.

Model

- Display letter frieze card **Ee.** Explain that the name of this letter is lowercase **e.**
- Describe the movement needed to form lowercase **e.**
- Say: *A lowercase* **e** *is slide right, circle left.* Match the timing of your speech with the action of modeling the letter formation.

✔ **QUICK-CHECK Distribute blackline master 1. Tell students to say the name of each picture in a row. Have them count the words in the row and write the number in the box.**

Independent Activities

Phonological Awareness

Ask students to draw a picture about a place they like to go. Then have them make up a sentence about their picture, such as "I like to go to the zoo." Instruct the other students to repeat the sentence while counting the words on their fingers.

Letter Identification/ Formation

Provide a model of a letter *e* made of pipe cleaners and have students make their own pipe-cleaner *e*s.

Have students fold a sheet of paper as many times as they can. Then tell them to unfold the paper and write the letter *e* in each of the sections.

Mix several sets of letter cards. Have students find all the *e*s.

Guided Practice

• Distribute letter cards **e, e, e,** and **e** and have students place them under the alphabet strips on their desks.
• Tell students to trace lowercase *e* and say the movement pattern and the letter name. Make sure students' words match their actions.

Write

• Have students practice writing lowercase *e* on their workmats.
• Remind them to say the movement pattern as they form the letter. Ask students to check their letter with the letter *e* on their alphabet strips.
• Distribute blackline master 2 and ask students to say the name of the letter. Then have them practice writing lowercase *e*. (The blackline master may be completed at this time or in a literacy center.)

Compare and Contrast

• Write lowercase *e* on the board. Write uppercase *E* next to it.
• Ask students to tell how the letters are alike and different. If they need help, say: *Both letters slide right. The lowercase* e *slides right first, then circles back. The uppercase* E *pulls down, lifts, then slides right on the top, middle, and bottom.*

Locate

• Have students locate *e* on their alphabet strips and name the letter and picture cue.
• Ask if anyone has the letter *e* in his or her name. Write the names on a sentence strip. Ask volunteers to frame the *e*s.

Sort

• Distribute letter cards **e, e, e, e, E, E, E,** and **E** to each student. Ask students to put all the lowercase *e*s in a row. Be sure that students find all the letters and that the letters they find are the correct ones.
• Repeat with the uppercase *E*s.

 QUICK-CHECK Use blackline master 3. Tell students to fill in the blanks with *e*s, then read the letters in each row.

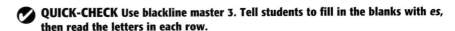
Small-Group Activities

The following small-group activities can be used to provide hands-on practice for students who need extra support.

WORD DISCRIMINATION

Pair students. Ask each pair to choose two words, either the same two words or two different words. Have each pair say its word to the group. Have the other students tell if the words are the same or different.

CONCEPT OF WORDS

Provide picture cards **apple, sandwich, nut, napkin, fork, pumpkin, olive, cup, egg, dish, lunchbox, vegetables, jam, cake, corn,** and **wheat.** One at a time, students are to select a card and tell in which of these categories the picture belongs: *My Favorite Foods, Things I Use to Eat, Foods That Grow.* The other students repeat the category name while counting the number of words in the category on their fingers.

LETTER IDENTIFICATION/FORMATION

Give each student a shallow box lined with salt or sand. Have students practice writing the letter *e* while saying the movement pattern.

Objectives

Students will:

- Discriminate whether words are the same or different
- Discriminate between short and long words
- Recognize and learn the name of the letter *F*
- Write uppercase *F*

Materials Needed

- Alphabet Chart
- Picture Word Cards: *queen, vegetables, van, vest, kangaroo, jump rope, jam, lunchbox, dinosaur, envelope, rug, box, helicopter, pan, notebook, nest*
- Letter Frieze Card *Ff*
- Letter Cards *F, F, F, F, e, e, e, e*
- Alphabet Strips
- BLMs *1, 2, & 3*
- Student Workmats

 # Phonological Awareness

Word Discrimination

- Post signs that say "1," "2," and "3." Ask students to listen to these words: **play, play, plum.**
- Point out that word number one and word number two are the same, but word number three is different. Say: *Word number three is different, so I am going to point to the 3.*
- Say the words **near, nail,** and **nail.** Say: *Word number one is different, so I am going to point to the 1.*
- Ask students to listen carefully to each set of words. Tell them to point to the 1 if word one is different, to the 2 if word two is different, and to the 3 if word three is different.
- Use these words: **robot/rocket/rocket, seal/seal/seven, front/frost/front, kite/kite/key, honey/hammer/hammer, barrel/basket/barrel.**

Short and Long Words

- Say: *Some words are longer than other words. We can listen to hear which words are longer. Listen to these words:* **tree, dinosaur.**
- Let students say which is the longer word. Explain that they know **dinosaur** is longer because it takes more time to say.
- Tell students that there is another way to check. Write **tree** and **dinosaur** on the board, one under the other. Show students that **dinosaur** is the longer word because it has more letters than **tree.**
- Repeat the process with these word pairs: **cat/ladybug, umbrella/bus, motorcycle/boat, truck/mosquito, car/crocodile, cage/cucumber.**

 # Letter Name Identification/ Formation F

Shared Reading of the Alphabet Chart

- Using a pointer, read the Alphabet Chart letter by letter with the class. (*A, a; B, b; C, c; D, d,* etc.)
- Read the chart again. Say the picture cue, then the uppercase letter. (*apple, A; ball, B,* etc.) Have students join you.

Model

- Display letter frieze card **Ff.** Explain that the name of this letter is uppercase **F.**
- Describe the movement needed to form uppercase **F.** Tell students to start at the top when forming this letter.
- Say: *An uppercase* **F** *is pull down, lift, on the top slide right, in the middle slide right.* Match the timing of your speech with the action of modeling the letter formation.

✓ **QUICK-CHECK** Distribute blackline master 1. Tell students to name the pictures in each row and then to color the picture whose name is different.

Independent Activities

Phonological Awareness

Use picture cards **queen, vegetables, van, vest, kangaroo, jump rope, jam, lunchbox, dinosaur, envelope, rug, box, helicopter, pan, notebook,** and **nest.** Have students name each picture and sort the cards into groups of short and long picture names.

Letter Identification/ Formation

Provide construction paper, glue, dry beans, and a model of the letter **F.** Have students write a large **F** on the construction paper with glue and attach beans to the glue.

Cut the letter **F** out of a sponge. Fill a shallow pan with tempera paint. Have students cover the bottom of the sponge with a thin layer of paint, then press the sponge onto a sheet of white drawing paper.

Provide several sets of magnetic letters. Have students sort through the letters and place all the uppercase **F**s on a cookie sheet.

Guided Practice
- Distribute letter cards **F, F, F,** and **F** and have students place them under the alphabet strips on their desks.
- Tell students to trace uppercase **F** and say the movement pattern and letter name. Make sure that students' words match their actions.

Write
- Have students practice writing uppercase **F** on their workmats.
- Remind them to say the movement pattern as they form the letter. Ask students to check their letter with the letter **F** on their alphabet strips.
- Distribute blackline master 2 and ask students to say the name of the letter. Then have them practice writing uppercase **F.** (The blackline master may be completed at this time or in a literacy center.)

Compare and Contrast
- Write uppercase **F** on the chalkboard. Write lowercase **e** next to it.
- Ask students to tell how the letters are alike and different. If they need help, say: *Both letters slide right. The uppercase **F** pulls down, lifts, then slides right on the top and in the middle. The lowercase **e** slides right first, then circles back.*

Locate
- Have students locate **F** on their alphabet strips and name the letter and picture cue.
- Ask if anyone has the letter **F** in his or her name. Write the names on a sentence strip. Ask volunteers to frame the **F**s.

Sort
- Distribute letter cards **F, F, F, F, e, e, e,** and **e** to each student. Ask students to find all the uppercase **F**s and put them in a row. Be sure that students find all the letters and that the letters they find are the correct ones.
- Repeat with the lowercase **e**s.

 QUICK-CHECK Use blackline master 3. Tell students to look at the letters on the page and color all the Fs that look right.

 # Small-Group Activities

Select from the following small-group activities to provide hands-on practice for students who need extra support.

WORD DISCRIMINATION

Give students smiley face stickers to put on their thumbs, or have them draw two eyes and a smile on their thumbs with a washable marker. Ask students to listen and decide whether two words are the same or different. If the words are the same, students are to hold up their smiley face thumbs. Read these pairs of words: *alphabet/ambulance, dancer/dancer, celery/cereal, hotel/ hotel, eraser/eraser, dolphin/donkey, salad/ salad, pebble/pencil.*

SHORT AND LONG WORDS

Say the following pairs of words: *pig/astronaut, hot/cauliflower, salt/doghouse, cliff/ handkerchief, day/seventeen, arm/porcupine.* Ask students to repeat the words with you while they show with their hands which is the short word (hands close together) and which is the long word (hands far apart).

LETTER IDENTIFICATION/FORMATION

Have students write uppercase **F**s on the board, using paintbrushes dipped in water. Encourage them to say the movement pattern as they write.

Objectives

Students will:

- Discriminate between words that rhyme and words that do not
- Determine the number of words in a sentence
- Recognize and learn the name of the letter *f*
- Write lowercase *f*

Materials Needed

- Alphabet Chart
- Picture Word Cards: *sub, king, frog, nest, van, tub, cat, fan, bat, ring, vest, dog*
- Letter Frieze Card *Ff*
- Letter Cards *f, f, f, f, F, F, F, F*
- Alphabet Strips
- BLMs *1, 2, & 3*
- Student Workmats
- StartUp Song & Rhyme CD

 # Phonological Awareness

Rhyme Recognition

- Say the following words: ***bark, cup, park.*** Slowly say each word again, emphasizing the rhyme. Ask: *Which two words rhyme? Which word does not belong?*
- If students have difficulty, say: **Bark** and **park** *go together because they rhyme. They have the same middle and ending sounds, but* **cup** *does not have the same middle and ending sounds.*
- Continue with these sets of words: ***ball/call/band, spill/now/fill, cast/bring/ring, bunk/junk/jar, dive/jet/five, bed/feet/sweet.***

Concept of Words

- Say this sentence: "I like dogs." Demonstrate how to count the words by dropping a counter into a cup for each word.
- Show how to take the counters out of the cup and count them to find out how many words were in the sentence.
- Distribute a cup and markers to each student. Say this sentence: "The boy ran and hid." As students repeat the sentence, have them drop one counter into an empty cup for each word they hear.
- Have students pour the counters into one hand and count how many there are. Say the sentence again to check.
- Repeat the process with the sentences in the box at right.

> *I am sad.*
> *She is a nice girl.*
> *I see four cars.*
> *Look at the big house.*
> *I can jump.*
> *The cat is soft.*

Letter Name Identification/ Formation f

Shared Reading of the Alphabet Chart

- Using a pointer, read the Alphabet Chart letter by letter with the class. Start by reading the uppercase letters together in a high voice and the lowercase letters in a low voice.
- Read the chart again, chanting the names of the letters and the names of the pictures. (*A, a, apple; B, b, ball*, etc.) Have students join you.

Model

- Display letter frieze card **Ff.** Explain that the name of this letter is lowercase ***f.***
- Describe the movement needed to form lowercase ***f.*** Tell students to start at the top when forming this letter.
- Say: *A lowercase* **f** *is curve back from the top, cross in the middle.* Match the timing of your speech with the action of modeling the letter formation.

✓ **QUICK-CHECK Distribute blackline master 1. Tell students to name the picture in each row and cross out the picture for the word in each row that does not rhyme.**

Phonological Awareness

Place picture cards **sub, king, frog, nest, van, tub, cat, fan, bat, ring, vest,** and **dog** in the literacy center. Have students say the name of each picture aloud and match the cards whose names rhyme.

Letter Identification/ Formation

Provide an assortment of felt letters. Have students sort through the letters and place all the *f*s on the feltboard.

Supply old magazines, glue, construction paper, and scissors. Tell students to search through the magazines for lowercase *f*, cut out the letters they find, and paste the letters on construction paper.

Place photocopies of a poem or song that has been shared in class in the center. Have students find and circle all the *f*s.

I'm a Little Teapot

I'm a little teapot, short and stout,
Here is my handle, here is my spout.
When I get all steamed up, hear me shout.
Tip me over and pour me out.

Guided Practice

- Distribute letter cards **f, f, f,** and **f** and have students place them under the alphabet strips on their desks.
- Tell students to trace lowercase *f* and say the movement pattern and the letter name. Listen and watch to make sure that students' words match their actions.

Write

- Have students practice writing lowercase *f* on their workmats.
- Remind them to say the movement pattern as they form the letter. Ask students to check their letter with the letter *f* on their alphabet strips.
- Distribute blackline master 2 and ask students to say the name of the letter. Then have them practice writing lowercase *f.* (The blackline master may be completed at this time or in a literacy center.)

Compare and Contrast

- Write lowercase *f* on the board. Write uppercase *F* next to it.
- Ask students to tell how the letters are alike and different. If they need help, say: *The lowercase* **f** *has a curved top and a straight line going down and crosses in the middle. The uppercase* **F** *has a straight line going down and straight lines that go right at the top and in the middle.*

Locate

- Have students locate *f* on their alphabet strips and name the letter and picture cue.
- Ask if anyone has the letter *f* in his or her name. Write the names on a sentence strip. Ask volunteers to frame the *f*s.

Sort

- Distribute letter cards **f, f, f, f, F, F, F,** and **F** to each student. Ask students to find all the lowercase *f*s and put them in a row. Be sure that students find all the letters and that the letters they find are the correct ones.
- Repeat with the uppercase *F*s.

 QUICK-CHECK Use blackline master 3. Tell students to look at the letters at the bottom of the page, cut out all the lowercase *f*s, and glue them in the boxes.

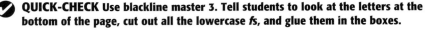 **Small-Group Activities**

Select from the following small-group activities to provide hands-on practice for students who need extra support.

RHYME RECOGNITION

Recite or listen to the recording of *I'm a Little Teapot,* pantomiming the actions. Then recite the rhyme, emphasizing the rhyming words. Repeat the rhyme. Stop after each pair of rhyming words and ask students to identify them. Finally, have students recite the rhyme and perform the actions.

CONCEPT OF WORDS

Invite students to take turns making up sentences about things they can do, such as "I can jump high" or "I can tie my shoes." Ask the other students to repeat the sentence while counting the number of words on their fingers.

LETTER IDENTIFICATION/FORMATION

Give each student a sheet of paper. Ask students to write the letter *f* in the middle and in each corner. Encourage them to say the movement pattern as they write.

Objectives
Students will:

- Discriminate whether words are the same or different
- Add words to sentences
- Recognize and learn the name of the letter *G*
- Write uppercase *G*

Materials Needed

- Alphabet Chart
- Picture Word Cards: *swing, train, wheat, shell, light, claw, block, skate, duck, ring, soap, horn*
- Letter Frieze Card *Gg*
- Letter Cards *G, G, G, G, f, f, f, f*
- Alphabet Strips
- BLMs *1, 2, & 3*
- Student Workmats
- StartUp Song & Rhyme CD

Phonological Awareness

Word Discrimination

- Ask students to listen to these words: ***tent, tent.*** Point out that the words are the same.
- Tell students to listen carefully to each pair of words you say. Say: *Stand up if the words are the same. Stay seated if the words are different.*
- Use these pairs of words: ***violin/vine, mix/mix, gold/gold, face/fish, ladder/lemon, sleep/sleep.***

Adding Words to Sentences

- Tell students that they will build some long sentences by adding words.
- Model by using your name and something you are doing. Say *[Your name] is reading.*
- Explain that you will make the sentence longer by adding words. Say: *[Your name] is reading a book. [Your name] is reading a book about birds.*
- Have a volunteer stand and perform an action, such as walking in place. Ask another volunteer to use the student's name and make a sentence that describes what he or she is doing. *([Student's name] is walking.)*
- Ask another student to add words to make the sentence longer. Prompt with questions. Ask: *Where could [student's name] be going? ([Student's name] is walking to the library.)* Have other students make more long sentences.

Letter Name Identification/ Formation G

Shared Reading of the Alphabet Chart

- Using a pointer, read the Alphabet Chart letter by letter with the class. Read the uppercase letters first. (*A, B, C,* etc.)
- Read the chart again, chanting the lowercase letters. (*a, b, c,* etc.) Have students join you.

Model

- Display letter frieze card **Gg.** Explain that the name of this letter is uppercase **G.**
- Describe the movement needed to form uppercase **G.** Tell students to start at the top when forming this letter.
- Say: *An uppercase **G** is circle back at the top, slide left in the middle.* Match the timing of your speech with the action of modeling the letter formation.

✓ **QUICK-CHECK Distribute blackline master 1. Tell students to look at each picture, make up a sentence about it, and color the picture that helps them make the longest sentence.**

Independent Activities

Phonological Awareness

Have pairs of students sing or listen to the recording of *Skip to My Lou*. Ask them to listen for and name words that are the same, such as **skip, skip, skip** and **shoo, shoo, shoo.**

Letter Identification/ Formation

Make an outline of the letter *G* on sheets of construction paper. Have students cut out the letters and decorate them with written *G*s.

Provide strips of adding machine paper and a model of the letter *G.* Tell students to write as many *G*s as they can on their paper strips.

Have students practice writing large *G*s on the board using different colors. Remind them to say the movement pattern as they write.

Guided Practice
- Distribute letter cards **G, G, G,** and **G** and have students place them under the alphabet strips on their desks.
- Tell students to trace uppercase *G* and say the movement pattern and the letter name. Listen and watch to make sure that students' words match their actions.

Write
- Have students practice writing uppercase *G* on their workmats.
- Remind them to say the movement pattern as they form the letter. Ask students to check their letter with the letter *G* on their alphabet strips.
- Distribute blackline master 2 and ask students to say the name of the letter. Then have them practice writing uppercase *G.* (The blackline master may be completed at this time or in a literacy center.)

Compare and Contrast
- Write uppercase *G* on the chalkboard. Write lowercase *f* next to it.
- Ask students to tell how the letters are alike and different. If they need help, say: *Both letters curve back at the top. The uppercase* **G** *slides left in the middle. The lowercase* **f** *crosses in the middle.*

Locate
- Have students locate *G* on their alphabet strips and name the letter and picture cue.
- Ask if anyone has the letter *G* in his or her name. Write the names on a sentence strip. Ask volunteers to frame the *G*s.

Sort
- Distribute letter cards **G, G, G, G, f, f, f,** and **f** to each student. Ask students to find all the uppercase *G*s and put them in a row. Be sure that students find all the letters and that the letters they find are the correct ones.
- Repeat with the lowercase *f*s.

 QUICK-CHECK Use blackline master 3. Tell students to color all the uppercase Gs.

 Small Group Activities

Select from the following small group activities to provide hands-on practice for students who need extra support.

WORD DISCRIMINATION
Have students listen and tell whether words are the same or different. If the words are the same, tell students to hop. Use these pairs of words: *flag/fin, horse/hose, spray/ spray, vase/van, web/web, neck/neck, wagon/wallet, zero/zero, nine/nose, wig/ leg, write/write, child/child.*

ADDING WORDS TO SENTENCES
Place these picture cards facedown: **swing, train, wheat, shell, light, claw, block, skate, duck, ring, soap, horn.** Ask a student to choose a card and make up a sentence about the picture. Then ask another student to repeat the sentence, adding words to it.

LETTER IDENTIFICATION/FORMATION
Have students see how many *G*s they can write on their workmats in one minute. Encourage them to say the movement pattern as they write. Have students circle their best letter. Then ask them to erase the letters. Repeat the activity.

Objectives
Students will:

- Identify and remember a sequence of sounds
- Add words to incomplete sentences
- Recognize and learn the name of the letter *g*
- Write lowercase *g*

Materials Needed

- Alphabet Chart
- Picture Word Cards: *mop, apple, sock, top, nut, igloo, fan, pan, ostrich, cat, helicopter, umbrella, skunk, envelope, guitar, wagon*
- Letter Frieze Card *Gg*
- Letter Cards g, g, *g, g*, G, G, G, *G*
- Alphabet Strips
- BLMs *1, 2, & 3*
- Student Workmats

 # Phonological Awareness

Activate Listening

- Have students close their eyes and listen carefully as you make a sound. Knock on your desk. Have students open their eyes. Ask them to identify the sound.
- Tell students to listen again. Explain that this time you will make more than one sound.
- Cough and drop a book. Ask students to open their eyes and identify the two sounds.
- Repeat with these pairs of sounds: sneeze/snap fingers, clap/stomp, blow a whistle/ring a bell, sniff/tap a pencil on a desk.

Sentence Completion

- Remind students that sentences are made up of smaller parts called words. Words are used to make sentences. Say: *I am a teacher*. Explain that this is a sentence.
- Ask students to listen to another group of words. Say: *I am a...* Explain that the words do not make sense, so they do not make a sentence.
- Ask volunteers to add more words, such as **girl, baseball player,** or **big brother,** to make the group of words into a sentence.
- Repeat with the sentence starters at the right.

I like to...
Look at the...
Here is my...
I have a lot of...
Mom saw a...
It is time to...

Letter Name Identification/ Formation g

Shared Reading of the Alphabet Chart

- Using a pointer, chant the name of the picture for each letter, then the uppercase letter, then the lowercase letter. (*apple, A, a; ball, B, b*, etc.) Have students join you.

Model

- Display letter frieze card **Gg.** Explain that the name of this letter is lowercase **g.**
- Describe the movement needed to form lowercase **g.** Tell students to start at the top when forming this letter.
- Say: *A lowercase* **g** *is circle back around, push up, pull down, curve in.* Match the timing of your speech with the action of modeling the letter formation.

✓ **QUICK-CHECK Distribute blackline master 1. Tell students to color each object that makes a sound.**

Phonological Awareness

Have partners take turns selecting one of these picture cards: **mop, apple, sock, top, nut, igloo, fan, pan, ostrich, cat, helicopter, umbrella, skunk, envelope, guitar, wagon.** One partner starts a sentence about the picture. The other partner finishes the sentence.

Letter Identification/ Formation

Write large *g*s on construction paper. Provide modeling clay and have students outline the letters with clay.

Provide newspaper shopping ads. Ask students to circle all the *g*s, using a brightly colored crayon or marker.

Put several sets of magnetic letters into a soup pot. Have students take turns ladling out several letters and locating the lowercase *g*s. When the pot is empty, have students refill it with the letters and start again.

Guided Practice
- Distribute letter cards **g, g, g,** and **g** and have students place them under the alphabet strips on their desks.
- Tell students to trace lowercase *g* and say the movement pattern and the letter name. Listen and watch to make sure that students' words match their actions.

Write
- Have students practice writing lowercase *g* on their workmats.
- Remind them to say the movement pattern as they form the letter. Ask students to check their letter with the letter *g* on their alphabet strips.
- Distribute blackline master 2 and ask students to say the name of the letter. Then have them practice writing lowercase *g*. (The blackline master may be completed at this time or in a literacy center.)

Compare and Contrast
- Write lowercase *g* on the chalkboard. Write uppercase **G** next to it.
- Ask students to tell how the letters are alike and different. If they need help, say: *Both letters circle back at the top. The lowercase* **g** *pushes up, pulls down, and curves in. The uppercase* **G** *slides left in the middle.*

Locate
- Have students locate *g* on their alphabet strips and name the letter and picture cue.
- Ask if anyone has the letter *g* in his or her name. Write the names on a sentence strip. Ask volunteers to frame the *g*s.

Sort
- Distribute letter cards **g, g, g, g, G, G, G,** and **G** to each student. Ask students to find all the lowercase *g*s and put them in a row. Be sure that students find all the letters and that the letters they find are the correct ones.
- Repeat with the uppercase **G**s.

 QUICK-CHECK Use blackline master 3. Tell students to find their way through the maze by circling all the *g*s.

 ## Small-Group Activities

Select from the following small-group activities to provide hands-on practice for students who need extra support.

LISTENING
Give each student a set of drumsticks or two unsharpened pencils. Ask students to listen while you hit your sticks together in a sound pattern. Then have them repeat the pattern. Let students take turns creating sound patterns for others to repeat.

SENTENCE COMPLETION
Have students complete the following sentence starters aloud: *I am…, I love…, I like to eat…, I see two…, I ride in the…, I can….*

LETTER IDENTIFICATION/FORMATION
Provide a variety of alphabet books and have students locate and compare the lowercase *g*s. Point out that lowercase *g* as well as other letters can be shown in print in different ways.

Objectives

Students will:

- Discriminate between words that rhyme and words that do not
- Discriminate between short and long words
- Recognize and learn the name of the letter *H*
- Write uppercase *H*

Materials Needed

- Alphabet Chart
- Picture Word Cards: *kangaroo, umbrella, leaf, dinosaur, gate, elephant, box, dog, helicopter, ostrich, iguana, pumpkin, sun, notebook, map, antelope*
- Letter Frieze Card *Hh*
- Letter Cards *H, H, H, H, g, g, g, g*
- Alphabet Strips
- BLMs *1, 2,* & *3*
- Student Workmats

 # Phonological Awareness

Rhyme Recognition

- Say: *A cat wore a hat.* Have students repeat the sentence. Ask: *Did any words rhyme?* Help students name the rhyming words **cat** and **hat.**
- Say: *A cat wore a coat.* Have students repeat the sentence. Ask: *Did any words rhyme in this sentence?* Point out that there are no rhyming words.
- Repeat with the sentences in the box at right. Have students clap two times and name the rhyming words if they hear a rhyme. Have them shake their heads *no* if they do not hear a rhyme.

> *A mouse is in my house.*
> *I like to sing on the swing.*
> *She stood on the stairs.*
> *The bug crawled on the rug.*
> *The bear swatted the bee.*
> *It's a good day to play.*

Short and Long Words

- Say: *Some words are longer than other words. We can hear which words are longer. Listen to these words:* **butterfly, bus.**
- Let students say which is the longer word. Explain that **butterfly** is longer because it takes more time to say.
- Tell students that there is another way to check. Write **butterfly** and **bus** on the board, one under the other. Show students that **butterfly** is longer because it has more letters than **bus.**
- Repeat with these word pairs: ***train/ambulance, grasshopper/snake, bumblebee/horse, car/caterpillar, house/photograph, harmonica/truck.***

Letter Name Identification/ Formation H

Shared Reading of the Alphabet Chart

- Using a pointer, read the Alphabet Chart letter by letter with the class, saying the uppercase letters. (*A, B, C, D,* etc.)
- Read the chart again, this time chanting the uppercase letters backward. (*Z, Y, X, W,* etc.) Have students join you.

Model

- Display letter frieze card **Hh.** Explain that the name of this letter is uppercase **H.**
- Describe the movement needed to form uppercase **H.** Tell students to start at the top when forming this letter.
- Say: *An uppercase* **H** *is pull down, lift, pull down, cross in the middle.* Match the timing of your speech with the action of modeling the letter formation.

✓ **QUICK-CHECK Distribute blackline master 1. Tell students to look at each pair of pictures, say the picture names, and color the picture that has the longer name.**

Independent Activities

Phonological Awareness

Let students work in small groups. Provide picture cards **kangaroo, umbrella, leaf, dinosaur, gate, elephant, box, dog, helicopter, ostrich, iguana, pumpkin, sun, notebook, map,** and **antelope.** Have students take turns choosing two cards and saying the picture names. Ask them to say which of the two words is longer or if the two words are about the same length. Have the other students say if they agree or disagree.

Letter Identification/ Formation

Provide short and long pretzel sticks. Let students make *H*s using two long sticks and one short stick.

Place photocopies of *Humpty Dumpty* in the literacy center. Ask students to say the rhyme if they know it. Then have them locate and circle the *H*s in the poem.

Supply old magazines, scissors, glue, and construction paper. Tell students to write an uppercase *H* on the construction paper, then search for *H*s to cut out and paste on the paper.

Guided Practice
- Distribute letter cards **H, H, H,** and **H** and have students place them under the alphabet strips on their desks.
- Tell students to trace uppercase *H* and say the movement pattern and the letter name. Listen and watch to make sure that students' words match their actions.

Write
- Have students practice writing uppercase *H* on their workmats.
- Remind them to say the movement pattern as they form the letter. Ask students to check their letter with the letter *H* on their alphabet strips.
- Distribute blackline master 2 and ask students to say the name of the letter. Then have them practice writing uppercase *H.* (The blackline master may be completed at this time or in a literacy center.)

Compare and Contrast
- Write uppercase *H* on the chalkboard. Write lowercase *g* next to it.
- Ask students to tell how the letters are alike and different. If they need help, say: *Both letters use a pull-down movement. The uppercase* **H** *pulls down twice, then crosses in the middle. The lowercase* **g** *pulls down, then curves in.*

Locate
- Have students locate *H* on their alphabet strips and name the letter and picture cue.
- Ask if anyone has the letter *H* in his or her name. Write the names on a sentence strip. Ask volunteers to frame the *H*s.

Sort
- Distribute letter cards **H, H, H, H, g, g, g,** and **g** to each student. Ask students to find all the uppercase *H*s and put them in a row. Be sure that students find all the letters and that the letters they find are the correct ones.
- Repeat with the lowercase *g*s.

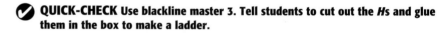 **QUICK-CHECK Use blackline master 3. Tell students to cut out the *H*s and glue them in the box to make a ladder.**

 # Small-Group Activities

Select from the following small-group activities to provide hands-on practice for students who need extra support.

RHYME RECOGNITION
Provide each student with a noisemaker, such as a bell or shaker. Tell students to use their noisemakers each time they hear rhyming words and hold them still when they do not. Have students identify the rhyming words they hear. Use these sentences: *We ate cake by the lake. The man had a plan. They played at the park. She ran in the race.*

SHORT AND LONG WORDS
Say these pairs of words, one pair at a time: ***tree/basketball, cat/ladybug, umbrella/ car, motorcycle/bear, toe/cheeseburger, marshmallow/kids.*** Ask students to repeat the words while they show with their hands which is the shorter word (hands close together) and which is the longer word (hands far apart).

LETTER IDENTIFICATION/FORMATION
Ask students to locate *H*s in the yellow pages of old telephone books. Tell them to circle the letters they find with a crayon or marker.

Objectives
Students will:

- Listen to and repeat a sequence of words
- Produce a rhyming word in response to a clue
- Recognize and learn the name of the letter *h*
- Write lowercase *h*

Materials Needed

- Alphabet Chart
- Picture Word Cards: *ant, wheat, stick, bell, kite, chick, coat, mop, skunk, shell, block, chain, frog, ski, swing, jar*
- Letter Frieze Card *Hh*
- Letter Cards *h, h, h, h, H, H, H, H*
- Alphabet Strips
- BLMs *1, 2, & 3*
- Student Workmats
- StartUp Song & Rhyme CD

Phonological Awareness

Listen and Repeat

- Say: *Listen to these words—***bat, cup, day.** *Say the words to me.* Have students repeat the words.
- Repeat with the words ***lake, ice,*** and ***farm.*** After students repeat the words, tell them that they are learning to be good listeners.
- Continue with the following sets of words: ***hat/kite/lock, win/two/swing, six/plant/nose, seed/log/chip, bee/cut/shark, plum/tape/slow.***

Produce Rhyme

- Say: *I am thinking of two words that rhyme. I will tell you one word. Then I will give you a clue for the other word.*
- Say: *I know a word that rhymes with* **hen** *and is a number larger than nine. What is my word?* (**ten**)
- Repeat with the clues in the box at the right.

I know a word that rhymes with. . .

. . . **toe** *and is something cold and white.* (**snow**)

. . . **fun** *and gives us light.* (**sun**)

. . . **nose** *and is a kind of flower.* (**rose**)

. . . **make** *and is what you eat on your birthday.* (**cake**)

. . . **lamp** *and is something you put on a letter.* (**stamp**)

. . . **nail** *and is something a dog wags.* (**tail**)

Letter Name Identification/ Formation h

Shared Reading of the Alphabet Chart

- Using a pointer, read the Alphabet Chart letter by letter with the class, saying every other lowercase letter starting with ***a.*** (*a, c, e, g,* etc.)
- Read the chart again, chanting every other lowercase letter, starting with ***b.*** (*b, d, f, h,* etc.) Have students join you.

Model

- Display letter frieze card **Hh.** Explain that the name of this letter is lowercase ***h.***
- Describe the movement needed to form lowercase ***h.*** Tell students to start at the top when forming this letter.
- Say: *A lowercase* **h** *is pull down, push up to the middle, curve forward, pull down.* Match the timing of your speech with the action of modeling the letter formation.

QUICK-CHECK Distribute blackline master 1. Tell students to name each picture and draw something whose name rhymes with the picture name.

Phonological Awareness

Provide picture cards **ant, wheat, stick, bell, kite, chick, coat, mop, skunk, shell, block, chain, frog, ski, swing,** and **jar.** Let students work in pairs. One partner draws three cards and says the picture names. The other partner repeats the picture names without looking at the cards.

Letter Identification/ Formation

Have students form lowercase *h* using cereal or raisins. Have them repeat the activity several times.

Provide construction paper, glue, sand, and a model of the letter *h.* Have students write a large *h* on the construction paper with glue and sprinkle sand onto the glue. After the glue dries, have them shake off the excess sand and trace the letter with their fingers.

Place a supply of felt letters in the literacy center. Have students sort through the letters and place all the *h*s on the feltboard.

Guided Practice
- Distribute letter cards **h, h, h,** and **h** and have students place them under the alphabet strips on their desks.
- Tell students to trace lowercase *h* and say the movement pattern and the letter name. Listen and watch to make sure that students' words match their actions.

Write
- Have students practice writing lowercase *h* on their workmats.
- Remind them to say the movement pattern as they form the letter. Ask students to check their letter with the letter *h* on their alphabet strips.
- Distribute blackline master 2 and ask students to say the name of the letter. Then have them practice writing lowercase *h.* (The blackline master may be completed at this time or in a literacy center.)

Compare and Contrast
- Write lowercase *h* on the chalkboard. Write uppercase *H* next to it.
- Ask students to tell how the letters are alike and different. If they need help, say: *Both letters start with a pull-down movement. The lowercase* **h** *pushes up to the middle, curves forward, and pulls down. The uppercase* **H** *lifts, pulls down again, and crosses in the middle.*

Locate
- Have students locate *h* on their alphabet strips and name the letter and picture cue.
- Ask if anyone has the letter *h* in his or her name. Write the names on a sentence strip. Ask volunteers to frame the *h*s.

Sort
- Distribute letter cards **h, h, h, h, H, H, H,** and **H** to each student. Ask students to find all the lowercase *h*s and put them in a row. Be sure that students find all the letters and that the letters they find are the correct ones.
- Repeat with the uppercase *H*s.

 QUICK-CHECK Use blackline master 3. Tell students to color each part that has *h* and then tell you what they have made.

 # Small-Group Activities

Select from the following small-group activities to provide hands-on practice for students who need extra support.

LISTEN AND REPEAT
Say the following sets of words to students and ask them to repeat the words: *arm/box/cry, fog/gray/last, shed/pole/night, wolf/sing/teeth, bone/cart/deer, hood/flour/drum, nine/push/rain, waves/talk/soup.*

PRODUCE RHYME
Recite or listen to the recording of the nursery rhyme *I Hop On My Horse.* Emphasize the meaning by pantomiming. Pretend to ride the horse, place your arms high and then low, put your hand on your head, and pull back on reins. Recite the poem again, this time stopping before *down* and *whoa* to let students supply the rhymes.

LETTER IDENTIFICATION/FORMATION
Have students write *h*s on several small self-stick notes. Let each student select his or her best *h* to stick on the board.

Objectives
Students will:

- Produce a rhyming word in response to a clue
- Segment words by syllables
- Recognize and learn the names of the letters *I* and *i*
- Write uppercase *I* and lowercase *i*

Materials Needed

- Alphabet Chart
- Picture Word Cards: *map, magnet, ant, sun, sandwich, tent, tiger, nut, nest, pumpkin, ox, car, house, umpire, guitar, web*
- Letter Frieze Card *Ii*
- Letter Cards *I, I, I, I, i, i, i, i*
- Alphabet Strips
- BLMs *1, 2, & 3*
- Student Workmats
- StartUp Song & Rhyme CD

 Phonological Awareness

Produce Rhyme

- Tell students you are thinking of two words that rhyme. You will tell them one word, then give them a clue for the other word.
- Say: *I know a word that rhymes with* **bat** *and is a furry animal that meows. What is my word?* (**cat**)
- Repeat using the clues in the box at the right.

Segment Words by Syllables

- Explain that words are made up of smaller parts called syllables. Say: *If we listen carefully to a word when we say it, we can hear the syllables, or parts, in the word.*
- Say a two-syllable name, such as **Rachel,** stressing each syllable. Tell students that **Rachel** is made up of two smaller parts, or syllables.
- Say **Rachel** again and clap once for each syllable.
- Repeat the name again. Have students say the name and clap the syllables with you.
- Use the activity in the box at the right to help students practice dividing words into syllables.

Letter Name Identification/ Formation Ii

Shared Reading of the Alphabet Chart

- Using a pointer, read the Alphabet Chart letter by letter with the class. (*A, a; B, b; C, c; D, d,* etc.)
- Read the chart again, chanting the names of the letters and the names of the pictures. (*A, a, apple; B, b, ball,* etc.) Have students join you.

Model

- Display letter frieze card **Ii.** Explain that the name of this letter is uppercase *I* and that the name of this letter is lowercase *i.*
- Describe the movement needed to form uppercase *I* and lowercase *i.* Tell students to start at the top when forming their letters.
- Say: *An uppercase* **I** *is pull down, across at the top, across at the bottom. A lowercase* **i** *is pull down, dot at the top.* Match the timing of your speech with the action of modeling the letter formations.

✔ **QUICK-CHECK Distribute blackline master 1. Tell students to say the name of each picture, clap the syllables, and tally or write the number of syllables they hear.**

I know a word that rhymes with . . .

. . . **fan** *and is something you use to cook food.* (**pan**)

. . . **meat** *and is something you put on your bed.* (**sheet**)

. . . **hug** *and is found on the floor.* (**rug**)

. . . **pie** *and is what birds can do.* (**fly**)

. . . **bear** *and is something you sit on.* (**chair**)

. . . **spool** *and is a place you go to learn.* (**school**)

Zippity, dippity, let's play a game.
Zippity, dippity, here's the name.
Rachel (Say the name, dividing it into syllables.)
Clap it. (Students say the name and clap the syllables.)
Whisper it. (Students whisper the name, emphasizing the syllables.)
Silently. (Students pantomime saying the name.)

Independent Activities

Phonological Awareness

Provide picture cards **map, magnet, ant, sun, sandwich, tent, tiger, nut, nest, pumpkin, ox, car, house, umpire, guitar,** and **web.** Have students say the name of each picture card and clap the number of syllables in the name.

Letter Identification/ Formation

Provide several sets of letter cards. Have students find all the uppercase *I*s and all the lowercase *i*s.

Place a Big Book or poetry poster in the literacy center. Have students look through the book or poem, use highlighter tape to mark the letters *I* and *i,* and tally how many letters they found on a sheet of paper.

Write a large uppercase *I* and a large lowercase *i* on construction paper. Have students outline the letters with modeling clay.

Guided Practice

- Distribute letter cards **I, I, I,** and **I,** and have students place them under the alphabet strips on their desks.
- Tell students to trace uppercase *I* and say the movement pattern and the letter name. Make sure that students' words match their actions.
- Repeat with lowercase *i.*

Write

- Have students practice writing uppercase *I* on their workmats.
- Remind them to say the movement pattern as they form the letter. Ask students to check their letter with the letter *I* on their alphabet strips.
- Repeat with lowercase *i.*
- Distribute blackline master 2 and ask students to say the names of the letters. Then have them practice writing uppercase *I* and lowercase *i.* (The blackline master may be completed at this time or in a literacy center.)

Compare and Contrast

- Write uppercase *I* on the chalkboard. Write lowercase *i* next to it.
- Ask students to tell how the letters are alike and different. If they need help, say: *Both letters start with a pull-down movement. The uppercase I goes across at the top and across at the bottom. The lowercase i has a dot at the top.*

Locate

- Have students locate *I* and *i* on their alphabet strips and name each letter and picture cue.
- Ask if anyone has the letter *I* or *i* in his or her name. Write the names on a sentence strip. Ask volunteers to frame the *I*s and *i*s.

Sort

- Distribute letter cards **I, I, I, I, i, i, i,** and **i** to each student. Ask students to find all the uppercase *I*s and put them in a row. Be sure that students find all the letters and that the letters they find are the correct ones.
- Repeat with the lowercase *i*s.

 QUICK-CHECK Use blackline master 3. Tell students to name the letters in each row and circle the uppercase *I*s and the lowercase *i*s.

 Small-Group Activities

The following small-group activities can be used to provide hands-on practice for students who need extra support.

PRODUCE RHYME

Say or listen to the recording of the nursery rhyme *Hey, Diddle Diddle* with students, pantomiming the actions. Recite the rhyme alone. Stop before *fiddle* and *spoon* to let students say the rhymes.

SEGMENT WORDS BY SYLLABLES

Have students take turns saying their first names. Then have them clap the syllables. Ask the rest of the group to silently count the number of claps, then say how many syllables they heard.

LETTER IDENTIFICATION/FORMATION

Provide a variety of alphabet books. Have students locate and compare the uppercase *I*s and lowercase *i*s. Point out that uppercase *I* does not always cross at the top and the bottom, and that the lowercase *i* may have a curve at the bottom.

Objectives

Students will:

- Identify rhyming words
- Segment words by syllables
- Recognize and learn the name of the letter **J**
- Write uppercase **J**

Materials Needed

- Alphabet Chart
- Picture Word Cards: *quarter, vest, bat, zipper, watch, zebra, ring, elbow, leaf, rabbit, goat, wagon, ant, mitten, cup, olive*
- Letter Frieze Card *Jj*
- Letter Cards *J, J, J, J, I, I, I, I*
- Alphabet Strips
- BLMs *1, 2, & 3*
- Student Workmats
- StartUp Song & Rhyme CD

Phonological Awareness

Rhyme Recognition

- Read or listen to the recording of the poem *Listening Time* and use the hand motions indicated by the words.
- Ask students to repeat the poem with you. Pause after the second line. Ask: *Which words rhyme?* (**side, hide**)
- Continue saying the poem, pausing after lines four, six, and eight to let students name the rhyming words.

Segment Words by Syllables

- Remind students that words are made up of smaller parts called syllables. Say: *If we listen carefully to a word when we say it, we can hear the smaller parts, or syllables.*
- Say a two-syllable name, such as **Jackson**, stressing each syllable.
- Point out to students that **Jackson** is made up of two smaller parts, or syllables.
- Say **Jackson** again and clap once for each syllable. Repeat the name again, and this time have students say the name and clap the syllables with you.
- Use the activity in the box at the right to help students practice dividing words into syllables.

Letter Name Identification/ Formation J

Shared Reading of the Alphabet Chart

- Using a pointer, read the Alphabet Chart letter by letter with the class, using only the uppercase letters. (*A, B, C, D,* etc.)
- Read the chart again, chanting the names of the pictures. (*apple, ball,* etc.) Have students join you.

Model

- Display letter frieze card **Jj.** Explain that the name of this letter is uppercase **J.**
- Describe the movement needed to form uppercase **J.** Tell students to start at the top when forming their letter.
- Say: *An uppercase* **J** *is pull down, curve back, across at the top.* Match the timing of your speech with the action of modeling the letter formation.

✓ **QUICK-CHECK** Distribute blackline master 1. Tell students to say the name of each picture and clap the syllables in the name. Have them draw a red line under a picture if they hear one syllable and a blue line if they hear two syllables.

Listening Time

Sometimes my hands are at my side.
Then behind my back they hide.
Sometimes I wiggle my fingers so;
Shake them fast, shake them slow.
Sometimes my hands go clap,
clap, clap;
Then I rest them on my lap.
Now they're quiet as quiet can be
Because it's listening time, you see!

Zippity, dippity, let's play a game.
Zippity, dippity, here's the name.
Jackson (Say the name, dividing it into syllables.)
Clap it. (Students say the name and clap the syllables.)
Whisper it. (Students whisper the name, emphasizing the syllables.)
Silently (Students pantomime saying the name.)

Independent Activities

Phonological Awareness

Provide picture cards **quarter, vest, bat, zipper, watch, zebra, ring, elbow, leaf, rabbit, goat, wagon, ant, mitten, cup,** and **olive.** Ask students to say each picture name and listen for the number of syllables. Have them sort the picture cards into those with one-syllable names and those with two-syllable names.

Letter Identification/ Formation

Let students form the letter *J* with cereal or raisins on a small plate. Have them repeat the activity several times.

Provide colored chalk, black construction paper, and a cup of water. Have students dip the chalk into the water and write *J*s on the construction paper until the paper is filled.

Place a model of a letter *J* made of pipe cleaners in the literacy center. Have students make their own *J* using pipe cleaners.

Guided Practice

- Distribute letter cards **J, J, J,** and **J** and have students place them under the alphabet strips on their desks.
- Tell students to trace uppercase *J* and say the movement pattern and the letter name. Listen and watch to make sure that students' words match their actions.

Write

- Have students practice writing uppercase *J* on their workmats.
- Remind them to say the movement pattern as they form the letter. Ask students to check their letter with the letter *J* on their alphabet strips.
- Distribute blackline master 2 and ask students to say the name of the letter. Then have them practice writing uppercase *J*. (The blackline master may be completed at this time or in a literacy center.)

Compare and Contrast

- Write uppercase *J* on the chalkboard. Write uppercase *I* next to it.
- Ask students to tell how the letters are alike and different. If they need help, say: *Both letters pull down and cross at the top. The uppercase* **J** *curves back at the bottom. The uppercase* **I** *crosses at the bottom.*

Locate

- Have students locate *J* on their alphabet strips and name the letter and picture cue.
- Ask if anyone has the letter *J* in his or her name. Write the names on a sentence strip. Ask volunteers to frame the *J*s.

Sort

- Distribute letter cards **J, J, J, J, I, I, I,** and **I** to each student. Ask students to find all the uppercase *J*s and put them in a row. Be sure that students find all the letters and that the letters they find are the correct ones.
- Repeat with the uppercase *I*s.

 QUICK-CHECK Use blackline master 3. Tell students to look at the letters on the page and color all the Js that look right.

 # Small Group Activities

Select from the following small group activities to provide hands-on practice for students who need extra support.

RHYME RECOGNITION

Say one of these sentences: "Don't rush when you brush." "I jump off the stump." "You may have one when you're done." "Come look at my new book." "I found this on the ground." "I wore my coat to the store." Have students repeat the sentence. Then say: *The rhyming words are _____.* Have students fill in the blank. Continue with the remaining sentences.

SEGMENT WORDS BY SYLLABLES

Have students take turns saying their last names. Then have them clap the syllables in the names. Ask the rest of the group to silently count the number of claps, then say how many syllables they heard.

LETTER IDENTIFICATION/FORMATION

Give each student a sheet of paper. Ask students to write the letter *J* in the middle and in each corner. Encourage them to say the movement pattern as they write.

Objectives

Students will:

- Identify changes in familiar spoken text
- Segment words by syllables
- Recognize and learn the name of the letter *j*
- Write lowercase *j*

Materials Needed

- Alphabet Chart
- Picture Word Cards: *magnet, mop, ox, cap, pen, mitten, king, apple, notebook, pumpkin, ostrich, kangaroo, umpire, dinosaur, envelope, umbrella*
- Letter Frieze Card *Jj*
- Letter Cards *j, j, j, j, J, J, J, J*
- Alphabet Strips
- BLMs *1, 2, & 3*
- Student Workmats
- StartUp Song & Rhyme CD

 Phonological Awareness

Listening for Changes

- Recite, sing, or listening to the recording to *The Itsy-Bitsy Spider* several times with students.
- Say: *I'm going to say the rhyme again, but I'm not sure if I can remember the words.* Ask students to listen carefully as you say the words in each line.
- Say the first two lines correctly. *(The itsy-bitsy spider climbed up the water spout.)* Say the lines again, but make a mistake *(The itsy-bitsy spider climbed down the water spout.)* Stop when you make the mistake, clap, say the correct word, and finish the line.
- Continue with the rest of the lines, but this time ask students to clap when you make a mistake. When they clap, pause and ask them to tell you the correct word.

Segment Words by Syllables

- Tell students that they are going to practice listening for syllables. Explain that they are to jump in place to indicate the number of syllables in a word.
- Show picture card **magnet** and have students identify it.
- Demonstrate how to jump twice for **magnet,** once for each syllable.
- Continue with these picture cards: one syllable—**mop, ox, cap, pen, king;** two syllables—**mitten, apple, notebook, pumpkin, ostrich;** three syllables—**kangaroo, umpire, dinosaur, envelope, umbrella.**

> ### The Itsy-Bitsy Spider
> *The itsy-bitsy spider
> climbed up the water spout;
> Down came the rain
> And washed the spider out.
> Out came the sun,
> And dried up all the rain.
> So the itsy-bitsy spider
> climbed up the spout again.*

Letter Name Identification/Formation j

Shared Reading of the Alphabet Chart

- Using a pointer, read the Alphabet Chart letter by letter with the class. Alternate using a loud and a quiet voice to say the lowercase letters. (*a* [loud], *b* [quiet], *c* [loud], etc.)
- Read the chart again, reversing the loud and quiet letters. (*a* [quiet], *b* [loud], *c* [quiet], etc.) Have students join you.

Model

- Display letter frieze card **Jj.** Explain that the name of this letter is lowercase *j.*
- Describe the movement needed to form lowercase *j.* Tell students to start at the top when forming this letter.
- Say: *A lowercase* **j** *is pull down, curve back, dot at the top.* Match the timing of your speech with the action of modeling the letter formation.

QUICK-CHECK Distribute blackline master 1. Have students cut out the pictures, name them, clap the syllables in the picture names, and glue the pictures under 1, 2, or 3 to show how many syllables they heard.

Phonological Awareness

Have students work in pairs. Each partner should select a book and find a favorite picture. One partner names an item in his or her picture, and the other partner claps the syllables in the name and tells how many syllable he or she heard. Then the partners trade roles.

Letter Identification/ Formation

Provide construction paper, glue, rice, and a model of the letter *j*. Have students write a large *j* on the construction paper with glue and attach rice to the glue.

Have students fold a sheet of paper as many times as they can. They then unfold the paper and write the letter *j* in each section.

Provide several sets of magnetic letters. Let students sort through the letters and place all the *j*s on a cookie sheet.

Guided Practice
• Distribute letter cards **j, j, j,** and **j** and have students place them under the alphabet strips on their desks.
• Tell students to trace lowercase *j* and say the movement pattern and the letter name. Listen and watch to make sure that students' words match their actions.

Write
• Have students practice writing lowercase *j* on their workmats.
• Remind them to say the movement pattern as they form the letter. Ask students to check their letter with the letter *j* on their alphabet strips.
• Distribute blackline master 2 and ask students to say the name of the letter. Then have them practice writing lowercase *j*. (The blackline master may be completed at this time or in a literacy center.)

Compare and Contrast
• Write lowercase *j* on the chalkboard. Write uppercase *J* next to it.
• Ask students to tell how the letters are alike and different. If they need help, say: *Both letters pull down and curve back. The lowercase* **j** *has a dot at the top. The uppercase* **J** *crosses at the top.*

Locate
• Have students locate *j* on their alphabet strips and name the letter and picture cue.
• Ask if anyone has the letter *j* in his or her name. Write the names on a sentence strip. Ask volunteers to frame the *j*s.

Sort
• Distribute letter cards **j, j, j, j, J, J, J,** and **J** to each student. Ask students to find all the lowercase *j*s and put them in a row. Be sure that students find all the letters and that the letters they find are the correct ones.
• Repeat with the uppercase *J*s.

 QUICK-CHECK Use blackline master 3. Tell students to find all the lowercase *j*s and color each one a different color.

 # Small Group Activities

Select from the following small group activities to provide hands-on practice for students who need extra support.

LISTENING FOR CHANGES
Sing or listen to the recording of *I'm a Little Teapot* several times, inviting students to sing along. Then recite the song, but use several incorrect words. Ask students to clap when they hear a mistake and tell you the correct word.

SEGMENT WORDS BY SYLLABLES
Put assorted school supplies, such as a book, pencil, paper, eraser, and scissors, into a bag. Take out the items one at a time. Have students name the items, clap the number of syllables in their names, and sort the items into groups according to the number of syllables.

LETTER IDENTIFICATION/FORMATION
Give each student a picture dictionary and ask students to locate lowercase *j*s.

Objectives

Students will:

- Segment the first sound in a word
- Identify a letter sound that is repeated
- Recognize and learn the names of the letters *K* and *k*
- Write uppercase *K* and lowercase *k*

Materials Needed

- Alphabet Chart
- Picture Word Cards: *plant, shell, fox, jar, stick, horn, truck, wheat, skate, king, light, top, vest, swing, soap, tree*
- Letter Frieze Card *Kk*
- Letter Cards *K, K, K, K, k, k, k, k*
- Alphabet Strips
- BLMs *1, 2, & 3*
- Student Workmats

Phonological Awareness

Segment Initial Sounds

- Point to your desk, say **desk,** and then say: *The first sound in* **desk** *is /***d***/.* (Be sure to emphasize both the /**d**/ in the word and the /**d**/ in isolation. When emphasizing, clip the vowel sound so that /**d**/ does not become /**duh**/.)
- Have students identify the beginning sound as you point to other objects in the room that have single beginning consonant sounds, such as a light, map, book, wall, and door.

Identify Repeated Sounds

- Say: *Silly Sally sips sodas.*
- Ask students to listen for the /**s**/ sound as you repeat the tongue twister. Stretch the phoneme in isolation when you are telling them the sound they are listening for.
- Say the tongue twisters in the box at the right. Ask students which sound is repeated. Stretch the phoneme that you want students to notice.

> Messy Martha makes monstrous mud pies.
> Nurse Nancy needs needles.
> Peter Piper picked a peck of pickled peppers.
> Barb bounces big beautiful balls.
> Dizzy Dan is a dancing dinosaur.

Letter Name Identification/Formation Kk

Shared Reading of the Alphabet Chart

- Using a pointer, read the Alphabet Chart letter by letter with the class. (*A, a; B, b; C, c; D, d,* etc.)
- Read the chart again, chanting the names of the letters and the names of the pictures. (*A, a, apple; B, b, ball,* etc.) Have students join you.

Model

- Display letter frieze card **Kk.** Explain that the name of this letter is uppercase *K* and that the name of this letter is lowercase *k.*
- Describe the movement needed to form uppercase *K* and lowercase *k.* Tell students to start at the top when forming their letters.
- Say: *An uppercase* **K** *is pull down, slant in, slant out. A lowercase* **k** *is pull down, slant in, slant out.* Match the timing of your speech with the action of modeling the letter formations.

✔ **QUICK-CHECK Distribute blackline master 1. Tell students to draw a line from each picture in column 1 to the picture in column 2 whose name begins with the same sound.**

Independent Activities

Phonological Awareness

Provide picture cards **plant, shell, fox, jar, stick, horn, truck, wheat, skate, king, light, top, vest, swing, soap** and **tree.** Have students work in pairs. One partner takes a picture and says: *The first sound in ___ is ___.* Then the other partner chooses a picture.

Letter Identification/ Formation

Supply old magazines, glue, construction paper, and scissors. Ask students to cut out uppercase *K*s and lowercase *k*s and paste them on the construction paper.

Provide watercolors, brushes, and paper. Have students paint the letters *K* and *k* several times.

Place long and short pretzel sticks in the literacy center. Tell students to make uppercase *K*s and lowercase *k*s using the long and short sticks.

Guided Practice

- Distribute letter cards **K, K, K,** and **K** and have students place them under the alphabet strips on their desks.
- Tell students to trace uppercase *K* and say the movement pattern and the letter name. Listen and watch to make sure that students' words match their actions.
- Repeat with lowercase *k.*

Write

- Have students practice writing uppercase *K* on their workmats.
- Remind them to say the movement pattern as they form the letter. Ask students to check their letter with the letter *K* on their alphabet strips.
- Repeat with lowercase *k.*
- Distribute blackline master 2 and ask students to say the names of the letters. Then have them practice writing uppercase *K* and lowercase *k.* (The blackline master may be completed at this time or in a literacy center.)

Compare and Contrast

- Write uppercase *K* on the chalkboard. Write lowercase *k* next to it.
- Ask students to tell how the letters are alike and different. If they need help, say: *Both letters have the same movement pattern. The slant lines on the uppercase* **K** *meet at the middle of the stick and are longer. The slant lines on the lowercase* **k** *meet lower on the stick and are shorter.*

Locate

- Have students locate *K* and *k* on their alphabet strips and name each letter and picture cue.
- Ask if anyone has the letter *K* or *k* in his or her name. Write the names on a sentence strip. Ask volunteers to frame the *K*s and *k*s.

Sort

- Distribute letter cards **K, K, K, K, k, k, k,** and **k** to each student. Ask students to find all the uppercase *K*s and put them in a row. Be sure that students find all the letters and that the letters they find are the correct ones.
- Repeat with the lowercase *k*s.

 QUICK-CHECK Use blackline master 3. Have students find all the uppercase Ks and color them red and find all the lowercase ks and color them blue.

 # Small Group Activities

Select from the following small group activities to provide hands-on practice for students who need extra support.

SEGMENT INITIAL SOUNDS

Provide an assortment of small objects, such as a can, ball, pen, rock, leaf, comb, cap, ring, bean, and key. Have students name the objects and say their beginning sounds.

IDENTIFY REPEATED SOUNDS

Read these titles: *Baby Bunnies, Mary Had a Little Lamb, Jack and Jill, Pease Porridge Hot, Lizards in a Log, Baby Bears, I Hop On My Horse.* Have students listen for beginning sounds that are repeated. Make sure to stretch the repeated sound.

LETTER IDENTIFICATION/FORMATION

Ask students to trace letter card **K.** Then have them write the letter *K* on their workmats several times. Encourage them to say the movement pattern as they write. Repeat with letter card **k.**

Objectives
Students will:

- Segment the first sound in a word
- Segment compound words by parts
- Recognize and learn the name of the letter *L*
- Write uppercase *L*

Materials Needed

- Alphabet Chart
- Picture Word Cards: *pan, mop, ball, map, sock, car, sun, tent, nut, nest, fox, top, pen, cat, box, fan*
- Letter Frieze Card *Ll*
- Letter Cards *L, L, L, L, K, K, K, K*
- Alphabet Strips
- BLMs *1, 2, & 3*
- Student Workmats

 Phonological Awareness

Segment Initial Sounds

- Hold up a book, say the word **book,** then say: *The first sound in* **book** *is /b/.* Emphasize both the **/b/** in the word and the **/b/** in isolation.
- Sing these words to the tune of *Mary Had a Little Lamb: What's the first sound that you hear, that you hear, that you hear? What's the first sound that you hear in* **book, book, book?** Let students answer.
- Repeat with the words **seal, cake, zoo, milk, fish, hot, jump, pink, run,** and **toy.**

Segment Compound Words

- Ask two students to come to the front of the room, stand side by side, and join hands. Tell them that they are the two words that make up the compound word **popcorn.** Let one student be the first word, **pop,** and the other student the second word, **corn**.
- Tell students that when they are holding hands, they are the whole word, **popcorn,** but when they are not holding hands, they are just part of that word.
- Say: *When I touch your shoulder, stop holding hands to divide the word, then say your part of the word.*
- Repeat with other pairs of students and the compound words **football, washcloth, snowball, homework, airport, sailboat,** and **doghouse.**

 Letter Name Identification/Formation L

Shared Reading of the Alphabet Chart

- Using a pointer, read the Alphabet Chart letter by letter with the class. Alternate using a loud and a quiet voice to say the uppercase letters. (*A* [loud], *B* [quiet], *C* [loud], etc.)
- Read the chart again, this time reversing the loud and quiet letters. (*A* [quiet], *B* [loud], *C* [quiet], etc.) Have students join you.

Model

- Display letter frieze card **Ll.** Explain that the name of this letter is uppercase **L.**
- Describe the movement needed to form uppercase **L.** Tell students to start at the top when forming their letter.
- Say: *An uppercase* **L** *is pull down, slide right.* Match the timing of your speech with the action of modeling the letter formation.

 QUICK-CHECK Distribute blackline master 1. Have students name each picture, then draw a line from a picture in column 1 to a picture in column 2 to make a compound word.

Independent Activities

Phonological Awareness

Provide picture cards **pan, mop, ball, map, sock, car, sun, tent, nut, nest, fox, top, pen, cat, box,** and **fan.** Have students name the pictures and pair them by their beginning sounds.

Letter Identification/ Formation

Write the outline of the letter *L* on sheets of construction paper. Have students cut out the letters and decorate them with written *L*s.

Provide several sets of magnetic letters. Have students sort through the letters and place all the *L*s on a cookie sheet.

Supply a stamp for the letter *L,* an ink pad, and white paper. Tell students to create a design by stamping the letter *L* on the paper.

Guided Practice
• Distribute letter cards **L, L, L,** and **L** and have students place them under the alphabet strips on their desks.
• Tell students to trace uppercase *L* and say the movement pattern and the letter name. Listen and watch to make sure that students' words match their actions.

Write
• Have students practice writing uppercase *L* on their workmats.
• Remind them to say the movement pattern as they form the letter. Ask students to check their letter with the letter *L* on their alphabet strips.
• Distribute blackline master 2 and ask students to say the name of the letter. Then have them practice writing uppercase *L*. (The blackline master may be completed at this time or in a literacy center.)

Compare and Contrast
• Write uppercase *L* on the board. Write uppercase *K* next to it.
• Ask students to tell how the letters are alike and different. If they need help, say: *Both letters start with a pull-down movement. The uppercase* L *slides right. The uppercase* K *slants in and slants out in the middle.*

Locate
• Have students locate *L* on their alphabet strips and name the letter and picture cue.
• Ask if anyone has the letter *L* in his or her name. Write the names on a sentence strip. Ask volunteers to frame the *L*s.

Sort
• Distribute letter cards **L, L, L, L, K, K, K,** and **K** to each student. Ask students to find all the uppercase *L*s and put them in a row. Be sure that students find all the letters and that the letters they find are the correct ones.
• Repeat with the uppercase *K*s.

 QUICK-CHECK Use blackline master 3. Have students color each part that has an L in it and tell you what they have made.

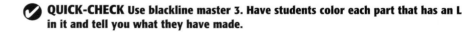 ## Small Group Activities

Select from the following small group activities to provide hands-on practice for students who need extra support.

SEGMENT INITIAL SOUNDS
Say: *I spy something that starts with /***m**/ [or any other consonant sound]. The student who correctly guesses the object gets to give the next clue.

SEGMENT COMPOUND WORDS
Select two students and whisper one part of a compound word to each student. Tell them to say their part of the word when you touch their shoulder. Ask the rest of the group to say what compound word is made when the two word parts are combined. Repeat with other student pairs and the compound words *inchworm, spacecraft, pancake, mailbox, scarecrow,* and *grapefruit.*

LETTER IDENTIFICATION/FORMATION
Ask students to locate *L*s in newspaper headlines and circle them using a crayon or marker.

Objectives

Students will:

- Produce a rhyming word
- Segment compound words by parts
- Recognize and learn the name of the letter *l*
- Write lowercase *l*

Materials Needed

- Alphabet Chart
- Picture Word Cards: *box, car, cup, cake, cat, fish, house, coat, sun, light, lunchbox, notebook*
- Letter Frieze Card *Ll*
- Letter Cards *l, l, l, l, L, L, L, L*
- Alphabet Strips
- BLMs *1, 2, & 3*
- Student Workmats
- StartUp Song & Rhyme CD

Phonological Awareness

Produce Rhyme

- Tell students you are thinking of two words that rhyme. You will tell them one word, then give them a clue for the other word.
- Say: *I know a word that rhymes with* **can** *and is something you cook in. What is my word?* (**pan**)
- Repeat with the clues in the box at the right.

Segment Compound Words

- Say the word *skateboard.* Then divide the word into its parts: *skate* (pause) *board.* Ask students to repeat the word and its parts.
- Say: *I am going to take away the first part of* **skateboard.** *Tell me the second part of the word.*
- Ask students to say the second part. Say: *That's right,* **skateboard** *without* **skate** *is just* **board**.
- Have students say each of the following compound words, pausing briefly between parts. Then have them say only the second part of each word. Use these words: *hairbrush, tiptoe, flagpole, eyebrow, baseball, mailbox.*

> *I know a word that rhymes with . . .*
> - . . . **seat** *and stands for things with ten toes.* (**feet**)
> - . . . **rug** *and is another word for* **insect.** (**bug**)
> - . . . **fly** *and is something blue above you.* (**sky**)
> - . . . **chair** *and is found on your head.* (**hair**)
> - . . . **school** *and is a place to swim.* (**pool**)

Letter Name Identification/Formation *l*

Shared Reading of the Alphabet Chart

- Using a pointer, read the Alphabet Chart letter by letter with the class. Have students pat their leg for each lowercase letter. (*A, a* [pat]; *B, b* [pat]; etc.)
- Read the chart again, this time patting for the uppercase letters. (*A* [pat], *a; B* [pat], *b;* etc.) Have students join you.

Model

- Display letter frieze card **Ll**. Explain that the name of this letter is lowercase *l*.
- Describe the movement needed to form lowercase *l*. Tell students to start at the top when forming this letter.
- Say: *A lowercase* **l** *is pull down.* Match the timing of your speech with the action of modeling the letter formation.

> **✓ QUICK-CHECK** Distribute blackline master 1. Tell students to cut out the pictures, put together two pictures whose names make a compound word pictured, and glue the pictures in place.

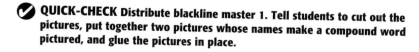

Phonological Awareness

Place picture cards **box, car, cup, cake, cat, fish, house, coat, sun, light, lunchbox,** and **notebook** in the literacy center. Tell students to find the picture names that are already compound words and put them in a stack. Then have students pair the remaining cards to make new compound words.

Letter Identification/ Formation

Supply game tiles from commercial letter games. Have students sort through the letters and find all the **l**s.

Provide multiple copies of the letter cards **a** through **l** and **A** through **L**. Have students sort through the cards and clip all the lowercase **l**s to a clothesline.

Place photocopies of *Lizards in a Log* in the literacy center. Ask students to circle all the **l**s in the rhyme.

Guided Practice

- Distribute letter cards **l, l, l,** and **l** and have students place them under the alphabet strips on their desks.
- Tell students to trace lowercase **l** and say the movement pattern and the letter name. Listen and watch to make sure that students' words match their actions.

Write

- Have students practice writing lowercase **l** on their workmats.
- Remind them to say the movement pattern as they form the letter. Ask students to check their letter with the letter **l** on their alphabet strips.
- Distribute blackline master 2 and ask students to say the name of the letter. Then have them practice writing lowercase **l.** (The blackline master may be completed at this time or in a literacy center.)

Compare and Contrast

- Write lowercase **l** on the chalkboard. Write uppercase **L** next to it.
- Ask students to tell how the letters are alike and different. If they need help, say: *Both letters pull down, but the uppercase* **L** *slides right at the bottom.*

Locate

- Have students locate **l** on their alphabet strips and name the letter and picture cue.
- Ask if anyone has the letter **l** in his or her name. Write the names on a sentence strip. Ask volunteers to frame the **l**s.

Sort

- Distribute letter cards **l, l, l, l, L, L, L,** and **L** to each student. Ask students to find all the lowercase **l**s and put them in a row. Be sure that students find all the letters and that the letters they find are the correct ones.
- Repeat with the uppercase **L**s.

 QUICK-CHECK Use blackline master 3. Tell students to write lowercase *l* in each box on the large *l*s and then color the large *l*s.

 # Small Group Activities

Select from the following small group activities to provide hands-on practice for students who need extra support.

PRODUCE RHYME

Recite or listen to the recording of the nursery rhyme *Teddy Bear, Teddy Bear* several times with students, pantomiming the actions in the rhyme. Recite the rhyme alone, this time stopping before ***ground, do, prayers,*** and ***light*** to let students say the rhymes.

SEGMENT COMPOUND WORDS

Say the following compound words one at a time: ***someone, toothpick, northwest, hallway, lighthouse, daytime, forehead, shoelace, yardstick, rainbow.*** Ask: *What part comes first?* Students should say only the first part of the word

LETTER IDENTIFICATION/FORMATION

Have students see how many **l**s they can write on their workmats in one minute. Encourage them to say the movement pattern as they write. Have students circle their best letter. Then ask them to erase their work. Repeat the activity.

Objectives

Students will:

- Produce rhyming words
- Segment the first sound in a word
- Recognize and learn the name of the letter *M*
- Write uppercase *M*

Materials Needed

- Alphabet Chart
- Picture Word Cards: *wheat, vest, tree, pan, ring, kite, mop, feet, gate, box, cake, coat, bat, chick, frog, rope*
- Letter Frieze Card *Mm*
- Letter Cards *M, M, M, M, l, l, l, l*
- Alphabet Strips
- BLMs *1, 2, & 3*
- Student Workmats

 # Phonological Awareness

Produce Rhyme

- Have students sit in a circle on the floor with you. Tell them they will play a rhyming game in which they will say rhyming words as fast as they can.
- Explain that you will say a word and roll a ball to someone. That person says a word that rhymes with your word and passes the ball quickly to someone else. That person says another rhyming word and passes the ball.
- Use the words *play, man, car, hen, sun, pan, hat, red, sky*, and *light*.

Segment Initial Sounds

- Show students how to pat their legs and clap their hands in a pat/pat/clap rhythm.
- Say: *I will say an animal name:* **cat.** *You say the beginning sound twice and the animal name once while patting and clapping:* /c/, /c/, **cat.** Pat your legs twice for the letters and clap once for the word.
- Continue with these animal names: *dog, horse, cow, bear, deer, goat, fox, toad, duck, lamb, goose, bird.*

Letter Name Identification/ Formation M

Shared Reading of the Alphabet Chart

- Using a pointer, read the Alphabet Chart letter by letter with the class. (*A, a; B, b; C, c; D, d,* etc.)
- Read the chart again, chanting the names of the uppercase letters and the names of the pictures. (*A, apple; B, ball,* etc.) Have students join you.

Model

- Display letter frieze card **Mm.** Explain that the name of this letter is uppercase **M.**
- Describe the movement needed to form uppercase **M.** Tell students to start at the top when forming their letter.
- Say: *An uppercase* **M** *is pull down, lift, slant right, slant up, pull down.* Match the timing of your speech with the action of modeling the letter formation.

 QUICK-CHECK Distribute blackline master 1. Tell students to name the pictures in each row. Have them circle the smiley face if the names begin with the same sound or circle the frowning face if the names begin with different sounds.

Independent Activities

Phonological Awareness

Provide picture cards **wheat, vest, tree, pan, ring, kite, mop, feet, gate, box, cake, coat, bat, chick, frog,** and **rope.** Let partners take turns drawing a card, naming the picture, and saying a word that rhymes with the picture name.

Letter Identification/ Formation

Place several sets of magnetic letters in the literacy center. Have students sort through the letters and place all the *M*s on a cookie sheet.

Have students practice writing large *M*s on the board in different colors. Remind them to say the movement pattern as they write.

Have students search the room for the letter *M.* Ask them to highlight the letters they find with highlighter tape.

Guided Practice

- Distribute letter cards **M, M, M,** and **M** and have students place them under the alphabet strips on their desks.
- Tell students to trace uppercase *M* and say the movement pattern and the letter name. Listen and watch to make sure that students' words match their actions.

Write

- Have students practice writing uppercase *M* on their workmats.
- Remind them to say the movement pattern as they form the letter. Ask students to check their letter with the letter *M* on their alphabet strips.
- Distribute blackline master 2 and ask students to say the name of the letter. Then have them practice writing uppercase *M.* (The blackline master may be completed at this time or in a literacy center.)

Compare and Contrast

- Write uppercase *M* on the chalkboard. Write lowercase *l* next to it.
- Ask students to tell how the letters are alike and different. If they need help, say: *Both letters start with a pull-down movement. The uppercase* **M** *then lifts, slants right, slants up, and pulls down.*

Locate

- Have students locate *M* on their alphabet strips and name the letter and picture cue.
- Ask if anyone has the letter *M* in his or her name. Write the names on a sentence strip. Ask volunteers to frame the *M*s.

Sort

- Distribute letter cards **M, M, M, M, l, l, l,** and **l** to each student. Ask students to find all the uppercase *M*s and put them in a row. Be sure that students find all the letters and that the letters they find are the correct ones.
- Repeat with the lowercase *l*s.

 QUICK-CHECK Use blackline master 3. Tell students to connect the dots in alphabetical order and tell you what letter they have made.

 Small Group Activities

Select from the following small group activities to provide hands-on practice for students who need extra support.

PRODUCE RHYME

Tell students that they can make up a fun, new name using rhyming words. Say: *I am Terry. My name rhymes with* **berry.** *My new name is Terry Berry.* Have students take turns making up rhyming names in this way.

SEGMENT INITIAL SOUNDS

Tell students that you are going on a pretend trip and need to pack your bag. Say: *First I need to pack things that begin with /s/. I'll take /s/ /s/ socks. What else can I pack?* Have students suggest other /s/ items, saying the initial sound and then the whole word. Continue with other initial sounds.

LETTER IDENTIFICATION/FORMATION

Have students write *M*s on several small self-stick notes. Let each student select the best one to stick on the board.

Objectives

Students will:

- Listen to and repeat a sequence of words
- Produce rhyming words
- Recognize and learn the name of the letter *m*
- Write lowercase *m*

Materials Needed

- Alphabet Chart
- Picture Word Cards: *cat, swing, tree, frog, shell, fox, snake, jar, goat, skate, top, vest, sail, ox, yak, zoo*
- Letter Frieze Card *Mm*
- Letter Cards *m, m, m, m, M, M, M, M*
- Alphabet Strips
- BLMs *1, 2, & 3*
- Student Workmats

 ## Phonological Awareness

Listen and Repeat

- Say: *Listen to these words:* **all, girl, plane, lock.** *Can you say them, too?* Have students chant the words back to you.
- Repeat with these sets of words: ***hush/lamp/rope/wood, clock/turn/star/ cage, game/jump/pin/toe, bath/light/spoon/hill, corn/smile/help/lunch.***

Produce Rhyme

- Tell students you will say a sentence, but you will leave off the last word.
- Say: *It is your job to think of a rhyming word to finish the sentence. Here is the first sentence: I drove far in my ___.* Be sure to emphasize the word that the students' word is supposed to rhyme with.
- Have students say a word that rhymes with *far* and makes sense in the sentence (*car*).
- Continue with the sentence starters in the box at the right.

> Don't bounce the **ball** in the ___.
> (*hall*)
> I use my **nose** to smell the ___.
> (*rose*)
> Take a **look** at my new ___.
> (*book*)
> I like to **bake** a birthday ___.
> (*cake*)
> My cousin **came** to play a ___.
> (*game*)

Letter Name Identification/ Formation m

Shared Reading of the Alphabet Chart

- Using a pointer, read the Alphabet Chart letter by letter with the class, saying the uppercase letters in a high voice and the lowercase letters in a low voice.
- Read the chart again, chanting the names of the letters and the names of the pictures. (*A, a, apple; B, b, ball*, etc.) Have students join you.

Model

- Display letter frieze card **Mm.** Explain that the name of this letter is lowercase ***m.***
- Describe the movement needed to form lowercase ***m.*** Tell students to start at the top when forming this letter.
- Say: *A lowercase* **m** *is pull down, push up, curve forward, pull down, push up, curve forward, pull down.* Match the timing of your speech with the action of modeling the letter formation.

✓ **QUICK-CHECK Distribute blackline master 1. Tell students to name each picture and draw something that rhymes with the picture name.**

Independent Activities

Phonological Awareness

Provide picture cards **cat, swing, tree, frog, shell, fox, snake, jar, goat, skate, top, vest, sail, ox, yak,** and **zoo.** Let students work in pairs. One partner selects three cards and says the picture names. The other partner repeats the words without looking at the cards. Then the partners trade roles.

Letter Identification/ Formation

Provide multiple copies of various letter cards. Have students sort through the cards and pull out all the *m*s.

Have students form the letter *m* with cereal or raisins on a small plate. Ask them to repeat the activity several times.

Ask students to write lowercase *m* on a large sheet of white paper with a red crayon or marker. Then have them trace the letter using green, blue, orange, yellow, and purple crayons or markers.

GUIDED PRACTICE

- Distribute letter cards **m, m, m,** and **m** and have students place them under the alphabet strips on their desks.
- Tell students to trace lowercase *m* and say the movement pattern and the letter name. Listen and watch to make sure that students' words match their actions.

WRITE

- Have students practice writing lowercase *m* on their workmats.
- Remind them to say the movement pattern as they form the letter. Ask students to check their letter with the letter *m* on their alphabet strips.
- Distribute blackline master 2 and ask students to say the name of the letter. Then have them practice writing lowercase *m.* (The blackline master may be completed at this time or in a literacy center.)

COMPARE AND CONTRAST

- Write lowercase *m* on the chalkboard. Write uppercase *M* next to it.
- Ask students to tell how the letters are alike and different. If they need help, say: *Both letters pull down at the beginning and at the end. The lowercase* **m** *pushes up and curves forward twice in the middle. The uppercase* **M** *lifts, slants right, and slants up in the middle.*

LOCATE

- Have students locate *m* on their alphabet strips and name the letter and picture cue.
- Ask if anyone has the letter *m* in his or her name. Write the names on a sentence strip. Ask volunteers to frame the *m*s.

SORT

- Distribute letter cards **m, m, m, m, M, M, M,** and **M** to each student. Ask students to find all the lowercase *m*s and put them in a row. Be sure that students find all the letters and that the letters they find are the correct ones.
- Repeat with the uppercase *M*s.

 QUICK-CHECK Use blackline master 3. Tell students to name each letter and color each lowercase m a different color.

Small Group Activities

Select from the following small group activities to provide hands-on practice for students who need extra support.

LISTEN AND REPEAT

Say: *Hop two times.* Ask students to repeat exactly what you said, then do it. Continue with these instructions: *Touch your toes. Hold up your hands. Sit on the floor. Blink your eyes. Stretch out your arms. Run in place. Clap your hands.*

PRODUCE RHYME

Tell students that you have some unusual school supplies in your bag. Reach inside for the first item, but don't display it. Say: *I have a* **wencil** *in my bag.* Have students tell you what rhymes with **wencil** (**pencil**). Show the pencil. Continue with other supplies, calling them by nonsense rhyming names. Challenge students to guess the objects.

LETTER IDENTIFICATION/FORMATION

Give each student a sheet of paper. Ask students to write lowercase *m* in the middle and in each corner. Encourage them to say the movement pattern as they write.

Objectives
Students will:

- Identify rhyming words
- Segment the first sound in a word
- Recognize and learn the name of the letter *N*
- Write uppercase *N*

Materials Needed

- Alphabet Chart
- Picture Word Cards: *ant, plant, ski, tree, chain, train, duck, truck, house, blouse, kite, light, ring, king, mitten, kitten*
- Letter Frieze Card *Nn*
- Letter Cards *N, N, N, N, m, m, m, m*
- Alphabet Strips
- BLMs *1, 2, & 3*
- Student Workmats
- StartUp Song & Rhyme CD

Phonological Awareness

Rhyme Recognition

- Tell students you will name three words and they are to tell you which two words rhyme. Say: *Rhyming is fun. I do it all the time.* **Fall, mat, ball.** *Which words rhyme?* (**fall, ball**)
- If students have difficulty, repeat the three words more slowly, emphasizing the two that rhyme.
- Repeat with the following sets of words: ***gate/red/head, back/sack/cart, bag/save/wag, mop/run/sun, five/hive/fog, big/mug/dig.***

Segment Initial Sounds

- Ahead of time, put such objects as a rock, a nut, a doll, a sock, a key, a nail, a bead, a fan, a jar, and a leaf into a bag.
- Say: *I have a bag of things. I will give you clues to help you guess each thing. The first clue will always be the first sound of the word: I have something that begins with /r/.*
- Let students make some guesses. As they try different words, they should segment the initial sound. For example: *Is it a /r/ /ug/?*
- If students need help, offer another clue. Say: *You can find one on the ground.*
- Keep adding clues until students guess the correct word, ***rock.***
- Continue with other objects in the bag.

Letter Name Identification/ Formation N

Shared Reading of the Alphabet Chart

- Using a pointer, read the Alphabet Chart letter by letter with the class, saying the uppercase letters from ***Z*** to ***A.*** (*Z, Y, X, W,* etc.)
- Read the chart again, saying the names of the lowercase letters from *z* to *a.* (*z, y, x, w,* etc.) Have students join you.

Model

- Display letter frieze card **Nn.** Explain that the name of this letter is uppercase ***N.***
- Describe the movement needed to form uppercase ***N.*** Tell students to start at the top when forming their letter.
- Say: *An uppercase* **N** *is pull down, lift, slant right, push up.* Match the timing of your speech with the action of modeling the letter formation.

 QUICK-CHECK Distribute blackline master 1. Tell students to cut out the pictures, name each one, match the rhyming picture names, and glue the pictures with rhyming names in the boxes.

Independent Activities

Phonological Awareness

Provide picture cards **ant, plant, ski, tree, chain, train, duck, truck, house, blouse, kite, light, ring, king, mitten,** and **kitten.** Have partners scramble the cards, place them face down in four rows, and play a matching game. Players turn over two cards at a time. If the words rhyme, they keep the cards. If the words do not rhyme, they turn the cards over again. Play continues until all cards are matched. The player with the most matches wins.

Letter Identification/ Formation

Provide old newspapers and red markers. Ask students to circle *N*s they find in the headlines.

Supply strips of adding machine tape and a model of the letter *N.* Have students write as many *N*s on their strips as they can.

Have students practice writing large *N*s on the board in different colors. Remind them to say the movement pattern as they write.

Guided Practice

- Distribute letter cards **N, N, N,** and **N** and have students place them under the alphabet strips on their desks.
- Tell students to trace uppercase *N* and say the movement pattern and the letter name. Listen and watch to make sure that students' words match their actions.

Write

- Have students practice writing uppercase *N* on their workmats.
- Remind them to say the movement pattern as they form the letter. Ask students to check their letter with the letter *N* on their alphabet strips.
- Distribute blackline master 2 and ask students to say the name of the letter. Then have them practice writing uppercase *N.* (The blackline master may be completed at this time or in a literacy center.)

Compare and Contrast

- Write uppercase *N* on the board. Write lowercase *m* next to it.
- Ask students to tell how the letters are alike and different. If they need help, say: *Both letters begin with a pull-down movement. The uppercase* **N** *lifts, slants right, and pushes up. The lowercase* **m** *pushes up and curves forward and pulls down twice.*

Locate

- Have students locate *N* on their alphabet strips and name the letter and picture cue.
- Ask if anyone has the letter *N* in his or her name. Write the names on a sentence strip. Ask volunteers to frame the *N*s.

Sort

- Distribute letter cards **N, N, N, N, m, m, m,** and **m** to each student. Ask students to find all the uppercase *N*s and put them in a row. Be sure that students find all the letters and that the letters they find are the correct ones.
- Repeat with the lowercase *m*s.

 QUICK-CHECK Use blackline master 3. Tell students to circle all the *N*s to make their way through the maze.

 Small Group Activities

Select from the following small group activities to provide hands-on practice for students who need extra support.

RHYME RECOGNITION

Sing or listen to the recording of *Rock-a-Bye Baby* with students. Say the first two lines again and ask if the ending words (**top, rock**) rhyme. Then say the last two lines and ask if the ending words (**fall, all**) rhyme. Let students name other words that rhyme **fall** and **all.**

SEGMENT INITIAL SOUNDS

Say: *Guess who I am thinking of.* Secretly choose the name of one of the students and repeat the initial sound, for example, /t/ /t/ /t/. After students have correctly guessed the name, ask them to segment its initial sound. Continue with other students' names.

LETTER IDENTIFICATION/FORMATION

Have students see how many *N*s they can write on their workmats in one minute. Encourage them to say the movement pattern as they write. Have students circle their best letter. Then ask them to erase their work. Repeat the activity.

Objectives

Students will:

- Discriminate initial sounds
- Segment words by syllables
- Recognize and learn the name of the letter *n*
- Write lowercase *n*

Materials Needed

- Alphabet Chart
- Picture Word Cards: *quarter, sock, zipper, fork, zero, lunchbox, map, bell, kangaroo, envelope, zebra, ox, dinosaur, watch, guitar, elephant*
- Letter Frieze Card *Nn*
- Letter Cards *n, n, n, n, N, N, N, N*
- Alphabet Strips
- BLMs *1, 2, & 3*
- Student Workmats
- StartUp Song & Rhyme CD

 # Phonological Awareness

Sound Discrimination

- Tell students they will play a game in which they match the first sound of a word with a name.
- Have two students, each with a different beginning sound in his or her name, such as **Mario** and **Sarah,** come to the front of the room. Say each name, stretching the beginning sound.
- Say the poem in the box at the right. Ask students to answer with the correct sound and name, such as **/m/ Mario.**
- Continue until all students have had a chance to come forward.

> Mario and Sarah
> are our friends.
> Say their names with me.
> **/m/ /m/ Mario, /s/ /s/ Sarah.**
> One starts with **/m/.**
> I wonder who it can be?

Segment Words by Syllables

- Say or listen to the recording of *Baby Bunnies* with students several times.
- Have students say the rhyme again, replacing the words **bunny** and **bunnies** with claps. Ask students how many claps are needed to show the number of syllables, or parts, in **bunny** and **bunnies**.
- Chant and clap the words as shown in the box at the right.
- Repeat the rhyme again, choosing other words to clap, such as **another, bouncy,** or **sleepyheads**.

> ### Baby Bunnies
>
> *Baby (clap-clap) dressed in blue,*
> *Met another. Then there were two.*
> *Bouncy (clap-clap) to the left.*
> *Bouncy (clap-clap) to the right.*
> *Bouncy (clap-clap) get in bed.*
> *Off to bed, you sleepyheads.*

Letter Name Identification/ Formation n

Shared Reading of the Alphabet Chart

- Using a pointer, read the Alphabet Chart letter by letter with boys saying the lowercase letters and girls saying the picture cues.
- Read the chart again, this time having students reverse roles with the girls reading the lowercase letters and the boys reading the picture cues.

Model

- Display letter frieze card **Nn.** Explain that the name of this letter is lowercase **n.**
- Describe the movement needed to form lowercase **n.** Tell students to start at the top when forming this letter.
- Say: *A lowercase **n** is pull down, push up, curve forward, pull down.* Match the timing of your speech with the action of modeling the letter formation.

✓ **QUICK-CHECK Distribute blackline master 1. Tell students to say the name of each picture, clap the syllables in the name, and draw a circle around 1, 2, or 3 to show how many syllables they heard.**

Independent Activities

Phonological Awareness

Place picture cards **quarter, sock, zipper, fork, zero, lunchbox, map, bell, kangaroo, envelope, zebra, ox, dinosaur, watch, guitar,** and **elephant** in the literacy center. Have students say the name of each picture and clap the number of syllables in the name. Then have them sort the pictures into groups according to the number of syllables in the picture names.

Letter Identification/ Formation

Supply game titles from commercial board games. Have students sort through the letters and find all the *n*s.

Place construction paper, glue, strips of yarn, and a model of the letter *n* in the center. Have students write a large *n* on the construction paper with glue and attach strips of yarn.

Provide a stamp for the letter *n*, an ink pad, and white paper. Have students create a design by stamping the letter *n*.

Guided Practice
- Distribute letter cards **n, n, n,** and **n** and have students place them under the alphabet strips on their desks.
- Tell students to trace lowercase *n* and say the movement pattern and the letter name. Listen and watch to make sure that students' words match their actions.

Write
- Have students practice writing lowercase *n* on their workmats.
- Remind them to say the movement pattern as they form the letter. Ask students to check their letter with the letter *n* on their alphabet strips.
- Distribute blackline master 2 and ask students to say the name of the letter. Then have them practice writing lowercase *n*. (The blackline master may be completed at this time or in a literacy center.)

Compare and Contrast
- Write lowercase *n* on the chalkboard. Write uppercase *N* next to it.
- Ask students to tell how the letters are alike and different. If they need help, say: *Both letters start with a pull-down movement. The lowercase* **n** *has a push up, curve forward, and pull down. The uppercase* **N** *has a lift, slant right, and push up.*

Locate
- Have students locate *n* on their alphabet strips and name the letter and picture cue.
- Ask if anyone has the letter *n* in his or her name. Write the names on a sentence strip. Ask volunteers to frame the *n*s.

Sort
- Distribute letter cards **n, n, n, n, N, N, N,** and **N** to each student. Ask students to find all the lowercase *n*s and put them in a row. Be sure that students find all the letters and that the letters they find are the correct ones.
- Repeat with the uppercase *N*s.

 QUICK-CHECK Use blackline master 3. Tell students to look at the letters on the page and color all the *n*s that look right.

 # Small-Group Activities

Select from the following small-group activities to provide hands-on practice for students who need extra support.

SOUND DISCRIMINATION
Sing or listen to the recording of *London Bridge* with students several times. Have students listen for initial */f/* words in the first stanza (***falling, fair***), initial */b/* words in the second and third stanzas (***build, bars, bend***), and one */s/* word in the last stanza (***silver***).

SEGMENT WORDS BY SYLLABLES
Choose an object that students can see in the classroom. Say: *I see a* ___. Clap the number of syllables in the word, but don't say the word. Students can make guesses by saying an appropriate word while clapping the syllables. The student who guesses correctly chooses the next object.

LETTER IDENTIFICATION/FORMATION
Ask students to trace the letter *n* card. Then have them write the lowercase *n* on their workmats several times. Encourage them to say the movement pattern as they write.

Objectives
Students will:

- Discriminate initial sounds
- Segment words by syllables
- Recognize and learn the names of the letters *O* and *o*
- Write uppercase and lowercase *O* and *o*

Materials Needed

- Alphabet Chart
- Picture Word Cards: *mop, map, sub, sock, tub, tent, nut, nest, fox, fork, pan, pen, car, cup, house, hat*
- Letter Frieze Card *Oo*
- Letter Cards *o, o, o, o, O, O, O, O*
- Alphabet Strips
- BLMs *1, 2, & 3*
- Student Workmats

 Phonological Awareness

Produce Rhyme

- Sit with students in a circle on the floor. Explain that almost any word can be rhymed, and sometimes rhymes are nonsense words.
- Show a large rubber ball. Say: *I will say a word and roll the ball to a student. That student will say a word that rhymes with my word. The class will decide whether it is a real word or a nonsense word. Then the student will roll the ball to another student.*
- Start with the word **hat.** Students might choose real words, such as **bat, fat, mat, cat, that, brat, flat, sat, or pat,** or nonsense words, such as **crat, dat,** or **jat.**

Segment Initial Sounds

- Display a puppet. Tell students his name is Choppy and that he chops the first sound off a word before he finishes it.
- As Choppy, say: **/h/ /ôrs/.** Have students identify the word. (**horse**) Say: *A cowboy rides a horse.*
- Say each of the following words separating it into its onset (initial sound) and its rime (the other sounds): **park, bath, lamp, night, cage, face, wing, tool, help, note, duck, girl.** Have students identify each word and use it in a sentence.

 Letter Name Identification/ Formation Oo

Shared Reading of the Alphabet Chart

- Using a pointer, read the uppercase letters on the Alphabet Chart letter by letter with the class. Use a sound pattern, such as *A, B, C* (pause), *D, E, F* (pause), and so on.
- Repeat with the lowercase letters. Have students join you.

Model

- Display letter frieze card **Oo.** Explain that the name of this letter is uppercase **O** and the name of this letter is lowercase **o.**
- Describe the movement needed to form uppercase **O** and lowercase **o.** Tell students to start at the top when forming their letters.
- Say: *An uppercase* **O** *is circle around. A lowercase* **o** *is circle around.* Match the timing of your speech with the action of modeling the letter formations.

✓ **QUICK-CHECK** Distribute blackline master 1. Tell students to name each picture and draw something whose name rhymes with the picture name.

Independent Activities

Phonological Awareness

Distribute picture cards **mop, map, sub, sock, tub, tent, nut, nest, fox, fork, pan, pen, car, cup, house,** and **hat** to students. Ask a student to say the name of the picture on his or her card, segmenting the initial sound, for example, */c/ /ar/.* The student with the picture with the same initial phoneme then calls out */c/ /up/,* and the two students stand together. Continue until all cards are matched.

Letter Identification/ Formation

Have students sort through a supply of commercial word game tiles and find all the uppercase *O*s and lowercase *o*s.

Make an outline of *O* and *o* on the floor with masking tape. Have students drive over the letter outlines using toy cars.

Have students write *O* and *o* on a sheet of construction paper with glue and attach strips of yarn.

Provide stamps for uppercase *O* and lowercase *o,* an ink pad, and white paper. Have students create a design by stamping *O*s and *o*s.

Have students look through familiar books and use highlighter tape to mark uppercase *O*s and lowercase *o*s. Have them tally on a sheet of paper the number of *O*s and the number of *o*s they find.

Guided Practice

- Distribute letter cards **O, O, O, O, o, o, o,** and **o** and have students place them under the alphabet strips on their desks.
- Tell students to trace uppercase *O* and say the movement pattern and the letter name. Listen and watch to make sure that students' words match their actions.
- Repeat with lowercase *o.*

Write

- Have students practice writing uppercase *O* on their workmats.
- Remind them to say the movement pattern as they form the letter. Ask students to check their letter with the letter *O* on their alphabet strips.
- Repeat with lowercase *o.*
- Distribute blackline master 2 and ask students to say the names of the letters. Then have them practice writing uppercase *O* and lowercase *o.* (The blackline master may be completed at this time or in a literacy center.)

Compare and Contrast

- Write uppercase *O* on the chalkboard. Write lowercase *o* next to it.
- Ask students to tell how the letters are alike and different. If they need help, say: *Both letters are formed by circling around, but the uppercase* O *is taller than the lowercase* o.

Locate

- Have students locate *O* and *o* on their alphabet strips and name each letter and the picture cue.
- Ask if any students have the letter *O* or *o* in their names. Write the names on a sentence strip. Ask volunteers to frame the *O*s and *o*s.

Sort

- Distribute letter cards **O, O, O, O, o, o, o,** and **o** to each student. Ask students to find all the uppercase *O*s and put them in a row. Be sure that students find all the letters and that the letters they find are the correct ones.
- Repeat with the lowercase *o*s.

 QUICK-CHECK Use blackline master 3. Have students find all the uppercase Os and color them red and find all the lowercase os and color them blue.

 # Small-Group Activities

Select from the following small-group activities to provide hands-on practice for students who need extra support.

PRODUCE RHYME

Sit in a circle. Tell students to imagine going to the store and buying items that rhyme. Say: *I'm going shopping to buy a* **pup** *and a* **cup.** Go around the circle and give each student a turn. If students need help, suggest words, such as **box, cake, ring, mop, bat,** or **car.**

SEGMENT INITIAL SOUNDS

Say the following rhyme, using phonemes from students' names and having students fill in the blank. Say: *Begin with* **/k/** *and end with* **/im/.** *Put them together and they say ___.* Continue until all student names have been used.

LETTER IDENTIFICATION/FORMATION

Have students write uppercase *O*s and lowercase *o*s on the board using paintbrushes dipped in water. Encourage them to say the movement patterns as they form the letters.

Objectives

Students will:

- Discriminate words that begin with the same sound
- Segment words into syllables
- Recognize and learn the names of the letters *P* and *p*
- Write uppercase *P* and lowercase *p*

Materials Needed

- Alphabet Chart
- Picture Word Cards: *iguana, ox, ostrich, sandwich, mop, antelope, hat, apple, napkin, duck, yolk, envelope, kitten, quarter, zoo, olive*
- Letter Frieze Card *Pp*
- Letter Cards *P, P, P, P, p, p, p, p*
- Alphabet Strips
- BLMs *1, 2, & 3*
- Student Workmats
- StartUp Song & Rhyme CD

Phonological Awareness

Sound Discrimination

- Read the poem *Lizards in a Log* aloud. Have students chant with you and perform the actions.
- Tell students you will say each line of the poem and they are to listen for words that begin with the same sound.
- Tally the number of /l/ words students hear (**lizards, log, live, left, little, lizard, living, lonely**) Challenge them to think of other words that begin with the same sound.

Segment Words into Syllables

- Have a student pantomime an action such as climbing for the class. Have the class guess the action the student is performing.
- When the action is guessed, the student says, "Yes, I am climbing." Ask the class to repeat the word **climbing,** clap the syllables in the word, and say the number of syllables.
- Suggest in a whisper the following actions for students who need help: skateboarding, wiggling, marching, nodding, reading, bowing, tiptoeing, digging, hopping, waving.

> ### Lizards in a Log
>
> *Five lizards live in a log.*
> *One left to live with a frog.*
> *One left to live with a dog.*
> *Two left to live with a hog.*
> *One little lizard living in the bog.*
> *It's a little lonely living in a log.*

Letter Name Identification/ Formation Pp

Shared Reading of the Alphabet Chart

- Using a pointer, read the Alphabet Chart letter by letter with the class. (*A, a; B, b; C, c; D, d,* etc.)
- Read the chart again, chanting the names of the letters and the names of the pictures (*A, a, apple; B, b, ball,* etc.) Have students join you.

Model

- Display letter frieze card **Pp.** Explain that the name of this letter is uppercase *P* and the name of this letter is lowercase *p.*
- Describe the movement needed to form uppercase *P* and lowercase *p.* Tell students to start at the top when forming their letters.
- Say: *An uppercase **P** is pull down, push up, circle forward. A lowercase **p** is pull down, push up, circle forward.* Match the timing of your speech with the action of modeling the letter formation.

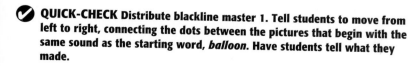

QUICK-CHECK Distribute blackline master 1. Tell students to move from left to right, connecting the dots between the pictures that begin with the same sound as the starting word, *balloon.* Have students tell what they made.

Independent Activities

Phonological Awareness

Provide old catalogs, construction paper, scissors, and glue. Have students cut out pictures and glue them onto the paper. Ask them to name each picture, clap the number of syllables in the name, and write the numeral next to the picture.

Letter Identification/ Formation

Write a large **P** and **p** in the center of a sheet of butcher paper. Have students write the letters several times on the paper.

Write large **P**s and **p**s on construction paper "mats." Provide modeling clay and have students outline the letters with the clay.

Have students form the letters **P** and **p** with cereal or raisins on a small plate. Ask them to repeat the activity several times.

Provide sets of felt letters. Have students find all the **P**s and **p**s and place them on a feltboard.

Have students circle **P**s and **p**s they find in newspaper shopping ads with a bright crayon or marker.

Guided Practice
- Distribute letter cards **P, P, P, P, p, p, p,** and **p** and have students place them under the alphabet strips on their desks.
- Tell students to trace uppercase **P** and say the movement pattern and the letter name. Make sure that students' words match their actions.
- Repeat with lowercase **p.**

Write
- Have students practice writing uppercase **P** on their workmats.
- Remind them to say the movement pattern as they form the letter. Ask students to check their letter with the letter **P** on their alphabet strips.
- Repeat with lowercase **p.**
- Distribute blackline master 2 and ask students to say the names of the letters. Then have them practice writing uppercase **P** and lowercase **p.** (The blackline master may be completed at this time or in a literacy center.)

Compare and Contrast
- Write uppercase **P** on the board. Write lowercase **p** next to it.
- Ask students to tell how the letters are alike and different. If they need help, say: *Both letters are formed the same way.*

Locate
- Have students locate **P** and **p** on their alphabet strips and name each letter and the picture cue.
- Ask if any students have the letter **P** or **p** in their names. Write the names on a sentence strip. Ask volunteers to frame the **P**s and **p**s.

Sort
- Distribute letter cards **P, P, P, P, p, p, p,** and **p** to each student. Ask students to put all the uppercase **P**s in a row. Be sure that students find all the letters and that the letters they find are the correct ones.
- Repeat with the lowercase **p**s.

 QUICK-CHECK Use blackline master 3. Tell students to name the letters in each row and color the uppercase Ps **and lowercase p**s.

 ## Small-Group Activities

Select from the following small-group activities to provide hands-on practice for students who need extra support.

SOUND DISCRIMINATION
Have students sit in a circle. Tell them you will say a name. If the students have the same sound at the beginning of their own names, they jump up. If the beginning sounds are not the same, the students stay seated. Continue until all students are standing.

SEGMENT WORDS INTO SYLLABLES
Make three necklaces, one each with the numeral 1, 2, or 3. Provide picture cards **iguana, ox, ostrich, sandwich, mop, antelope, hat, apple, napkin, duck, yolk, envelope, kitten, quarter, zoo,** and **olive.** Select three students and give each one a necklace. Have the other students name each picture, clap the number of syllables in the name, and hand the card to the person whose necklace has that number.

LETTER IDENTIFICATION/FORMATION
Give each student a shallow box lined with salt or sand. Have students write **P**s and **p**s with their fingers while saying the movement patterns.

Objectives

Students will:

- Listen to and perform steps in sequence
- Identify rhyming words in a song
- Recognize and learn the name of the letter *Q*
- Write uppercase *Q*

Materials Needed

- Alphabet Chart
- Picture Word Cards: *plant, ant, ski, tree, chain, train, light, kite, skunk, trunk, chick, stick, bat, fox, swing, truck*
- Letter Frieze Card *Qq*
- Letter Cards *Q, Q, Q, Q, P, P, P, P*
- Alphabet Strips
- BLMs *1, 2,* & *3*
- Student Workmats
- StartUp Song & Rhyme CD

 ## Phonological Awareness

Perform Steps in Sequence

- Choose one student to be "Action Kid." Tell him or her to listen carefully and follow your directions. Tell the other students to listen and see if "Action Kid" follows directions correctly.
- Give a set of instructions such as "Clap your hands, walk to the sink, and smile at the class." Have the class give a thumbs-up or thumbs-down signal to show whether "Action Kid" followed the instructions correctly.
- Choose a new "Action Kid" and repeat with new instructions, such as those shown in the box at the right.

Identify Rhyming Words

- Prepare index cards with numerals from 2 to 10.
- Sing or listen to the recording of *This Old Man* several times with students.
- Hold up the card with the numeral 2. Ask students to recall the word from the song that rhymes with *two.* If they need help, repeat the relevant lines, leaving out the last word.
- Continue with the other numeral cards until all the rhyming words are named.

 ## Letter Name Identification/ Formation Q

Shared Reading of the Alphabet Chart

- Using a pointer, read the uppercase letters on the Alphabet Chart letter by letter with the class. Use a sound pattern, such as saying four letters loudly and four letters softly.
- Read the chart again, this time starting with four letters softly, then four letters loudly. Have students join you.

Model

- Display letter frieze card **Qq.** Explain that the name of this letter is uppercase **Q.**
- Describe the movement needed to form uppercase **Q.** Tell students to start at the top when forming this letter.
- Say: *An uppercase* **Q** *is circle around, lift, slant right at the bottom.* Match the timing of your speech with the action of modeling the letter formation.

✓ **QUICK-CHECK Distribute blackline master 1. Tell students to name the pictures in each row and circle the smiley face if the names rhyme or the frowning face if they do not rhyme.**

Crawl to the table, stand up, and hop on one foot.
Stand by the easel, take three skips to the bookshelf, and rub your head.
Pat a friend on the back, walk backward two steps, and point to the window.
Jump two times, write your name on the board, and take a bow.

This old man, he played **one;**
He played knick-knack on my **thumb.**
With a knick-knack paddy-whack, give the dog a bone.
This old man came rolling home.
two/shoe
three/knee
four/door
five/hive
six/sticks
seven/heaven
eight/gate
nine/spine
ten/again

Independent Activities

Phonological Awareness

Provide picture cards **plant, ant, ski, tree, chain, train, light, kite, skunk, trunk, chick, stick, bat, fox, swing,** and **truck.** Have students put the cards that rhyme into one group and the cards that don't rhyme into another group.

Letter Identification/ Formation

Make the outline of the letter *Q* on sheets of construction paper. Have students cut out the letters and decorate them with written *Q*s.

Have students write a large *Q* on a sheet of construction paper with glue and attach beans to the glue.

Have students practice writing large *Q*s on the board in different colors. Have them say the movement pattern as they form the letter.

Have students sort through magnetic letters and place all the *Q*s in a group on a cookie sheet.

Guided Practice
- Distribute letter cards **Q, Q, Q,** and **Q** and have students place them under the alphabet strips on their desks.
- Tell students to trace uppercase *Q* and say the movement pattern and the letter name. Listen and watch to make sure that students' words match their actions.

Write
- Have students practice writing uppercase *Q* on their workmats.
- Remind them to say the movement pattern as they form the letter. Ask students to check their letter with the letter *Q* on their alphabet strips.
- Distribute blackline master 2 and ask students to say the name of the letter. Then have them practice writing uppercase *Q.* (The blackline master may be completed at this time or in a literacy center.)

Compare and Contrast
- Write uppercase *Q* on the board. Write uppercase *P* next to it.
- Ask students to tell how the letters are alike and different. If they need help, say: *Both letters circle. The uppercase* Q *circles around, lifts, and slants right at the bottom. The uppercase* P *pulls down, pushes up, then circles forward.*

Locate
- Have students locate *Q* on their alphabet strips and name the letter and picture cue.
- Ask if any students' names begin with the letter *Q.* Write the names on a sentence strip. Ask volunteers to frame the *Q*s.

Sort
- Distribute letter cards **Q, Q, Q, Q, P, P, P,** and **P** to each student. Ask students to find all the uppercase *Q*s and put them in a row. Be sure that students find all the letters and that the letters they find are the correct ones.
- Repeat with the uppercase *P*s.

 QUICK-CHECK Use blackline master 3. Tell students to color the circles of the *Q*s red and the slants blue.

 ## Small-Group Activities

Select from the following small-group activities to provide hands-on practice for students who need extra support.

PERFORM STEPS IN SEQUENCE
Give each student three blocks in three different colors. Give some instructions. For example, say: *Put the green and blue blocks over the red block. Put the red block over the blue block and the green block under the blue block.* Have students compare to see if they all followed the instructions correctly.

IDENTIFY RHYMING WORDS
Give students a smiley sticker to put on their thumbs. Have them listen to see if the following sets of words rhyme: *cherry/berry, mother/brother, finish/forest, trouble/bubble, circle/circus, bunny/honey, number/lumber, penny/pencil, robin/robot, cable/stable.* Tell students to hold up their smiley thumbs if the two words rhyme.

LETTER IDENTIFICATION/FORMATION
Have students write *Q*s on chart paper using paintbrushes dipped in water. Encourage them to say the movement pattern as they form the letter.

Objectives

Students will:

- Segment the first sound in a word
- Segment words into syllables
- Recognize and learn the name of the letter *q*
- Write lowercase *q*
- Alphabet Chart

Materials Needed

- Picture Word Cards: *bell, box, cake, car, dog, duck, feet, fox, gate, goat, horn, house, mop, map, ring, rope*
- Letter Frieze Card *Qq*
- Letter Cards *q, q, q, q, Q, Q, Q, Q*
- Alphabet Strips
- BLMs *1, 2, & 3*
- Student Workmats

 # Phonological Awareness

Segment Initial Sounds

- Call on a student and ask: *Do* **mom** *and* **mat** *begin the same?* After the student responds, ask: *How do you know?* Guide the student to respond that both begin with **/m/**.
- Have the other students clap once if they agree and twice if they do not.
- Repeat with the words **seed** and **jar,** taking time to model if students have difficulty.
- Continue with the word pairs in the box at right.

vine/vase	cab/bib
sun/tail	wax/watch
bear/bed	face/fall
point/sink	fork/four
tail/lake	feet/cook
tub/toys	pink/gift

Segment Words by Syllables

- Say the word **magnet.** Divide the word into its syllables: **mag** (pause) **net.**
- Say: **Magnet** *without* **mag** *is just* **net.**
- Repeat with the words in the box at right.
- Say each word. Have students divide the word into its syllables, pausing briefly between them. Then have students say only the last part of each word.

ankle	paper
ribbon	people
music	window
bottle	gravy
danger	breakfast
pencil	second

Letter Name Identification/ Formation q

Shared Reading of the Alphabet Chart

- Using a pointer, read the uppercase letters on the Alphabet Chart letter by letter with the class. (*A, B, C, D,* etc.)
- Read the chart again, chanting the names of the lowercase letters and the names of the pictures. (*a, apple; b, ball,* etc.) Have students join you.

Model

- Display letter frieze card **Qq.** Explain that the name of this letter is lowercase **q.**
- Describe the movement needed to form lowercase **q.** Tell students to start at the top when forming their letters.
- Say: *A lowercase* **q** *is circle back around, push up, pull down.* Match the timing of your speech with the action of modeling the letter formation.

QUICK-CHECK Distribute blackline master 1. Tell students to cut out the pictures, name each picture, clap the syllables in the name, and glue the pictures under 1, 2, or 3 to show how many syllables they heard.

Independent Activities

Phonological Awareness

Provide picture cards **bell, box, cake, car, dog, duck, feet, fox, gate, goat, horn, house, mop, map, ring,** and **rope.** Have partners scramble the cards, place them face down, and turn over two cards at a time. If the picture names begin with the same sound, partners say, for example: *These cards match because both words begin with /g/.* If the words do not begin with the same sound, they say, for example, *These cards don't match because one word begins with /b/ and one word begins with /h/.*

Letter Identification/ Formation

Make a model of the letter *q* with pipe cleaners. Have students make their own *q*s with pipe cleaners.

Have students fold a sheet of paper as many times as they can. Then ask them to unfold the paper and write the letter *q* in each section.

Have students use watercolors or fingerpaints to write the letter *q* several times on a large sheet of white construction paper.

Have students sort through sets of magnetic letters and place all the *q*s in a group on a cookie sheet.

Guided Practice
- Distribute letter cards **q, q, q,** and **q** and have students place them under the alphabet strips on their desks.
- Tell students to trace lowercase *q* and say the movement pattern and the letter name. Listen and watch to make sure that students' words match their actions.

Write
- Have students practice writing lowercase *q* on their workmats.
- Remind them to say the movement pattern as they form the letter. Ask students to check their letter with the letter *q* on their alphabet strips.
- Distribute blackline master 2 and ask students to say the name of the letter. Then have them practice writing lowercase *q.* (The blackline master may be completed at this time or in a literacy center.)

Compare and Contrast
- Write lowercase *q* on the chalkboard. Write uppercase *Q* next to it.
- Ask students to tell how the letters are alike and different. If they need help, say: *Both letters circle. The lowercase* q *circles back around, pushes up, then pulls down. The uppercase* Q *circles around, lifts, then slants right at the bottom.*

Locate
- Have students locate *q* on their alphabet strips and name the letter and the picture cue.
- Ask if any students have the letter *q* in their names. Write the names on a sentence strip. Ask volunteers to frame the *q*s.

Sort
- Distribute letter cards **q, q, q, q, Q, Q, Q,** and **Q** to each student. Ask students to find all the lowercase *q*s and put them in a row. Be sure that students find all the letters and that the letters they find are the correct ones.
- Repeat with the uppercase *Q*s.

 QUICK-CHECK Use blackline master 3. Tell students to look at the letters at the bottom of the page, cut out all the lowercase *q*s, and glue them in the boxes.

 ## Small-Group Activities

Select from the following small-group activities to provide hands-on practice for students who need extra support.

SEGMENT INITIAL SOUNDS
Select a student to be the leader. Have the leader think of the name of another student and ask: *Guess who I am thinking of?* Tell the leader to say the initial sound of the name, for example, */t/ /t/ /t/* or */vvvvvv/.* Tell students whose names begin with that sound to stand. Have the leader give more clues until the correct name is guessed. Have that student think of and give clues for the next name.

SEGMENT WORDS BY SYLLABLES
Say each of the following two-syllable words: *apple, honey, letter, number, onion, robot, supper, turtle, rooster, puppy, bubble, elbow.* Call on a student to help you divide the word into syllables. Then ask: *What comes first?* Have students say the first syllable in unison.

LETTER IDENTIFICATION/FORMATION
Have students see how many *q*s they can write on their workmats in one minute. Encourage them to say the movement pattern as they form each letter. Have students circle their best letter. Then have them erase their letters and repeat the activity.

Objectives

Students will:

- Segment the first sound in a word
- Segment words into syllables
- Recognize and learn the name of the letter *R*
- Write uppercase *R*

Materials Needed

- Alphabet Chart
- Picture Word Cards: *mitten, magnet, tiger, antelope, apple, sandwich, notebook, napkin, igloo, iguana, pumpkin, ostrich, dinosaur, helicopter, umbrella, umpire*
- Letter Frieze Card *Rr*
- Letter Cards *R, R, R, R, q, q, q, q*
- Alphabet Strips
- BLMs *1, 2, & 3*
- Student Workmats

Phonological Awareness

Segment Initial Sounds

- Say the word *fair*. Ask students to say the beginning sound in the word (/**f**/).
- Repeat using the words in the box at right.
- Repeat the activity several times. Have students segment the first sound faster each time.

Segment Words into Syllables

- Show students a puppet or stuffed animal and explain that it has an unusual way of talking. Have the puppet say its name in syllables: /**hen**/ /**rē**/. Then say the name naturally, **Henry.** Have students count the syllables by clapping once for each syllable
- Explain that Henry will name his favorite foods. Say the words in the box at right. Have students segment each word, clap its syllables, count the syllables, and then say the word naturally.

seat	/s/	Bill	/b/
way	/w/	phone	/f/
hate	/h/	fear	/f/
same	/s/	nice	/n/
Max	/m/	heart	/h/
land	/l/		

apples	popcorn
potatoes	frankfurters
carrots	hamburgers
strawberries	spaghetti
raisins	macaroni
pizza	oranges

Letter Name Identification/ Formation R

Shared Reading of the Alphabet Chart

- Using a pointer, read the Alphabet Chart letter by letter with the class. (*A, a, B, b, C, c, D, d,* etc.)
- Read the chart again, chanting the uppercase letters from *Z* to *A* and the names of the pictures. Have students join you.

Model

- Display letter frieze card **Rr.** Explain that the name of this letter is uppercase **R.**
- Describe the movement needed to form uppercase **R.** Tell students to start at the top when forming this letter.
- Say: *An uppercase **R** is pull down, lift, curve forward, slant right.* Match the timing of your speech with the action of modeling the letter formation.

✓ **QUICK-CHECK Distribute blackline master 1. Tell students to say the name of each animal, clap the syllables, and then draw a bar on the cage for each syllable they hear.**

Independent Activities

Phonological Awareness

Provide picture cards **mitten, magnet, tiger, antelope, apple, sandwich, notebook, napkin, igloo, iguana, pumpkin, ostrich, dinosaur, helicopter, umbrella,** and **umpire.** Place them face down on the table. Have students take turns choosing a card without showing it to the others and saying the picture name by dividing it into syllables. Have the other students figure out the word and say it naturally.

Letter Identification/ Formation

Have students use red markers to circle *R*s they find in the headlines of old newspapers.

Give each student a strip of adding machine tape and a model of the letter *R.* Have students write as many *R*s on the strips as they can.

Have students form the letter *R* with cereal or raisins on a plate. Ask them to repeat the activity several times.

Have students sort through the letter tiles of a commercial board game and find all the *R*s.

Make a model of the letter *R* with pipe cleaners. Have students make their own *R*s with pipe cleaners.

Guided Practice
- Distribute letter cards **R, R, R,** and **R** and have students place them under the alphabet strips on their desks.
- Tell students to trace uppercase *R* and say the movement pattern and the letter name. Listen and watch to make sure that students' words match their actions.

Write
- Have students practice writing uppercase *R* on their workmats.
- Remind them to say the movement pattern as they form the letter. Ask students to check their letter with the letter *R* on their alphabet strips.
- Distribute blackline master 2 and ask students to say the name of the letter. Then have them practice writing uppercase *R.* (The blackline master may be completed at this time or in a literacy center.)

Compare and Contrast
- Write uppercase *R* on the board. Write lowercase *q* next to it.
- Ask students to tell how the letters are alike and different. If they need help, say: *Both letters have a pull-down movement. The uppercase* **R** *pulls down first, then lifts, curves forward, and slants right. The lowercase* **q** *circles back around, pushes up, then pulls down.*

Locate
- Have students locate *R* on their alphabet strips and name the letter and the picture cue.
- Ask if any students' names begin with the letter *R.* Write the names on a sentence strip. Ask volunteers to frame the *R*s.

Sort
- Distribute letter cards **R, R, R, R, q, q, q,** and **q** to each student. Ask students to find all the uppercase *R*s and put them in a row. Be sure that students find all the letters and that the letters they find are the correct ones.
- Repeat with the lowercase *q*s.

 QUICK-CHECK Use blackline master 3. Tell students to color each section that has an *R* and tell you what they have made.

 ## Small-Group Activities

Select from the following small-group activities to provide hands-on practice for students who need extra support.

SEGMENT INITIAL SOUNDS
Ask each student to think of a favorite thing that begins with the same letter as his or her name. Pair students and have partners whisper their favorites to each other. Then have students tell what their partner chose by segmenting the initial sounds. For example, /m/ /m/ /m/ /at/ *likes* /m/ /m/ /m/ /ilk/, /s/ /s/ /s/ /andē/ *likes to* /s/ /s/ /s/ /ing/.

SEGMENT WORDS INTO SYLLABLES
Have students introduce themselves to Henry the puppet by saying their names and dividing them into syllables. Tell the other students to repeat each name while clapping the syllables and then say it naturally. Provide support as needed.

LETTER IDENTIFICATION/FORMATION
Have students write *R*s on several small self-stick notes. Have each student select his or her best *R* to stick on the board.

Objectives

Students will:

- Produce rhyming words
- Segment words into syllables
- Recognize and learn the name of the letter *r*
- Write lowercase *r*

Materials Needed

- Alphabet Chart
- Picture Word Cards: *zipper, quarter, X ray, kitten, yo-yo, jump rope, zebra, wagon, lunchbox, guitar, elbow, rabbit, under, olive, igloo, umpire*
- Letter Frieze Card *Rr*
- Letter Cards *r, r, r, r, R, R, R, R*
- Alphabet Strips
- BLMs *1, 2, & 3*
- Student Workmats
- StartUp Song & Rhyme CD

Phonological Awareness

Produce Rhyme

- Say: *I had to clean the garage. I was wishing I could go ___.* Ask students to think of an action word for the sentence that rhymes with **wishing** (**fishing**).
- Continue with the sentences in the box at right. Emphasize the word with which the students' suggested word is supposed to rhyme.

Segment Words into Syllables

- Say the word **window** and then divide it into syllables: **win** (pause) **dow.**
- Say: **Window** *without* **dow** *is just* **win.**
- Repeat with the words in the box (below right).
- Say each word. Have students divide the word into its syllables, pausing briefly between them. Then have students say only the first part of the word.

Letter Name Identification/ Formation r

Shared Reading of the Alphabet Chart

- Using a pointer, read the lowercase letters on the Alphabet Chart letter by letter with the class. Use a sound pattern such as *loud, soft, soft.* (*a*, *b*, *c*, *d*, *e*, *f*, etc.)
- Read the chart again, using the opposite pattern: *soft, loud, loud.* (*a*, **b**, **c**, *d*, **e**, **f**, etc.) Have students join you.

Model

- Display letter frieze card **Rr**. Explain that the name of this letter is lowercase *r*.
- Describe the movement needed to form lowercase *r*. Tell students to start at the top when forming their letters.
- Say: *A lowercase* **r** *is pull down, push up, curve forward.* Match the timing of your speech with the action of modeling the letter formation.

✓ **QUICK-CHECK Distribute blackline master 1. Tell students to say the name of each picture, clap the syllables in the picture name, and tally or write the number of syllables they hear.**

While Mom was *parking,* the dog was ___. (**barking**)
While we were *dining,* the sun was ___. (**shining**)
As we were *walking,* we were also ___. (**talking**)
The weather is *freezing,* and I am ___. (**sneezing**)
The lambs are *playing,* and the horses are ___. (**neighing**)
I'm hungry! I'll start *looking* to see what's ___. (**cooking**)

---

blanket	chicken
building	whisper
kettle	winter
meadow	painting
zipper	berry
candy	fifteen
cousin	zebra

Phonological Awareness

Have students draw pictures of two objects whose names rhyme, such as a **purse** and a **nurse.** Display the pairs of drawings in the room.

Letter Identification/ Formation

Give each student a small notebook. Have students write a letter **r** each time they spot an **r** in classroom print (posters, name tags, and so on).

Have students form the letter **r** with coins or buttons. Then have them scramble the objects and repeat the activity several times.

Have students use watercolors or fingerpaints to paint the letter **r** several times on a large sheet of white construction paper.

Put sets of magnetic letters into a soup pot. Have students take turns ladling out several letters and locating the lowercase **r**s. When the pot is empty, refill it with the letters and begin again.

Have students sort through familiar books and use highlighter tape to locate **r**s. Have them tally on a sheet of paper how many **r**s they found.

Guided Practice
- Distribute letter cards **r, r, r,** and **r** and have students place them under the alphabet strips on their desks.
- Tell students to trace lowercase **r** and say the movement pattern and the letter name. Make sure that students' words match their actions.

Write
- Have students practice writing lowercase **r** on their workmats.
- Remind them to say the movement pattern as they form the letter. Ask students to check their letter with the letter **r** on their alphabet strips.
- Distribute blackline master 2 and ask students to say the name of the letter. Then have them practice writing lowercase **r.** (The blackline master may be completed at this time or in a literacy center.)

Compare and Contrast
- Write lowercase **r** on the board. Write uppercase **R** next to it.
- Ask students to tell how the letters are alike and different. If they need help, say: *Both letters start with a pull-down movement. The lowercase* **r** *then pushes up and curves forward. The uppercase* **R** *then lifts, curves forward, and slants right.*

Locate
- Have students locate **r** on their alphabet strips and name the letter and the picture cue.
- Ask if any students have the letter **r** in their names. Write the names on a sentence strip. Ask volunteers to frame the **r**s.

Sort
- Distribute letter cards **r, r, r, r, R, R, R,** and **R** to each student. Have students put all the lowercase **r**s in a row.
- Repeat with the uppercase **R**s.

 QUICK-CHECK Use blackline master 3. Tell students to name each letter, circle each **r**, and tally the number of **r**s in each row.

 ## Small-Group Activities

Select from the following small-group activities to provide hands-on practice for students who need extra support.

PRODUCE RHYME
Chant or listen to the recording of *Hey, Diddle Diddle.* Discuss the meaning of **fiddle** and explain that **diddle** is a nonsense word that rhymes with **fiddle.** Ask students to think of other musical instruments and make up new nonsense rhymes. For example: *Hey bumpet bumpet, the cat and the trumpet* or *Hey joot joot, the cat and the flute.*

SEGMENT WORDS INTO SYLLABLES
Provide picture cards **zipper, quarter, X ray, kitten, yo-yo, jump rope, zebra, wagon, lunchbox, guitar, elbow, rabbit, under, olive, igloo,** and **umpire.** Have students take turns saying a picture name and dividing it into syllables. Ask: *What comes last?* Tell students to say only the last syllable in unison.

LETTER IDENTIFICATION/FORMATION
Have students write as many **r**s as possible on their workmats in one minute, saying the movement pattern as they write each letter. Have them circle their best letter, erase all their letters, and repeat the activity.

Objectives

Students will:

- Blend syllables to form a word
- Segment the first sound in a word
- Recognize and learn the names of the letters *S* and *s*
- Write uppercase *S* and lowercase *s*

Materials Needed

- Alphabet Chart
- Picture Word Cards: *apple, tiger, sandwich, notebook, iguana, ostrich, helicopter, umpire, guitar, yo-yo, envelope, wagon, dinosaur, vegetables, zebra, kitten*
- Letter Frieze Card *Ss*
- Letter Cards *S, S, S, S, s, ,s, s, s*
- Alphabet Strips
- BLMs *1, 2, & 3*
- Student Workmats
- StartUp Song & Rhyme CD

Phonological Awareness

Blend Syllables

- Show students Henry the puppet and remind them that he talks only in syllables. Ask the puppet to tell students what his favorite toy is. As the puppet, say: **ro/bot.** Then say the word **robot** naturally.
- Repeat with the words in the box at the right. Have the puppet segment each word into syllables. Have students blend the syllables to make the word.

mar/bles	*pup/pet*
rock/et	*sol/diers*
sub/ma/rine	*doll/house*
bas/ket/ball	*dom/i/noes*

Segment Initial Sounds

- Call on a student and ask: *Do* **sad** *and* **sock** *begin the same?* After the student answers, ask: *How do you know?* Guide the student to respond that both words begin with **/s/.**
- Tell the other students to clap once if they agree and twice if they don't.
- Repeat, asking another student: *Do* **weed** *and* **farm** *begin the same?*
- Continue with the word pairs in the box at the right. Model segmenting initial sounds if students need help.

van/vest	*cave/bed*
six/toe	*wig/worm*
belt/bike	*fork/foot*
purse/sand	*pole/pie*
tack/lake	*fire/read*
team/tire	*hide/cake*

Letter Name Identification/ Formation Ss

Shared Reading of the Alphabet Chart

- Divide the class into two teams.
- Using a pointer, lead one team to say the uppercase letters on the Alphabet Chart from *A* to *Z*. Lead the other team to say the lowercase letters from *a* to *z*. Then reverse.

Model

- Display letter frieze card **Ss**. Explain that the name of this letter is uppercase **S** and the name of this letter is lowercase **s**.
- Describe the movement needed to form uppercase **S** and lowercase **s**. Tell students to start at the top when forming their letters.
- Say: *An uppercase* **S** *is curve back, curve forward. A lowercase* **s** *is curve back, curve forward.* Match the timing of your speech with the action of modeling the letter formations.

✔ **QUICK-CHECK** Distribute blackline master 1. Tell students to name each picture and draw a picture of something whose name begins with the same sound as the picture name.

Independent Activities

Phonological Awareness

Provide picture cards **apple, sandwich, tiger, notebook, iguana, ostrich, helicopter, umpire, guitar, yo-yo envelope, wagon, dinosaur, vegetables, zebra,** and **kitten.** Have students say the name of each picture, divide the picture name into its syllables, and then say the word naturally.

Letter Identification/ Formation

Have students sort through letter tiles from commercial board games and find all the uppercase **S**s and lowercase **s**s.

Place a Big Book or poetry poster in the literacy center. Have students use highlighter tape to locate the letters **S** and **s.** Have them tally on a sheet of paper the numbers of **S**s and **s**s they find.

Write large **S**s and **s**s on construction paper "mats." Provide modeling clay and have students outline the letters with the clay.

Make outlines of the letters **S** and **s** on the floor with masking tape. Have students drive over the outlines using toy cars.

Distribute photocopies of the song *I'm a Little Teapot.* Sing or listen to the recording of the song together. Then have students circle the **S**s and **s**s on their photocopies.

Guided Practice

- Distribute letter cards **S, S, S, S, s, s, s,** and **s** and have students place them under the alphabet strips on their desks.
- Tell students to trace uppercase **S** and say the movement pattern and the letter name. Listen and watch to make sure that students' words match their actions.
- Repeat with lowercase **s.**

Write

- Have students practice writing uppercase **S** on their workmats.
- Remind them to say the movement pattern as they form the letter. Ask students to check their letter with the letter **S** on their alphabet strips.
- Repeat with lowercase **s.**
- Distribute blackline master 2 and ask students to say the names of the letters. Then have them practice writing uppercase **S** and lowercase **s.** (The blackline master may be completed at this time or in a literacy center.)

Compare and Contrast

- Write uppercase **S** on the board. Write lowercase **s** next to it.
- Ask students to tell how the letters are alike and different. If they need help, say: *Both letters are formed the same, but uppercase S is taller, and lowercase s is shorter.*

Locate

- Have students locate **S** and **s** on their alphabet strips and name each letter and the picture cue.
- Ask if any students have the letter **S** or **s** in their names. Write the names on a sentence strip. Ask volunteers to frame the **S**s and **s**s.

Sort

- Distribute letter cards **S, S, S, S, s, s, s,** and **s** to each student. Ask students to find all the uppercase **S**s and put them in a row. Be sure that students find all the letters and that the letters they find are the correct ones.
- Repeat with the lowercase **s**s.

 QUICK-CHECK Use blackline master 3. Tell students to cut out the letters, sort them into uppercase **S**s and lowercase **s**s, and glue them into the correct boxes.

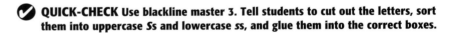 **Small-Group Activities**

Select from the following small-group activities to provide hands-on practice for students who need extra support.

SEGMENT SYLLABLES

Ask students to introduce their pets to Henry the puppet. Have them say the pets' names and divide the names into syllables. Have the other students repeat each name while clapping the syllables and then say it naturally. Students who do not have a pet can make up a name.

SEGMENT INITIAL SOUNDS

Provide picture cards **apple, sandwich, tiger, notebook, iguana, ostrich, helicopter, umpire, guitar, envelope, yo-yo, wagon, dinosaur, vegetables, zebra,** and **kitten.** Have students take turns naming the pictures. Tell the other students to stand on their left foot as they say the initial sound and to stand on their right foot as they say the rest of the word.

LETTER IDENTIFICATION/FORMATION

Have students write **S**s and **s**s on chart paper using paintbrushes dipped in water. Encourage them to say the movement pattern as they form each letter.

Objectives

Students will:

- Blend syllables to form a word
- Segment words by syllables
- Recognize and learn the name of the letter *T*
- Write uppercase *T*

Materials Needed

- Alphabet Chart
- Picture Word Cards: *pumpkin, sandwich, helicopter, magnet, antelope, umbrella, wagon, elephant, elbow, yo-yo, envelope, umpire, zebra, vegetables, quarter*
- Letter Frieze Card *Tt*
- Letter Cards *T, T, T, T, S, S, S, S*
- Alphabet Strips
- BLMs *1, 2, & 3*
- Student Workmats

Phonological Awareness

Blend Syllables

- Prepare a bag of objects that have two- or three-syllable names, using, for example, the objects listed in the box at right.
- Say the name of an object syllable by syllable, for example, **pen/cil.** Have students blend the syllables to say the word naturally. Take the object out of the bag so that students can confirm its name.

Segment Words by Syllables

- Show students three blocks.
- Say **garden** and then say its syllables: **gar/den.** Put down one block as you say **gar.** Stack a second block as you say **den.** Count the blocks to find out how many syllables are in the word.
- Give blocks to each student. Have students stack and count the blocks as they segment the words in the box at right.

pencil	handkerchief
newspaper	ribbon
marble	lemon
penny	toothbrush
marshmallow	candle
glasses	banana

Letter Name Identification/ Formation T

Shared Reading of the Alphabet Chart

- Using a pointer, read the Alphabet Chart letter by letter with the class. March in place as you say the uppercase letters. Step with your left foot for **A**, right foot for **B**, and so on.
- Repeat, starting on your right foot. Have students join you.

Model

- Display letter frieze card **Tt.** Explain that the name of this letter is uppercase **T.**
- Describe the movement needed to form uppercase **T.** Tell students to start at the top when forming this letter.
- Say: *An uppercase* **T** *is pull down, cross at the top.* Match the timing of your speech with the action of modeling the letter formation.

basket	carefully
because	dinner
camel	ship
center	forever
anywhere	kids
crayon	tornado
could	invention
together	year
happy	beautiful

✓ **QUICK-CHECK Distribute blackline master 1. Tell students to name the pictures in each row and clap the syllables in the picture names. They are to circle the smiley face if both picture names have the same number of syllables, and the frowning face if they do not.**

Independent Activities

Phonological Awareness

Ask students to make three columns labeled 1, 2, and 3 on a sheet of construction paper. Have them search through an old catalog, cut out items whose names have one, two, or three syllables, and glue each picture in the appropriate column.

Letter Identification/ Formation

Make the outline of the letter *T* on sheets of construction paper. Have students cut out the letters and decorate them with written *T*s.

Provide a stamp for the letter *T,* an ink pad, and white paper. Have students create a design by stamping the letter *T.*

Have students sort through sets of magnetic letters and place all the uppercase *T*s in a group on a cookie sheet.

Place a Big Book or poetry poster in the literacy center. Have students use high-lighter tape to locate the letter *T.* Then have them tally the number of *T*s they found on a sheet of paper.

Provide long and short pretzel sticks. Have students make *T*s using one long pretzel stick and one short pretzel stick.

Guided Practice
- Distribute letter cards **T, T, T,** and **T** and have students place them under the alphabet strips on their desks.
- Tell students to trace uppercase *T* and say the movement pattern and the letter name. Listen and watch to make sure that students' words match their actions.

Write
- Have students practice writing uppercase *T* on their workmats.
- Remind them to say the movement pattern as they form the letter. Ask students to check their letter with the letter *T* on their alphabet strips.
- Distribute blackline master 2 and ask students to say the name of the letter. Then have them practice writing the uppercase *T.* (The blackline master may be completed at this time or in a literacy center.)

Compare and Contrast
- Write uppercase *T* on the board. Write uppercase *S* next to it.
- Ask students to tell how the letters are alike and different. If they need help, say: *No parts of these letters are alike. The uppercase* **T** *pulls down, then crosses at the top. The uppercase* **S** *curves back, then curves forward.*

Locate
- Have students locate *T* on their alphabet strips and name the letter and the picture cue.
- Ask if any students' names begin with the letter *T.* Write the names on a sentence strip. Ask volunteers to frame the *T*s.

Sort
- Distribute letter cards **T, T, T, T, S, S, S,** and **S** to each student. Ask students to find all the uppercase *T*s and put them in a row. Be sure that students find all the letters and that the letters they find are the correct ones.
- Repeat with the uppercase *S*s.

 QUICK-CHECK Use blackline master 3. Tell students to color the pieces, cut them out, and glue them onto the paper to build some *T*s.

 # Small-Group Activities

Select from the following small-group activities to provide hands-on practice for students who need extra support.

BLEND SYLLABLES

Provide picture cards **pumpkin, sandwich, helicopter, magnet, antelope, umbrella, wagon, elephant, elbow, yo-yo, envelope, umpire, zebra, vegetables,** and **quarter.** Segment the picture names one at a time without showing the pictures. Have students blend the syllables to say the words. Show the cards so that students can confirm the words.

SEGMENT WORDS BY SYLLABLES

Have each student draw a picture of someone in his or her family, then show the picture, saying the name of the person. Tell the other students to clap the syllables in the name and tell how many they hear. Then have students sort all their pictures according to the number of syllables in the names.

LETTER IDENTIFICATION/FORMATION

Have students see how many *T*s they can write on their workmats in one minute. Encourage them to say the movement pattern as they write each letter. Have students circle their best letter, then erase their work, and repeat the activity.

Objectives
Students will:

- Discriminate words with the same initial sound
- Blend syllables to form words
- Recognize and learn the name of the letter *t*
- Write lowercase *t*

Materials Needed

- Alphabet Chart
- Picture Word Cards: *map, mop, mitten, magnet, duck, dog, dinosaur, dish, ring, rabbit, rug, rope, sock, sun, sub, sandwich*
- Letter Frieze Card *Tt*
- Letter Cards *t, t, t, t, T, T, T, T*
- Alphabet Strips
- BLMs *1, 2, & 3*
- Student Workmats
- StartUp Song & Rhyme CD

 # Phonological Awareness

Discriminate Initial Sounds

- Chant or listen to the recording of the poem *Baby Bears* with students. Have them perform the actions indicated.
- Say the lines of the poem one at a time. Tell students to listen for words that begin with the same sound.
- Tally the number of */b/* words students hear.
- Challenge students to think of other words that begin with the */b/* sound.
- Have students listen for phrases with repeated initial sounds, such as *hit his head* and *got to go.*

Blend Syllables

- Show students Henry the puppet and remind them that he speaks only in syllables. Have the puppet tell students what his favorite zoo animal is, for example, ***mon/key.*** Demonstrate how to say the word naturally.
- Have the puppet segment the words in the box at right. Have students blend the syllables to make the words.

> Five baby bears in the bed.
> One rolled over and hit his head.
> Four baby bears in the bed.
> One left to go and eat some
>   bread.
> Three baby bears in the bed.
> "I've got to go," one baby bear
>   said.
> Two baby bears in the bed.
> "I want my pajamas that are red!"
> One baby bear in the bed.
> He's so comfortable with the
>   whole bedspread.

camel	elephant
rhinoceros	tiger
panda	gorilla
ostrich	lion
leopard	hippopotamus
crocodile	tortoise

Letter Name Identification/ Formation t

Shared Reading of the Alphabet Chart

- Using a pointer, read the Alphabet Chart letter by letter with the class. Say the lowercase letters, chanting each one four times. (*a, a, a, a, b, b, b, b,* etc.)
- Have students join you.

Model

- Display letter frieze card **Tt.** Explain that the name of this letter is lowercase *t.*
- Describe the movement needed to form lowercase *t.* Tell students to start at the top when forming their letters.
- Say: *A lowercase* **t** *is pull down, cross near the top.* Match the timing of your speech with the action of modeling the letter formation.

 QUICK-CHECK Distribute blackline master 1. Tell students to say each picture name, then color the picture red if it starts like *heart* and yellow if it starts like *sun.*

Independent Activities

Phonological Awareness

Have each student draw a picture of at least two objects or activities that begin with the same sound as his or her name.

Letter Identification/ Formation

Have students dip colored chalk into a cup of water and write *t*s on a sheet of construction paper until the paper is filled.

Provide a stamp for the letter *t*, an ink pad, and white paper. Have students create a design by stamping the letter *t*.

Provide multiple sets of letter cards. Have students sort through the cards and clip all the lowercase *t*s onto a clothesline.

Distribute photocopies of the poem *Humpty Dumpty* to students. Read the poem aloud or listen to the recording. Have students circle the *t*s on their photocopies.

Have students label a sheet of construction paper with the letter *t*. Have them search for *t*s in old magazines, cut out the letters, and paste them on the paper.

Guided Practice

- Distribute letter cards **t, t, t,** and **t** and have students place them under the alphabet strips on their desks.
- Tell students to trace lowercase *t* and say the movement pattern and the letter name. Listen and watch to make sure that students' words match their actions.

Write

- Have students practice writing lowercase *t* on their workmats.
- Remind them to say the movement pattern as they form the letter. Ask students to check their letter with the letter *t* on their alphabet strips.
- Distribute blackline master 2 and ask students to say the name of the letter. Then have them practice writing the lowercase *t*. (The blackline master may be completed at this time or in a literacy center.)

Compare and Contrast

- Write lowercase *t* on the board. Write uppercase *T* next to it.
- Ask students to tell how the letters are alike and different. If they need help, say: *Both letters pull down and cross. The lowercase* t *crosses near the top. The uppercase* T *crosses at the top.*

Locate

- Have students locate *t* on their alphabet strips and name the letter and the picture cue.
- Ask if any students have the letter *t* in their names. Write the names on a sentence strip. Ask volunteers to frame the *t*s.

Sort

- Distribute letter cards **t, t, t, t, T, T, T,** and **T** to each student. Ask students to find all the lowercase *t*s and put them in a row. Be sure that students find all the letters and that the letters they find are the correct ones.
- Repeat with the uppercase *T*s.

 QUICK-CHECK Use blackline master 3. Tell students to write *t* in each box in the large *t*.

 # Small-Group Activities

Select from the following small-group activities to provide hands-on practice for students who need extra support.

DISCRIMINATE INITIAL SOUNDS

Have students sit in a circle. Hand out picture cards **map, mop, mitten, magnet, duck, dog, dinosaur, dish, ring, rabbit, rug, rope, sock, sun, sub,** and **sandwich.** Say */m/, /d/, /r/,* or */s/.* Tell students whose picture name begins with that sound to "pop up" and take turns showing and naming their pictures. Continue until all pictures have been shown. Then have students swap cards and play again.

BLEND SYLLABLES

Ask students to name their favorite foods and divide the names into syllables. Have the other students blend the syllables and say the words naturally. Then have those students give a thumbs-up or thumbs-down signal to show whether or not they like the food.

LETTER IDENTIFICATION/FORMATION

Have students write as many *t*s as possible on their workmats in one minute, saying the movement pattern as they write each letter. Have students circle their best letter, erase their letters, and repeat the activity.

Objectives
Students will:

- Segment the first sound in a word
- Segment words into syllables
- Recognize and learn the name of the letters *U* and *u*
- Write uppercase *U* and lowercase *u*

Materials Needed

- Alphabet Chart
- Picture Word Cards: *helicopter, mop, iguana, pumpkin, nest, ostrich, yo-yo, napkin, guitar, ring, envelope, elbow, kangaroo, legs, van, zipper*
- Letter Frieze Card *Uu*
- Letter Cards *U, U, U, U, u, u, u, u*
- Alphabet Strips
- BLMs *1, 2, & 3*
- Student Workmats

 Phonological Awareness

Segment initial Sounds

- Bring out the puppet called Choppy and remind students that he chops the first sound off a word before finishing it.
- Have the puppet say */p/ /ark/*. Ask students to identify the word. Then use the word in a sentence. Say: *I like to play in the park.*
- Say each word in the box at the right. Have students say the word, segmenting the initial sound. Then have them use the word in a sentence.

jump	pet
sink	tent
goal	peach
bath	hen
van	worm
lap	fight

Segment Words into Syllables

- Have students sit in a circle. Remind them that words are made up of smaller parts called syllables. Say a two-syllable word such as **arrow,** stressing the syllables.
- Have students repeat the word, clap once for each syllable, and tell how many syllables they heard.
- Say a three-syllable word such as **animal.** Have students repeat the word and clap and count the syllables.
- Ask students to give a thumbs-up or thumbs-down signal to show whether the two words have the same number of syllables.
- Repeat with the pairs of words in the box at the right.

water/painting	mother/funny
vacation/lovely	chair/flower
marker/jumping	poster/jog
clock/jeans	pizza/cousin
following/container	
furniture/racquetball	

 Letter Name Identification/ Formation Uu

Shared Reading of the Alphabet Chart

- Using a pointer, lead students in reading the Alphabet Chart letter by letter. Have the boys name the uppercase and lowercase letters and the girls name the corresponding picture cues.
- Have students switch roles and read the chart again.

Model

- Display letter frieze card **Uu.** Explain that the name of this letter is uppercase **U** and the name of this letter is lowercase **u.**
- Describe the movement needed to form uppercase **U** and lowercase **u.** Tell students to start at the top when forming their letters.
- Say: *An uppercase* **U** *is pull down, curve forward, push up. A lowercase* **u** *is pull down, curve forward, push up, pull down.* Match the timing of your speech with the action of modeling the letter formations.

✔ **QUICK-CHECK Distribute blackline master 1. Tell students to say the name of each picture, clap the syllables in the picture name, and circle 1, 2, or 3 to show how many syllables they heard.**

Phonological Awareness

Provide picture cards **helicopter, mop, iguana, pumpkin, nest, ostrich, yo-yo, napkin, guitar, envelope, ring, elbow, kangaroo, legs, van,** and **zipper.** Have students say the name of each picture card, clap the syllables in the picture name, and sort the cards into groups of one-, two-, and three-syllable words.

Letter Identification/ Formation

Have students use watercolors or fingerpaints to paint uppercase *U* and lowercase *u* several times on a large sheet of white construction paper.

Have partners practice writing *U*s and *u*s on each other's back with their fingers and identifying which letter was written.

Have students sort through a supply of felt letters and place all the *U*s and *u*s on the board.

Give each student a strip of adding machine tape and models of the letters *U* and *u.* Have students write as many *U*s and *u*s as they can on their strips, alternating the uppercase and the lowercase forms.

Place a Big Book or poetry poster in the literacy center. Have students use highlighter tape to locate the letters *U* and *u.* Have them tally on a sheet of paper the numbers of *U*s and *u*s they find.

Guided Practice

- Distribute letter cards **U, U, U, U, u, u, u,** and **u** and have students place them under the alphabet strips on their desks.
- Ask them to trace uppercase *U* and say the movement pattern and the letter name. Listen and watch to make sure that students' words match their actions.
- Repeat with lowercase *u.*

Write

- Have students practice writing uppercase *U* on their workmats.
- Remind them to say the movement pattern as they form the letter. Ask students to check their letter with the letter *U* on their alphabet strips.
- Repeat with lowercase *u.*
- Distribute blackline master 2 and ask students to say the names of the letters. Then have them practice writing uppercase *U* and lowercase *u.* (The blackline master may be completed at this time or in a literacy center.)

Compare and Contrast

- Write uppercase *U* on the board. Write lowercase *u* next to it.
- Ask students to tell how the letters are alike and different. If they need help, say: *Both letters pull down, curve forward, and push up, but lowercase* **u** *then pulls down.*

Locate

- Have students locate *U* and *u* on their alphabet strips and name the letter and the picture cue.
- Ask if any students have the letter *U* or *u* in their names. Write the names on a sentence strip. Ask volunteers to frame the *U*s and *u*s.

Sort

- Distribute letter cards **U, U, U, U, u, u, u,** and **u** to each student. Ask students to find all the uppercase *U*s and put them in a row. Be sure that students find all the letters and that the letters they find are the correct ones.
- Repeat with the lowercase *u*s.

✓ **QUICK-CHECK Use blackline master 3. Tell students to find all the uppercase *U*s and color them red and all the lowercase *u*s and color them blue.**

 # Small-Group Activities

Select from the following small-group activities to provide hands-on practice for students who need extra support.

SEGMENT INITIAL SOUNDS

Say the words *rain, tail, hall, land, back, cart, horn, wash, lock, guess, hop,* and *joke.* Ask students to stand on their left foot as they say the initial sound and on their right foot as they say the rest of the word.

SEGMENT WORDS INTO SYLLABLES

Have students take turns naming a person or place they like to visit. They may choose whether to clap, snap, or tap the syllables. Ask the rest of the class to silently count the number of claps, snaps, or taps and then say how many syllables they heard.

LETTER IDENTIFICATION/FORMATION

Have students write *U* on their workmats several times, saying the movement pattern as they write each letter. Repeat with lowercase *u.*

Objectives

Students will:

- Produce a real or nonsense rhyming word
- Segment the first sound in a word
- Recognize and learn the names of the letters *V* and *v*
- Write uppercase *V* and lowercase *v*

Materials Needed

- Alphabet Chart
- Picture Word Cards: *bat, bell, ring, rope, fan, fox, horn, house, saw, soap, mop, map, coat, corn, top, tub*
- Letter Frieze Card *Vv*
- Letter Cards *V, V, V, V, v, v, v, v*
- Alphabet Strips
- BLMs *1, 2, & 3*
- Student Workmats

 # Phonological Awareness

Produce Rhyme

- Point out that almost any word can be rhymed and that rhymes are sometimes nonsense words.
- Have students sit in a circle with you on the floor and show them a large ball. Say: *I will name a word and roll the ball to one of you. You will say a word that rhymes with my word, and the class will decide if it is a real word or a nonsense word. Then you will roll the ball to another student.*
- Start with the word **cake.** Students might choose real words, such as **bake, shake, fake, lake, flake, make,** or **rake,** or nonsense words, such as **dake, gake,** or **zake.**
- Continue the game with additional starting words, such as **dad, draw, bell, play, king, pet, vest, hook,** and **wave.**

Segment Initial Sounds

- Show students how to pat their legs and clap their hands in a pat/pat/clap pattern.
- Tell students you will say an action word, then everyone will say the beginning sound twice and the action word once while patting and clapping.
- Demonstrate with the word **catch.** Say: **catch, /k/ /k/ catch** while patting your legs twice and clapping once. Have students try it with you.
- Try to keep the rhythm going as you call out the following action words: **laugh, paint, hide, cut, talk, dig, wash, run, dance.**

Letter Name Identification/ Formation Vv

Shared Reading of the Alphabet Chart

- Using a pointer, read the Alphabet Chart letter by letter with the class, saying every other letter, starting with **A, a.** (A, a; C, c; E, e, etc.)
- Read the chart again, chanting every other letter, starting with **B, b.** (B, b; D, d; F, f, etc.) Have students join you.

Model

- Display letter frieze card **Vv.** Explain that the name of this letter is uppercase **V** and the name of this letter is lowercase **v.**
- Describe the movement needed to form uppercase **V** and lowercase **v.** Tell students to start at the top when forming their letters.
- Say: *An uppercase* **V** *is slant right, slant up. A lowercase* **v** *is slant right, slant up.* Match the timing of your speech with the action of modeling the letter formations.

✓ **QUICK-CHECK Distribute blackline master 1. Tell students to name each picture and to draw something whose name rhymes with the picture name.**

Independent Activities

Phonological Awareness

Provide picture cards **bat, bell, ring, rope, fan, fox, horn, house, saw, soap, mop, map, coat, corn, top,** and **tub.** Partners place the picture cards face up. One partner points to and names a picture and then segments the initial sound: */b/ /at/.* The other partner points to and names another picture whose name has the same initial phoneme and segments the initial sound: */b/ /el/.* Both cards are then removed from play.

Letter Identification/ Formation

Have students form **V**s and **v**s with coins or buttons. Ask them to scramble the objects and repeat the activity.

Ask students to write **V** and **v** on a large sheet of white paper with a red crayon or marker. Have them trace each letter with two other colors of their own choosing.

Make the outline of the letters **V** and **v** on sheets of construction paper. Have students trace and then decorate the letters.

Guided Practice
- Distribute letter cards **V, V, V,** and **V** and have students place them under the alphabet strips on their desks.
- Tell students to trace uppercase **V** and say the movement pattern and the letter name. Listen and watch to make sure that students' words match their actions.
- Repeat with lowercase **v.**

Write
- Have students practice writing uppercase **V** on their workmats.
- Remind them to say the movement pattern as they form the letter. Ask students to check their letter with the letter **V** on their alphabet strips.
- Repeat with lowercase **v.**
- Distribute blackline master 2 and ask students to say the names of the letters. Then have them practice writing uppercase **V** and lowercase **v.** (The blackline master may be completed at this time or in a literacy center.)

Compare and Contrast
- Write uppercase **V** on the board. Write lowercase **v** next to it.
- Ask students to tell how the letters are alike and different. If they need help, say: *Both letters are formed the same, but uppercase **V** is taller and lowercase **v** is shorter.*

Locate
- Have students locate **V** and **v** on their alphabet strips and name each letter and the picture cue.
- Ask if anyone has the letter **V** or **v** in his or her name. Write the names on a sentence strip. Ask volunteers to frame the **V**s and **v**s.

Sort
- Distribute letter cards **V, V, V, V, v, v, v,** and **v** to each student. Ask students to find all the uppercase **V**s and put them in a row. Be sure that students find all the letters and that the letters they find are the correct ones.
- Repeat with the lowercase **v**s.

 QUICK-CHECK Use blackline master 3. Tell students to color all the uppercase Vs and lowercase vs that look right.

 Small-Group Activities

Select from the following small-group activities to provide hands-on practice for students who need extra support.

PRODUCE RHYME

Tell students that they will take an imaginary walk and that they must look for things that rhyme. For example, say: *I'm going walking. I see a pool and a school.* If a student has difficulty thinking of rhyming words, give him or her a starting word, such as **pup, frog, hen, sand, bug,** or **car.** Students may use nonsense words that rhyme.

SEGMENT INITIAL SOUNDS

Say the following rhyme with phonemes from number words and have students fill in the blank: *Begin with /t/ and end with /$\overline{oo}$/. Put them together and they say ___.* Continue with **seven, ten, four, eight, nine, six,** and **five.**

LETTER IDENTIFICATION/FORMATION

Have students write **V**s and **v**s on the board using different colors. Encourage them to say the movement pattern as they write.

Objectives

Students will:

- Blend syllables to form words
- Segment the first sound in a word
- Recognize and learn the names of the letters *W* and *w*
- Write uppercase *W* and lowercase *w*

Materials Needed

- Alphabet Chart
- Picture Word Cards: *pan, pen, sock, sun, hat, house, yarn, yak, ring, rope, goat, gate, watch, web, jacks, jam*
- Letter Frieze Card *Ww*
- Letter Cards *W, W, W, W, w, w, w, w*
- Alphabet Strips
- BLMs *1, 2, & 3*
- Student Workmats

Phonological Awareness

Blend Syllables

- Say: *I will name a sport by saying the word in syllables, or parts. You are to put the word back together by blending the syllables and then naming the sport.*
- Segment the syllables in **tennis,** pausing between the syllables: **ten** (pause) **nis.**
- Demonstrate how to blend the syllables and then say the name of the sport naturally.
- Divide other sports names and ask students to blend the syllables and say the word. Use these words: **basketball, swimming, football, soccer, karate, fishing, hockey.**

Segment Initial Sounds

- Give each student a two-inch and a four-inch strip of paper.
- Push your two strips together and say a word, such as **fort.** Then pull out the short piece with your left hand as you say **/f/** and the long piece with your right hand as you say **/ôrt/.**
- Model how to put the strips together as you say **fort.**
- Ask students to join you in segmenting the initial sounds in the following words: **page, bath, road, juice, boot, jeep, tight, cage, pick, phone.**

Letter Name Identification/ Formation Ww

Shared Reading of the Alphabet Chart

- Using a pointer, read the Alphabet Chart letter by letter with the class, as everyone marches in place. (*A, a; B, b; C, c,* etc.)

Model

- Display letter frieze card **Ww.** Explain that the name of this letter is uppercase *W* and the name of this letter is lowercase *w.*
- Describe the movement needed to form uppercase *W* and lowercase *w.* Tell students to start at the top when forming their letters.
- Say: *An uppercase* **W** *is slant right, slant up, slant right, slant up. A lowercase* **w** *is slant right, slant up, slant right, slant up.* Match the timing of your speech with the action of modeling the letter formations.

QUICK-CHECK Distribute blackline master 1. Have students name each picture pair and say the beginning sound in each picture name. Tell them to color both pictures if both words begin with the same sound and to cross out both pictures if they do not.

Independent Activities

Phonological Awareness

Provide picture cards **pan, pen, sock, sun, hat, house, yarn, yak, ring, rope, goat, gate, watch, web, jacks,** and **jam.** Have partners scramble the cards, place them face down in four rows, and play a matching game. Players turn over two cards at a time and segment the initial sounds in the picture names. If the words begin with the same sound, players keep the cards. If the words do not begin with the same sound, they turn the cards over again.

Letter Identification/ Formation

Place a Big Book or a poetry poster in the literacy center. Let students use highlighter tape to locate uppercase *W*s and lowercase *w*s. Students can use a sheet of paper to tally how many of each letter they found.

Provide pretzel sticks that students can use to make uppercase *W*s and lowercase *w*s.

Use masking tape to make the outline of a *W* and a *w* on the floor. Have students drive over the letter outlines using toy cars.

Guided Practice
- Distribute letter cards **W, W, W,** and **W** and have students place them under the alphabet strips on their desks.
- Tell students to trace uppercase *W* and say the movement pattern and the letter name. Listen and watch to make sure that students' words match their actions.
- Repeat with lowercase *w.*

Write
- Have students practice writing uppercase *W* on their workmats.
- Remind them to say the movement pattern as they form the letter. Ask students to check their letter with the letter *W* on their alphabet strips.
- Repeat with lowercase *w.*
- Distribute blackline master 2 and ask students to say the names of the letters. Then have them practice writing uppercase *W* and lowercase *w.* (The blackline master may be completed at this time or in a literacy center.)

Compare and Contrast
- Write uppercase *W* on the board. Write lowercase *w* next to it.
- Ask students to tell how the letters are alike and different. If they need help, say: *Both letters are formed the same, but uppercase* W *is taller and lowercase* w *is shorter.*

Locate
- Have students locate *W* and *w* on their alphabet strips and name each letter and the picture cue.
- Ask if anyone has the letter *W* or *w* in his or her name. Write the names on a sentence strip. Ask volunteers to frame the *W*s and *w*s.

Sort
- Distribute letter cards **W, W, W, W, w, w, w,** and **w** to each student. Ask students to find all the uppercase *W*s and put them in a row. Be sure that students find all the letters and that the letters they find are the correct ones.
- Repeat with the lowercase *w*s.

 QUICK-CHECK Use blackline master 3. Tell students to name the letters in each row and circle the uppercase *W*s and lowercase *w*s.

 # Small-Group Activities

Select from the following small-group activities to provide hands-on practice for students who need extra support.

BLEND SYLLABLES
Ask students to draw a picture of their favorite thing. Then have them take turns segmenting the picture name into syllables. Let the other students blend the syllables and then say the word naturally. The pictures may be shown so that students can check their responses.

SEGMENT INITIAL SOUNDS
Provide an assortment of small objects, some of which begin with the same sound, such as a bean, pen, rock, ball, leaf, bolt, book, ring, can, pencil, card, key, comb, lock, and cup. Have students name the objects and sort them by segmenting the initial sounds.

LETTER IDENTIFICATION/FORMATION
Have students write the letter *W* on their workmats several times. Encourage them to say the movement pattern as they write. Repeat with lowercase *w.*

Objectives

Students will:

- Blend syllables to form a word
- Segment the first sound in a word
- Recognize and learn the names of the letters *X* and *x*
- Write uppercase *X* and lowercase *x*

Materials Needed

- Alphabet Chart
- Picture Word Cards: *dinosaur, umpire, kitten, vegetables, quarter, mitten, umbrella, iguana, helicopter, magnet, antelope, zebra, pumpkin, ostrich, yo-yo*
- Letter Frieze Card *Xx*
- Letter Cards *X, X, X, X, x, x, x, x*
- Alphabet Strips
- BLMs *1, 2,* & *3*
- Student Workmats

Phonological Awareness

Blend Syllables

- Say: *I will name something you might find in a backyard. I will say the word in syllables. You are to put the word back together and tell me what it names.*
- Segment the syllables in **garden,** pausing between the syllables: **gar** (pause) **den.** Demonstrate how to blend the syllables to make the word. Then say the word naturally.
- Tell students you will name more backyard objects in syllables. Ask them to blend the syllables and say the words naturally. Use these words: **mower, caterpillar, ladder, flowers, shovel, sprinkler, robin.**

Segment Initial Sounds

- Say: *Listen for the first sound in this word:* **jar.** Be sure to emphasize */j/* in the word and */j/* in isolation. Ask: *What's the sound?*
- Sing the song in the box at right to the tune of *Mary Had a Little Lamb.*
- Continue with these words: **tent, bite, knee, rhyme, voice, luck, march, home, ditch, cage, wood, lamb.**

Letter Name Identification/ Formation Xx

Shared Reading of the Alphabet Chart

- Using a pointer, read the Alphabet Chart letter by letter with the class. Ask students to jump each time a lowercase letter is read. (*A, a* [jump]; *B, b* [jump]; *C, c* [jump], etc.)

Model

- Display letter frieze card **Xx.** Explain that the name of this letter is uppercase *X* and the name of this letter is lowercase *x.*
- Describe the movement needed to form uppercase *X* and lowercase *x.* Tell students to start at the top when forming their letters.
- Say: *An uppercase* **X** *is slant right, lift, slant left. A lowercase* **x** *is slant right, lift, slant left.* Match the timing of your speech with the action of modeling the letter formations.

> *What's the first sound that you hear, that you hear, that you hear?*
> *What's the first sound that you hear in the word* **jar, jar, jar***?*
> (Students should answer */j/.*)

✓ **QUICK-CHECK** Distribute blackline master 1. Tell students to name each picture and draw a picture of something whose name begins with the same sound as the picture name.

Phonological Awareness

Put picture cards **dinosaur, umpire, kitten, vegetables, quarter, mitten, umbrella, iguana, helicopter, magnet, antelope, zebra, pumpkin, ostrich,** and **yo-yo** in a bag. Tell students that you will choose a picture and say its name syllable by syllable. Tell students to blend the syllables and say the word naturally. Then show the card so that students can see if they were right.

Letter Identification/ Formation

Have students form uppercase **X** and lowercase **x** with cereal or raisins on a small plate. Ask them to repeat the activity several times.

Cut uppercase **X** and lowercase **x** out of a sponge. Fill a shallow pan with tempera paint. Tell students to cover the bottom of the sponges with a thin layer of paint and press the sponges onto a sheet of white drawing paper to form a design.

Provide a supply of magnetic letters. Have students sort through the letters and place all the uppercase **X**s and lowercase **x**s in separate groups on a cookie sheet.

Guided Practice

- Distribute letter cards **X, X, X,** and **X** and have students place them under the alphabet strips on their desks.
- Tell students to trace uppercase **X** and say the movement pattern and the letter name. Listen and watch to make sure that students' words match their actions.
- Repeat with lowercase **x.**

Write

- Have students practice writing uppercase **X** on their workmats.
- Remind them to say the movement pattern as they form the letter. Ask students to check their letter with the letter **X** on their alphabet strips.
- Repeat with lowercase **x.**
- Distribute blackline master 2 and ask students to say the names of the letters. Then have them practice writing uppercase **X** and lowercase **x.** (The blackline master may be completed at this time or in a literacy center.)

Compare and Contrast

- Write uppercase **X** on the board. Write lowercase **x** next to it.
- Ask students to tell how the letters are alike and different. If they need help, say: *Both letters are formed the same, but uppercase* **X** *is taller and lowercase* **x** *is shorter.*

Locate

- Have students locate **X** and **x** on their alphabet strips and name each letter and the picture cue.
- Ask if anyone has the letter **X** or **x** in his or her name. Write the names on a sentence strip. Ask volunteers to frame the **X**s and **x**s.

Sort

- Distribute letter cards **X, X, X, X, x, x, x,** and **x** to each student. Ask students to find all the uppercase **X**s and put them in a row. Be sure that students find all the letters and that the letters they find are the correct ones.
- Repeat with the lowercase **x**s.

 QUICK-CHECK Use blackline master 3. Tell students to cut out the letter cards, sort them into uppercase *X*s and lowercase *x*s, and glue them in the correct boxes.

 # Small-Group Activities

Select from the following small-group activities to provide hands-on practice for students who need extra support.

BLEND SYLLABLES

Say the names of objects—such as ***apple, umbrella, pencil, hammer, butterfly, bucket,*** and ***caterpillar***—by segmenting the words into syllables. For example: **ham/mer.** Have students blend the syllables and say the word.

SEGMENT INITIAL SOUNDS

Have students think of an object and a describing word that begin with the same sound and draw a picture of the object. As students share their drawings, the rest of the class guesses the words by segmenting the first sound of each word. For example: *Is it a* /r/ **ed** /r/ **abbit?** *Is it a* /b/ **umpy** /b/ **ox?**

LETTER IDENTIFICATION/FORMATION

Give each student a shallow box lined with salt or sand. Have them practice writing uppercase **X** and lowercase **x** while saying the movement pattern.

Objectives

Students will:

- Blend syllables to form words
- Segment the first sound in a word
- Recognize and learn the names of the letters *Y* and *y*
- Write uppercase *Y* and lowercase *y*

Materials Needed

- Alphabet Chart
- Picture Word Cards: *mitten, apple, notebook, sandwich, ostrich, umbrella, guitar, umpire, elbow, dinosaur, vegetables, quarter, zipper, magnet, kitten*
- Letter Frieze Card *Yy*
- Letter Cards *Y, Y, Y, Y, y, y, y, y*
- Alphabet Strips
- BLMs *1, 2, & 3*
- Student Workmats

Phonological Awareness

Blend Syllables

- Invite students to sing *This Old Man* with you.
- Slowly chant the first two lines, but replace **knick-knack** with a word segmented into syllables, as shown in the box at the right. Ask students to blend the syllables and then say the word naturally.
- Continue with the other verses.

Segment Initial Sounds

- Ask two students to come to the front of the room, stand side by side, and join hands. Segment the initial sound and the rest of the sounds in the word **cat.** Have one student be **/k/** and the other student be **/at/.**
- Tell students that when they are holding hands, they are the whole word, **cat,** but when they are not holding hands, they are each just a part of the word.
- Say: *When I touch your shoulder, stop holding hands to break the word apart, then say your part of the word.*
- Ask the two students to hold hands again as you say the whole word to model how the sounds are put together again.
- Repeat with other pairs of students and the words **back, van, rest, lap, hush, page, joke, dad, cold,** and **boat.**

Letter Name Identification/ Formation Yy

Shared Reading of the Alphabet Chart

- Using a pointer, read the Alphabet Chart letter by letter with the class. (*A, a; B, b; C, c; D, d,* etc.)
- Read the chart again, chanting the names of the letters and the names of the pictures. (*A, a, apple; B, b, ball,* etc.) Have students join you.

Model

- Display letter frieze card **Yy.** Explain that the name of this letter is uppercase **Y** and the name of this letter is lowercase **y.**
- Describe the movements needed to form uppercase **Y** and lowercase **y.** Tell students to start at the top when forming their letters.
- Say: *An uppercase **Y** is slant right to the middle, slant left to the middle, pull down to the bottom. A lowercase **y** is slant right to the middle, slant left to the bottom.* Match the timing of your speech with the action of modeling the letter formations.

✔ **QUICK-CHECK** Distribute blackline master 1. Have students name each pair of pictures. Tell them to color the pictures if the picture names begin with the same sound and to cross out the pictures if they do not.

---

*This old man, he played one,
He played bas (pause) ket
(pause) ball on my thumb.*

*This old man, he played two,
He played vid (pause) e
(pause) os on my shoe.*

*This old man, he played three,
He played base (pause) ball
on my knee.*

*This old man, he played four,
He played bag (pause) pipes
on my door.*

*This old man, he played five,
He played soc (pause) cer on
my hive.*

*This old man, he played six,
He played mu (pause) sic on
my sticks.*

*This old man, he played seven,
He played ban (pause) jo up
in heaven.*

*This old man, he played eight,
He played check (pause) ers
on my gate.*

*This old man, he played nine,
He played sax (pause) o
(pause) phone on my spine.*

*This old man, he played ten,
He played yo (pause) yo once
again.*

Independent Activities

Phonological Awareness

Provide picture cards **mitten, apple, notebook, sandwich, ostrich, umbrella, guitar, umpire, elbow, dinosaur, vegetables, quarter, zipper, magnet** and **kitten.** Have partners place the cards face down in a stack. One partner takes a card and says the syllables in the picture name. The other partner says the name naturally and looks at the card to check his or her answer.

Letter Identification/ Formation

Have partners practice writing *Y*s and *y*s on each other's back with their fingers and identifying which letter was written.

Provide models of *Y* and *y* made of pipe cleaners. Have students make their own pipe-cleaner *Y*s and *y*s.

Have students practice writing large *Y*s and *y*s on the board in different colors. Remind them to say the movement patterns as they write.

Guided Practice
- Distribute letter cards **Y, Y, Y,** and **Y** and have students place them under the alphabet strips on their desks.
- Tell students to trace uppercase *Y* and say the movement pattern and the letter name. Listen and watch to make sure that students' words match their actions.
- Repeat with lowercase *y.*

Write
- Have students practice writing uppercase *Y* on their workmats.
- Remind them to say the movement pattern as they form the letter. Ask students to check their letter with the letter *Y* on their alphabet strips.
- Repeat with lowercase *y.*
- Distribute blackline master 2 and ask students to say the names of the letters. Then have them practice writing uppercase *Y* and lowercase *y.* (The blackline master may be completed at this time or in a literacy center.)

Compare and Contrast
- Write uppercase *Y* on the board. Write lowercase *y* next to it.
- Ask students to tell how the letters are alike and different. If they need help, say: *Both letters start with slant right to the middle, but the uppercase* **Y** *is slant left to the middle and pull down, while the lowercase* **y** *is slant left to the bottom.*

Locate
- Have students locate *Y* and *y* on their alphabet strips and name each letter and the picture cue.
- Ask if anyone has the letter *Y* or *y* in his or her name. Write the names on a sentence strip. Ask volunteers to frame the *Y*s and *y*s.

Sort
- Distribute letter cards **Y, Y, Y, Y, y, y, y,** and **y** to each student. Ask students to find all the uppercase *Y*s and put them in a row. Be sure that students find all the letters and that the letters they find are the correct ones.
- Repeat with the lowercase *y*s.

 QUICK-CHECK Use blackline master 3. Tell students to find all the uppercase *Y*s and put polka dots on them. Then tell students to find all the lowercase *y*s and put stripes on them.

 # Small-Group Activities

Select from the following small-group activities to provide hands-on practice for students who need extra support.

BLEND SYLLABLES
Say: *I'm thinking of something you can ride. It's a **bi** (pause) **cy** (pause) **cle**. What am I thinking of?* Students should blend the syllables and then say the word. Then have them think of something and give a clue that includes both the category and the segmented syllables.

SEGMENT INITIAL SOUNDS
Say these weather words one by one: ***rain, sun, heat, fog, hail, cold, dew, wind, mist.*** Tell students to stand on their left foot as they say the initial sound and on their right foot as they say the rest of the word.

LETTER IDENTIFICATION/FORMATION
Ask students to locate uppercase *Y*s and lowercase *y*s in a book they choose. Have them show several of the letters they find to the group.

Objectives

Students will:

- Segment the first sound in a word
- Segment words by syllables
- Recognize and learn the names of the letters *Z* and *z*
- Write uppercase *Z* and lowercase *z*

Materials Needed

- Alphabet Chart
- Picture Word Cards: *guitar, lunchbox, elephant, bell, ox, umbrella, yo-yo, sub, ostrich, apple, helicopter, tent, magnet, pumpkin, zipper, vegetables*
- Letter Frieze Card *Zz*
- Letter Cards *Z, Z, Z, Z, z, z, z, z*
- Alphabet Strips
- BLMs *1, 2, & 3*
- Student Workmats
- StartUp Song & Rhyme CD

Phonological Awareness

Segment Initial Sounds

- Give each student a two-inch and a four-inch strip of paper.
- Push your two strips together and say a word, such as **yard.** Then pull out the short piece with your left hand as you say */y/* and the long piece with your right hand as you say */ârd/*.
- Model how to put the strips together as you say **yard.**
- Ask students to join you in segmenting the initial sounds in the following words: **vet, beach, tank, safe, desk, rice, night, paint, face.**

Segment Words by Syllables

- Sing or listen to the recording of *The Itsy-Bitsy Spider* with students several times.
- Tell students to say the song's words and this time to replace *itsy-bitsy* with claps for the word's syllables. Ask students to segment the syllables in the word to show you how many claps are needed *(four)*.
- Chant the song's words as shown in the box at right.
- Repeat, this time clapping the syllable in the word **spider**.

Letter Name Identification/ Formation Zz

Shared Reading of the Alphabet Chart

- Using a pointer, read the Alphabet Chart letter by letter with the class. (*A, a; B, b; C, c; D, d,* etc.)
- Read the chart again, chanting all the uppercase and lowercase letters that are formed the same (C, c; O, o; S, s; V, v; W, w; X, x; Z, z). Have students join you.

Model

- Display letter frieze card **Zz.** Explain that the name of this letter is uppercase **Z** and the name of this letter is lowercase **z.**
- Describe the movement needed to form uppercase **Z** and lowercase **z.** Tell students to start at the top when forming their letters.
- Say: *An uppercase* **Z** *is slide right, slant left, slide right. A lowercase* **z** *is slide right, slant left, slide right.* Match the timing of your speech with the action of modeling the letter formations.

 QUICK-CHECK Distribute blackline master 1. Tell students to say the name of each picture, clap the syllables in the picture name, and circle 1, 2, or 3 to show how many syllables they hear.

The clap-clap-clap-clap spider
Climbed up the water spout.
Down came the rain
And washed the spider out.
Out came the sun
And dried up all the rain.
So the clap-clap-clap-clap spider
Climbed up the spout again!

Independent Activities

Phonological Awareness

Provide old magazines, construction paper, scissors, and glue. Have students cut out five pictures and glue them onto the paper. Ask students to name each picture, segment the syllables in the picture name, and tally or write the number of syllables they hear next to the picture.

Letter Identification/ Formation

Write a large uppercase *Z* and a large lowercase *z* on construction paper "mats." Provide modeling clay and have students outline the letters with the clay.

Put sets of magnetic letters into a soup pot. Have students take turns ladling out several letters and locating the *Z*s and *z*s. When the pot is empty, refill it with the letters and have students begin again.

Provide long and short pretzel sticks. Have students make *Z*s using one long stick and two short sticks and *z*s using three short sticks.

Guided Practice

- Distribute letter cards **Z, Z, Z,** and **Z** and have students place them under the alphabet strips on their desks.
- Tell students to trace uppercase *Z* and say the movement pattern and the letter name. Listen and watch to make sure that students' words match their actions.
- Repeat with lowercase *z*.

Write

- Have students practice writing uppercase *Z* on their workmats.
- Remind them to say the movement pattern as they form the letter. Ask students to check their letter with the letter *Z* on their alphabet strips.
- Repeat with lowercase *z*.
- Distribute blackline master 2 and ask students to say the names of the letters. Then have them practice writing uppercase *Z* and lowercase *z*. (The blackline master may be completed at this time or in a literacy center.)

Compare and Contrast

- Write uppercase *Z* on the board. Write lowercase *z* next to it.
- Ask students to tell how the letters are alike and different. If they need help, say: *Both letters are formed the same, but uppercase Z is taller and lowercase z is shorter.*

Locate

- Have students locate *Z* and *z* on their alphabet strips and name each letter and the picture cue.
- Ask if anyone has the letter *Z* or *z* in his or her name. Write the names on a sentence strip. Ask volunteers to frame the *Z*s and *z*s.

Sort

- Distribute letter cards **Z, Z, Z, Z, z, z, z,** and **z** to each student. Ask students to find all the uppercase *Z*s and put them in a row. Be sure that students find all the letters and that the letters they find are the correct ones.
- Repeat with the lowercase *z*s.

 QUICK-CHECK Use blackline master 3. Tell students to draw a line from each uppercase letter to its matching lowercase letter.

 ## Small Group Activities

Select from the following small group activities to provide hands-on practice for students who need extra support.

SEGMENT INITIAL SOUNDS

Say *Jack and Jill* together slowly or listen to the recording. Then say the rhyme again, raising your hand for the highlighted words. Say: *Jack and **Jill** went up the hill to **fetch** a **pail** of **water**. **Jack** fell **down** and broke **his** crown, and Jill came **tumbling** after.* When you raise your hand, students are to segment the word after the initial sound.

SEGMENT WORDS BY SYLLABLES

Provide picture cards **guitar, lunchbox, elephant, bell, ox, umbrella, yo-yo, sub, ostrich, apple, helicopter, tent, magnet, pumpkin, zipper,** and **vegetables.** Divide the group into teams. Each team takes turns drawing a card, naming it, and segmenting the picture name into syllables.

LETTER IDENTIFICATION/FORMATION

Have students write uppercase *Z*s and lowercase *z*s on self stick notes. Tell them to select their best letters and stick them on the board.